ASHGARDEN

Grow a Revolution with the other books in the **PLOTTING THE STARS** series:

1: *Moongarden*
2: *Seagarden*

PLOTTING THE STARS
ASHGARDEN

MICHELLE A. BARRY

PIXEL+INK

PIXEL+INK

Text copyright © 2024 by Michelle A. Barry
Jacket illustration copyright © 2024 by TGM Development Corp.
Jacket illustration by Sarah J. Coleman
All rights reserved

Pixel+Ink is an imprint of Holiday House Publishing, Inc.
www.pixelandinkbooks.com
Printed and bound in August 2024 at Sheridan, Chelsea, MI, USA.
Book design by Jay Colvin

Cataloging-in-Publication information is available from the Library of Congress.

Hardcover ISBN: 978-1-64595-132-2
E-book ISBN: 978-1-64595-133-9

First Edition

1 3 5 7 9 10 8 6 4 2

*To the writers waiting for that one yes. Keep going.
This book is proof that you never know what sort of magic
could be waiting for you tomorrow if you do.*

—*M.A.B.*

CHAPTER ONE

MYRA

Fifth Month, 2449

I PUSH UP FROM WHERE I'M STILL SPRAWLED UNDER the cockpit's passenger seat—or what used to be a cockpit, and what used to resemble a seat. Now it's mangled metal, warped plastic, and random bits of fluff from the cushions. How did I get here?

It only takes a few seconds for everything to come burning back.

The nav-screen glowing red as we burst through the atmosphere.

A smell like burnt rubber growing stronger and stronger as the ship spirals.

Caught in the Old World's gravity, tumbling down.

The shuttle creaking and moaning as we descend, or maybe it's Hannah and Bernard screaming?

I can't remember anything else except the dark ground

rushing up at us, first blue, then brown, then green and green and green.

And then there was only black.

"Where is everyone?" I murmur, blinking to clear my vision before realizing it's smoke, not a brain fog, clouding my view. Thankfully, my glasses seem to have survived the crash intact.

"Bernard?" I croak. "Hannah?" I pull myself forward, cringing as a chorus of pain erupts all over my body. As I shift debris out of my way, a bright flash makes me jump. *Is the shuttle on fire?* No. The red isn't flickering or smoking. I reach out and carefully pick up the flaky crimson material with two fingers, holding it closer to my face.

A leaf.

I drop it like it's ablaze and scuttle back, bumping into something soft and firm.

"Watch it," Hannah growls, then coughs as she sits up. "We survived the landing?"

"Looks like it." I yank my collar up over my mouth as if that will help. "But probably not for long. Where's Bernard?"

"Over here," comes a muffled reply from the other end of the mangled ship.

Hannah and I crawl toward the voice, pushing through the ship's shrapnel, and other debris, too. Sticks, branches, and more leaves—most of them shades of red, but some gold, umber, and honey—are scattered throughout what's left of the cabin. There's even a cluster the same shade as a daffodil.

"We shouldn't be inhaling this," I murmur to Hannah as we try to move the twisted metal shards that have settled on top of Bernard.

"No kidding." Hannah grunts as she shoves away the last piece—part of the engine by the looks of it. "Unless you have a way to not breathe, could you maybe not remind me?"

I help Bernard to sit up, swiping dust and dirt from his clothes. "Are you all right?"

"I feel about as good as you look," he says, pulling his sleeve down over his palm and touching it gently to my head.

I wince, both at the spike of pain and at the sight of his shirt coming away streaked burgundy.

"We should get outside," Hannah says, struggling to her feet. "I don't like the look of that smoke."

"But outside—"

"We've already been exposed," Bernard reminds me grimly. "Being poisoned has got to be better than being burned to death."

"Are you sure about that?" I ask, climbing unsteadily to my feet and following Hannah.

"Nope."

We push through another tangle of debris, and then sunlight streams over us. I stumble out of the shuttle and onto the soft ground outside. My breath hitches, but not from the smoke or poison or the shock of the landing.

It's more beautiful than I could have ever imagined.

Tall, minty grass higher than my waist streams ahead of us in a field dotted with a rainbow of wildflowers. Beyond the clearing, endless rows of trees reach so far into the sky, it looks like they might be holding up the clouds. The leaves are like a Venusian sunset, amber and crimson and copper. The same as the scattered leaves inside the shuttle, but out here in the light, they glitter like gold. Like treasure. Like something I've only seen in my dreams and am only just remembering.

Even though I've never set foot on Old World soil before, even though I should be terrified of the plants surrounding me, I can't help feeling like I've finally come home.

The ground curves away, rolling and dipping in a way that's almost like—and nothing like—Moon craters. Instead of chalky dust and gravel leached of color, the hills here are glossy and green. In the distance, mountains sparkle in the sunlight as if they're carved from emerald or jade. I look back up at the trees. Were these all green once, too?

"It's stunning, isn't it?" Bernard says softly beside me. I can only nod.

"Is this what the Old World looked like in your memories?" Hannah asks. She's focused straight ahead, unable to tear her gaze away from this mystifying sight. "In your original's memories?"

Bernard squints and shakes his head. "Not like this. There wasn't as much open space in my lifetime. See," he says, pointing. "That's the remnants of a building."

I follow his finger. Though it's covered in moss and weeds, I can just make out something sleek and shiny glinting in the light. A small tree winds through it. Maybe once it was a wall. "The plants took the planet back," I murmur.

Bernard nods. "Some of it's familiar, though. Like the bright shades of changing leaves. When the weather's about to turn, they shift from green, then fall to the ground and fertilize the earth for the next generation of plants."

I smile, remembering Bernie telling me something similar once. Still, it's so different seeing the process in person. Like magic. I hold my hand out, and even before I call my Botan powers, my fingers are tingling. The air shimmers, and flowers bloom in a perfect ring around us, consuming the grass faster than a flame. I turn, raising my other arm, and a tree bursts from the ground. Bernard and Hannah stumble back, but I don't move. I know it isn't going to hurt me. I grin up at my newest friend. Its leaves bob in response, as if silently laughing.

"Guess your magic works pretty well here," Hannah says, a slight edge to her voice. "Can you keep them from poisoning us?"

"The other Botans couldn't," I say, dropping my arms.

Bernard nods, reaching up to brush a leaf hanging off my tree. "Maybe they've evolved since then."

I close my eyes, trying to sense the plants. My magic stirs, along with something else. Something dark and ugly, like a stain or wound. "I think they're still deadly," I whisper. "I can feel it."

"Then we need a plan." Hannah takes a few steps toward the forest. "Where do you think the others went when they were exiled? Maybe they found a way to survive."

I know Hannah wants her sister to be alive more than anything, but I can't imagine Meredith is still here. We don't even know what part of the Old World her shuttle crashed into. This planet is huge. She could be on the other side of the continent or have landed in the middle of the ocean. Or she might not have landed at all.

"We could look around," I suggest after a moment. "Maybe we'll find some clues."

We set off across the field. It seems safer than heading toward the mountains somehow.

"We should be careful," Bernard warns. "There could be dangerous creatures hunting."

Hannah frowns. "Wouldn't they have died off, too?"

He shrugs. "Nature adapts."

"Humans didn't."

"Maybe they would have, if they'd stayed," I say softly.

The trees are farther away than they look, and I'm becoming painfully aware of my injuries as the newness of this place wears off. Or maybe it's still shock. Before long, I'm limping, and I'm not the only one.

"Break?" Bernard huffs, collapsing to the ground before we both nod and settle beside him.

"Too bad Lila's not here," I murmur, assessing our bruises and scrapes. "She could heal us in a nanosecond." A new shock wave of pain bursts in my chest, and not the kind Lila's powers could mend. I'll never see her again. Or Canter. Or Bin-ro . . .

I take a slow, steadying breath, trying to get my emotions under control, blinking furiously and hoping the others assume that the sudden wetness in my eyes is from the wound throbbing on my temple.

Rustling in the brush behind us makes me forget both. "What was that?"

In a second, we're on our feet, backs pressed together, scanning our surroundings.

"Did you summon one of your plague animals just by mentioning them?" Hannah hisses.

"Animals don't work that way," Bernard fires back, his posture tense.

"Unless plague-surviving animals do."

"Both of you, be quiet!" I snap. "Maybe it won't he—"

Something crashes through the bushes. A lot of somethings. Tall and lanky, with green plants wrapped around their bodies and faces, they approach us like predators stalking prey.

"Run!" Hannah yells, and we all bolt in different directions. I pump my arms, wishing we were already in the forest. It'd be easier to lose whatever these creatures are in there. Desperate, I call on my magic, and elm trees sprout around us like sentinels. Maybe we could climb them? My hand is closing around the rough bark of a branch when something hits me, sending me crashing to the ground.

I roll onto my back, a sharp pain sparking in my neck as eyes behind a mask of foliage blink down at me. I try to fight, to throw the creature off me, but my limbs are limp and useless.

Then, for the second time today, all I see is black.

CHAPTER TWO

MYRA

WHEN I WAKE UP WHO-KNOWS-HOW-MANY HOURS later, I don't dare open my eyes. I listen, trying not to move except to breathe. The best time to learn what people don't want you to know is to pay attention when they don't think you can hear.

Voices murmur just out of earshot, so I risk opening my eyes a little to take in my surroundings. I'm in some sort of room. There are walls and a ceiling, and dim light, though it's from some sort of lamp and not the sun. There are plants everywhere. Growing up from the floor and through the roof, a garden trickles in like water seeping through a basket. Vines wind their way around sparse furniture and along the walls. A peony's ruffled petals rest against my foot.

I turn my head slowly from side to side, and as I do, a lump on my forehead presses into the pillow. A bandage.

I shift, realizing I'm less sore than I remember being when we left the shuttle. My throat and mouth feel funny, like they're stuffed with itchy fabric.

Confident I'm alone, I lift my head slightly. Hannah and Bernard aren't here. I push myself to sitting, already brainstorming ways to find my friends and escape. When I move, the peony against my leg shudders as if it's been given an electric shock. An instant later, the voices in the other room fall silent, and then footsteps thud closer and closer.

I throw myself back down and squeeze my eyes shut, forcing my breathing back to an even, sleepy rhythm. A door creaks open, and I fight the urge to flinch.

"We know you're not sleeping," a male voice says, a hint of amusement tingeing his words.

The bed shifts as someone settles beside me. I don't move.

"My friend here alerted us you were awake," a gentle female voice says.

I let my eyes flutter open. A blond woman, maybe a decade or so older than me, smiles and points her chin at the peony lying across the bed.

I clear my still-itchy throat. "The flower told you?"

She nods, reaching out to tap my wrist, then tracing her fingers over a Botan Inscription of a vine. "Can't you hear them?"

I gape at her, and then at the young man hovering behind

her shoulder. They are around the same age, twentyish, with dark-blond hair and green eyes. Vines weave through their locks, flowers sprouting over their ears and across their heads like crowns. Their clothes are shades of green and brown and seem to be made out of woven grass and leaves. The fabric, if you can call it that, drapes over their shoulders, twisting around their torsos and down their legs.

"Who are you?" I ask, sitting up. "And where are my friends? If you hurt them—"

"Whoa," the man says, holding up his hands. "Why would we save you just to hurt you? Your friends are fine. They're still asleep in the other room. The serum can take a while to work."

"The what?" I glance between the strangers. "What do you mean, you saved us? You attacked us!" The two exchange a knowing smile, and fury surges through me. "And how long have you been here? How can you survive the—"

"Let me guess," the man says. "The big, bad plants?"

"Don't tease her," the woman scolds. "They all think that way when they arrive. And without the serum, they'd be right."

"What—"

"The plants here *are* poisonous," she interrupts, "but we have a serum, a medicine, that neutralizes the toxins. Our people invented it ages ago."

"Your people?"

She pats my arm. "Botans. Like you."

"The Botans are . . . you're alive?" I stare at the pair, waiting for them to burst out laughing. But the man just sighs.

"Well, clearly we're alive," he says, holding his hands out to the side. "I'm not a ghost. At least, not last I checked."

"You know that most of the Botans were left behind when humanity evacuated?" asks the woman, and I nod. "Not long after that, the Botans developed the serum."

"But how?"

"From the plants, silly." She grins like it's the most obvious thing in the world. "You don't really think the plants would release poison without also giving us a cure."

"So, all this time . . . you've been here." I shake my head. "Why didn't the Botans tell anyone? Contact the Settlements?"

The two exchange another knowing glance, this one far less amused. "Working equipment was taken for the Settlements. They didn't exactly leave much, seeing as they assumed the abandoned would be dead within weeks," the man explains.

I furrow my brow, wincing when the wound under the bandage twinges. "But an Elector could have repaired broken equipment. Or a Tekkie."

"There weren't any Electors or Tekkies," the woman replies. "They were all evacuated. And tinkering with communication tech isn't really a Botan specialty."

More thoughts crash through my mind like a meteor shower. "So the Botans exiled here in the years since must be alive, too! Do you know Fiona Weathers? Or Meredith Lee? Meredith was sent within the last year. Fiona in the last decade. Where are they?"

The woman shrugs. "Those names don't sound familiar, but it's a big planet."

Hope deflates in my chest like a balloon hemorrhaging air.

"We could contact the nearby regions," the woman muses. "They might have heard of them."

I scowl. "I thought you couldn't contact anyone."

"It's not as easy as a vid-call, or however you communicate these days," she says, "but we do have ways of getting word to one another."

"How?"

She gestures toward the traitorous peony. "The plants carry our messages."

I'm about to ask her to explain how that works when the flower vibrates again, tickling my ankle. The pair glances at it, then toward the door where low voices carry from down the hall.

"Looks like your friends are awake," the man says, heading for the door.

"I'm Ava," the woman adds, helping me to my feet, before leading me after him. "That's my brother, Avon."

"Myra." We make our way down a hallway adorned with more plants growing through the cracks in the walls, floor, and ceiling. A question bubbles up, and I blurt it out before I can stop myself. "Did the peony actually speak to you? With—with words?"

"In a way. It's like hearing another language but only understanding the general meaning. Like you forgot the specific words but still grasp what they're saying."

Hannah and Bernard are sitting up in beds on opposite sides of another room. Both look dazed, jumping at the sight of the strangers, but they relax a little when they spot me.

"Are you all right?" Bernard asks me, and I nod, even though I'm not really sure that's true.

"What's going on?" Hannah demands, rubbing her forehead. "Who are you? Why did you attack us?"

The man—Avon—sighs, clearly exhausted by the prospect of explaining himself again, so I jump in instead.

Hannah eyes the pair suspiciously. "You're telling me that Botans have been living here for hundreds of years, and no one knew?"

"People tend to ignore those things they'd like to forget," Ava says quietly.

"It's not just Botans," Avon adds. "When everyone else evacuated for the Settlements, there were maybe a few thousand Botans left behind, but that was generations ago. Of course, not everyone's born with Botan magic."

I nod. "If Creers were genetic, I'd be covered in algebra equations."

Bernard rubs his neck. "So, do you have Creer schools like out in the Settlements?"

Avon's expression darkens. "We could if we had teachers. Plenty of people here have inklings of other magics—electrical, mending magic—but there's no one to show them how to use it. Nothing for them to study."

"It's almost impossible to learn a Creer without a teacher," Ava adds. "And definitely impossible when you can't study the principles and theories."

"That sounds familiar," I murmur, and Ava looks at me quizzically.

"Was that how it was for you?" she asks quietly, sympathy flashing in her eyes when I nod. "Well, plenty of teachers for you here." She turns to Bernard and Hannah. "And for you both."

"Bernard's a Botan," Hannah says, her cheeks flushing. "But I'm not. I'm a Tekkie."

Avon's eyebrows shoot up. "Really? Maybe you could identify the Tekkies around here. Teach them."

Hannah's face burns crimson. "I'm not a trained Tekkie."

"Oh." Avon glances toward the door. "If you want us to send a message to see if anyone knows your friends, we'd better get going. It can take a long time to get a response."

Outside, I gasp. We're standing in the middle of a small

village, though the homes appear to be carved into the trunks of massive trees. Some of the houses even span several.

"You live *inside* the trees?" I ask. "Doesn't it kill them?"

Avon scoffs. "Do they look dead? They're large enough that they can handle being hollowed out a bit."

"We know a thing or two about growing plants," Ava adds with a wink. A young woman with dark hair and tawny skin walks by and nods at us. "Hi, Nina," Ava calls, then turns back to us. "She was in the group that found you lot."

"How did you know to come looking for us?" Bernard asks.

"We saw the shuttle and knew it was another exile," she says. "Not many have landed here, but we've heard of others. One of the neighboring communities might know about your friends."

"Sister," Hannah corrects.

Avon's expression softens slightly. "Your sister is here?" When Hannah nods, he stands a little taller. "We'll find her. Someone will know. Especially if her arrival was recent."

Hannah doesn't say anything, though her eyes look glassy. Just yesterday—could it really only have been yesterday—she'd been certain she'd be reunited with Meredith in a Mercurian prison cell. I'm sure she doesn't want to get her hopes up again.

"It was a good thing we found you when we did," Ava

says. "The toxins won't kill you immediately—that takes a few weeks—but they can make you very sick. And, unfortunately, our Mending magic isn't always effective."

"Then how did you make the serum?" Bernard asks.

"Botan magic," answers Ava, grinning. "I told you, the plants provide almost every solution we could ever need. Do you know, some even store and give off light? We use them in the evenings as lanterns. Anyway"—she brushes a strand of hair out of her eyes, tucking it beneath a vine—"the recipe involves a few plants, and a pretty long brewing process. Once the serum's ready, it's injected, and the effect is immediate."

I remember the stabbing pain in my neck and wince. "Thank you," I say, even though it feels sort of belated. "For saving us."

Bernard nods eagerly. Hannah just eyes the pair, her gaze suspicious.

Ava smiles, and Avon grunts something unintelligible. We walk in silence another few minutes until we reach a clearing at the very center of the village. A few onlookers mill around, watching us curiously. Our Settlement clothing is as conspicuous as a rainstorm on the Moon.

A ring of boulders covered in moss and other plants rests in the middle of the clearing. At its center is a compact, lush garden. The growth is so thick I can't even see the ground. Flowers, bushes, and small trees are clustered together. A thick network of vines overlays them and winds out of the circle and into the village, disappearing into the distance.

"How does it work?" I ask.

"I'll go into the center to send the message," Ava explains, turning to Hannah. "Tell me more about who you're looking for. Where they're from, what they look like. Anything that might help identify them."

We describe Meredith and Fiona as best we can. Ava nods, then disappears into the foliage. After a minute or two, the garden shudders, like all the plants are taking a collective breath; then the vibration travels down the vines, away from us like ripples in water.

Ava reemerges. "Now we wait."

Bernard tilts his head. "How long will it take?"

Avon shrugs. "Could be days. Could be weeks. The message will cross all the communication gardens we're linked to. If someone knows your friends, they'll answer. It all depends on how far away the message needs to travel."

"So, what do we do in the meantime?" Hannah asks, crossing her arms.

A glint sparks in Avon's eyes. "You said you aren't trained in Tekkie magic, but you must know basic principles, right?"

"I know some theory," Hannah says slowly.

"And other Creers?" Ava asks. "Do you know their theories, too?"

"A little," I say, sensing where this is going. "I don't know if it will be enough to help anyone harness their magic, though."

"It's worth a shot," Bernard says, surprising me. "And in the meantime, they can help Myra and me with our Botan abilities."

Ava beams. "It's a deal!"

All I can do is stare at the vines snaking from the communication garden, wondering when they'll vibrate with an answer.

A week goes by, and then another. I split my time between my two friends. Hannah and I teach the others all we know about Creers. It isn't much, but the others here hang on our every word. The rest of the time, Bernard and I study Botan magic. There's more to know than I could even imagine. We quickly learn that plants have all sorts of uses beyond food and cosmetic applications. The ways the Botans have learned to work with the world around them are endless.

One afternoon, we practice communing with the trees, a fancy word for talking to them. Like Ava said, they don't exactly speak to us, but now I can hear what they're saying. When they want more water or need less light or more space to spread their roots. I tell them my needs, too—when I need a branch to lean on or a place to hide when I can't bear talking to anyone.

Especially when the memories from the Mercurian prison come crashing back.

Bernard and I are laughing as the trees tickle us with their pine needles when someone rushes into the clearing—a small boy.

"Visitors are here!" he exclaims. "From another region!"

Bernard and I bolt to our feet. "We've got to find Hannah!" I say, but just as the words escape my mouth, she bursts from one of the tree homes, her cheeks flushed.

"Where are they?" she demands. "Is it Meredith?"

We follow the boy to the other side of the settlement, where other villagers stand talking with a small group of unfamiliar faces. Avon turns and points to us. One of the adults, a woman, rushes forward, then stops and glowers.

She pushes her long amber hair away from her face. "Where is he?" she demands. "He was supposed to be here."

"Wh-where's who?" I sputter, recognition blooming inside me.

"My son!" she snaps. "Where is Canter?"

CHAPTER THREE

CANTER

I TIPTOE TO THE KITCHEN, HESITATING ON THE threshold. Everything is quiet and dark, and I'm careful not to make much noise. I don't want to wake the Crumplers. Lila's mom works long early shifts, and Lila's dad usually catches the first shuttle to his Neptune work site, so they've been asleep for hours.

Silent as a shadow, I make my way to the cabinet and pull out a bag of Crispy Bites, empty the contents into one hand, then clench the bag in the other. I squeeze the wrapper emblazoned with the MFI logo so tight my knuckles turn white, then drop the crumpled plastic into the trash compactor. If I could, I'd stop eating MFI products altogether. I seriously considered it until Lila reminded me I'd starve since there isn't anything else to eat.

Because of him. Because of them.

Head pounding, I resist the urge to kick the bin and wake the whole house, instead stuffing the snacks into my mouth before pressing my palms to my throbbing temples.

"Can't sleep, either?" a voice whispers from behind me, and I jump. Lila leans against her door in rumpled pajamas, her tangled curls perched on top of her head like a crown.

"Shh," I hiss. "You'll wake your parents." Only the sympathetic kindness of the Crumplers spared me from having to move back in with my father after . . . everything that happened two weeks ago. I promised myself I'd be the best houseguest imaginable, bordering on invisible, so they'd let me stay as long as possible. Ideally, forever. I'd rather disappear than move home. Wherever that is now.

"Nothing will wake my parents apart from a nuclear bomb," Lila whispers back.

"Your brother—"

"Is entrenched in his holo-games. Complete with headphones. He can't hear us."

I glance down the hall. Light flickers from under Landon's door. The entry to Lila's parents' room is dark.

"But," Lila continues, "I kind of need to get out of here. Want to go up to the roof? I saw a stairway leading there when they moved us in."

Moved us in is a generous term. After hauling us out of the prison and off Mercury, the guards dumped us in a Venusian apartment. Lila's parents followed soon after. I have no idea where my father went. And I don't care. Thankfully, he didn't argue when I refused to go with him. It was the least he could do, after everything. A jolt hammers my forehead, and I clutch my skull again.

"Come on," Lila says softly, touching my elbow. I realize I never answered her. It doesn't matter. Of course I want to get out of here. Unfortunately, the *here* I want to get out of is my own head, filled with memories—horrible, awful memories. Seeing as I can't escape myself, I settle for following Lila out the door, down the hall, and up three flights of stairs. We reach a locked door secured with an electrical sensor, and a deep rage fills me like a storm. I stare at it, as big a nemesis to me in this moment as Jake Melfin.

"Let me," Lila says, before my anger can whip to a full frenzy. She pulls a sharp clip out of her hair and sets to work. After a few seconds, a panel pops off, exposing a nest of wires.

"I can do the rest." I grunt, then disconnect and reconnect wires until the panel glows green and the locking mechanism clicks.

Humid, salty air washes over me as the door springs open, and my chest immediately loosens, the tension in my shoulders slipping away. For a moment, I can breathe again. I lean over a ledge to stare at the water stretching in all directions. "Do you even know what sea we're on?"

Lila props her elbows on the wall. "No idea. I doubt it's the Sea of da Vinci, though."

The Sea of da Vinci. Where V.A.M.A. is. Where we went to school. Me and Lila.

And Myra.

My head throbs, and I press my fists into my temple. Lila puts an arm around my back and I stiffen, forcing my head up and my hands to my sides. Her forehead creases, and I don't know if it's from frustration or something else. The same something else that's making my head throb.

"They could have been bluffing," she whispers.

"Then where's my mother?" I snap, sounding harsher than I mean to. "Where are the other Botans? Hannah's sister. All of them."

"I don't know. But it doesn't mean—"

"It does. It means exactly what you think it means. Myra and Hannah and Bernard . . . they're dead. We couldn't save them. *I* couldn't save them."

Lila opens her mouth to argue, then snaps it shut before burying her face in her hands.

"I'm sorry. I'm so sorry, Lila. I—" Crashing comets, I can't do anything right.

"Don't be," she says through tears. "You're right. We should have done more. We should have saved them."

"I keep playing it back in my head, over and over." I

stare out across the waves as Lila wipes her eyes. "What we could have done differently. How we could have changed things."

"Me too," Lila says. "And I can't find anything. It all went wrong so fast."

I close my eyes as the whole scene flashes through my mind again. A guard dragging me from the room, even as my plants and magic fought to keep me there. Myra trying to stop me with her own magic, except she couldn't. Not alone. I didn't realize what was happening until it was too late. Bernard had joined his Botan abilities with hers and overwhelmed mine. I fought my father every step from that room to the shuttle. Once we were on board, he shut me in a supply closet, and I beat on the door until my knuckles bled. But I couldn't escape, and I couldn't help her. I failed her.

I failed her as a friend.

The last time we were together, I screamed terrible things. Things I can never take back. I'll never be able to make it better or tell her I'm sorry, and that I didn't mean it. It was such a stupid thing to be that furious about, anyway. So what that she knew what my father had done. *So what.* It was ancient history. My knowing wouldn't have changed anything.

But what I said changed our friendship. Forever.

Lila and I are both quiet, the only sound the waves

crashing below, spraying salty water against the side of the crumbling apartment building.

"Myra would hate this," I finally say. "She'd hate us up here moping."

The ghost of a smile crosses Lila's lips. "She'd say something like 'Do you guys need me to do *everything*? What's next? How do we get back at Melfin?'"

A strange chuckle bubbles up in my chest, and I'm not sure if it's a laugh or a sob. "No, she'd say something like 'Really, hotshot? Are you going to make me avenge myself?'"

Lila snorts. "That does sound like her." She wipes her face on her sleeve. "And she's right."

"Maybe that's our way forward," I say, turning back to the water. "We just think of what Myra would tell us to do, then we do it."

"It'll definitely keep us motivated."

"I wish we'd helped her more back at V.A.M.A.," I say suddenly. "She was ready to track down the group of Reps on day one, and we just blew her off."

"I figured we'd have more time. But now . . ." Lila sighs. "We could've been spending that time with her. We could have found another way, besides going to Mercury."

"Quit playing that autoloop!" I say, slapping my hand down on the ledge. "What's next?"

Lila smiles. "Are you being Myra again?"

I force a grin. "How'd I do?"

"Not bad."

"So, what *is* next?"

A clatter on the other side of the roof makes us both jump. Lila and I exchange a look and together creep around the building.

A pile of machinery—tools, batteries, and wires—rests in a heap. A boy probably no older than eight or nine crouches over it.

"What are you doing up here?" I ask. I expect to startle the kid, clearly engrossed in whatever he's doing with the pile of junk, but he doesn't flinch.

He barely even blinks, looking up as if he was expecting us. "Trying to assemble a refrigeration unit. Ours is on the fritz, and my parents can't afford a new one right now."

"Do you—do you work up here a lot?" Lila asks, eyeing him like a puzzle she's trying to assemble upside down.

He turns back to the pile of parts. "Depends on what you call a lot." He brushes a strand of red hair out of his face. "Wanna help? It's hard to build the frame. My arms aren't long enough to hold all the pieces together." He gestures toward what looks like a half-built metal skeleton with frayed wires winding around every inch of it.

I raise an eyebrow. "Do you have Elector magic?"

"Nah," he says, twisting two wires together. They spark and he grins. "I'm a non-Creer."

"You're too young to know that," Lila says. "You can't have taken a Creer test yet."

He shrugs. "I just know. I don't want one, anyway."

"What do you mean you don't want one?" I rub at my arm. Inscriptions cover the skin beneath my shirt. I eye the nest of wires and piles of batteries with a longing that lodges a deep ache in my chest. "Everyone wants magic."

"Not me." The boy props the frame up again. "Can you hold this while I reconnect this circuit?"

"We were heading back inside, actually," I say.

Lila looks like she wants to add something, but I motion toward the stairs. We've got more important things to discuss than a refurbished refrigeration unit, and we can't talk in front of this kid. She sighs and follows me.

"Bye!" the boy calls. Lila waves. I just keep walking.

"Who doesn't want magic?" I grumble as we reach the door leading to the stairs.

Lila shrugs. "My dad says he doesn't mind not having a Creer. He likes what he does."

"But that's not the same as *not wanting* magic," I argue. She doesn't answer. "Bernard almost got himself killed trying to get his back. Hey." I stop midstair. "Maybe that's what we do next."

Lila pauses beside me. "What do you mean?"

"We take back what we can."

A light goes on in her eyes. "We find Perennial's group."

I study the Inscriptions creeping down over my wrist. Old Elector ones. My Botan markings are mostly covered from all the Elector magic I used for the V.A.M.A. production, and I haven't gotten a new Inscription, Botan or Elector, since.

Because of that day on Mercury. Because of Melfin. Because I failed my friend.

I look at Lila, her fingers tracing her Mender Inscriptions, also unchanged since we left the Mercurian prison. "And when we do, we take our magic back, too."

CHAPTER FOUR

MYRA

THE WOMAN GLARES AT ME LIKE I'VE GOT CANTER hidden behind my back.

"You're Fiona Weathers." Who else could this fiery-haired woman be? She even has Canter's eyes. But I need to hear her say it.

"What? Yes." Her expression softens, but a moment later, her eyes flash again, this time with desperation. "Who are you?"

"Myra. Myra Hodger."

I see a flicker of recognition, but how could she know who I am?

"Where's Canter?" she asks. "He's with you, isn't he?"

I shake my head.

"That's impossible." Her blue eyes are like ice. "He was supposed to be on that shuttle!"

I frown. "What?"

She starts pacing, her fingers tangled in her hair, pulling the auburn locks tight. Flowers sprout from the earth behind her, like a trail of footprints, all a dark, bloody red with thorns covering every inch of their stems.

A gray-haired man emerges from the huddle, glancing at me and then Hannah and Bernard before stopping at her side. He juts his chin. "I take it that's not your son?"

Fiona whirls around as if Canter just jumped out from behind a tree, but her eyes only find Bernard, who swipes his dark hair nervously out of his eyes.

"No," she says. "That's not him."

"What did you mean, he was supposed to be on the shuttle?" Hannah asks from behind me.

Fiona and the man exchange a look.

"What's your name?" the man asks Hannah.

She tells him, then repeats her question.

"I need to talk to Sandra," Fiona says. "Find out what went wrong."

"The next communication window isn't for several days," the man says. "We'll have to wait."

"I've waited for more than a decade!" Fiona doubles over as if she's going to be sick, but instead drops to her knees. The crimson flowers circle her like a bull's-eye.

The man wades through them, somehow dodging the

thorns, and rests a hand on her shoulder. I clench mine at my side.

"You—you planned this," I say, my voice low. "With Ms. Curie?"

Fiona peers up at me, her face pale. "It wasn't supposed to be you. Any of you. It was just supposed to be Canter and Sandra."

The three of us look at one another, confusion bleeding into shock and then anger.

"You told her to plant the seeds on him?" Hannah asks, horrified.

"It was the only way I could get him here," Fiona replies without a trace of remorse in her voice.

"He could've been killed in the crash," Bernard insists, shaking his head. "You'd really risk that? We barely survived."

Fiona scoffs. "With two Electors on board? They would've been able to repair the shuttle and pilot it easily. Besides, exile shuttles land in my region all the time. Mostly in the ocean, but ships today are made to withstand the impact."

Hannah steps forward. "Was my sister on one? Her name is Meredith Lee. She was exiled a year ago."

The man nods slowly. "Yes, I remember her."

"Where is she now?" Hannah asks eagerly. "Is she back in your region? How far is it?"

"She's not there anymore," he says. "She left shortly after arriving."

Hannah's face falls. "Left? Where'd she go?"

The man glances at Fiona, but she's glaring at the ground. "There are many communities here. She joined another."

Before Hannah can press him further, Fiona's pacing again.

"What went wrong?" she asks.

"Everything!" I reply angrily. "And you did this? How? Why?" Something the man said flashes through my mind. "What window were you talking about? You can't communicate with the Settlements from here."

"Sandra found a way. She'd been experimenting for some rebel group. Bouncing signals off old satellites still orbiting the Old World." Fiona waves her hand dismissively. "Through the group, she discovered what happens to Botan exiles, but she couldn't accept that I was gone, so she decided to try crashing a satellite onto the Old World surface. See if she could ping to it. Open up a communication line. It took months, but she finally got it to work."

I shake my head. "So, you've been talking to her since . . ."

"It's been almost a year."

"You've been plotting to kidnap Canter for a year?" Hannah asks.

"Not kidnap. Bring him home. And it hasn't been a year. Only since I realized he couldn't stay with *him* another second."

"Do you mean Director Weathers?" I ask.

Fury flashes in her eyes. "I thought Canter would be safe with his father. Protected. When I negotiated my deal with the Governing Council, I thought I could give them normal lives. But when I found out all Robert had done . . ." She closes her eyes. "I couldn't leave Canter with him."

"What did he do?"

She glares at me. "I thought you'd know better than most. Sandra's told me everything. He destroyed my garden after telling me he wouldn't. He promised to protect Bernie, then had him killed."

Bernard stiffens beside me, and I squeeze his arm.

"And when he discovered Canter had my talent, instead of helping him, he tried to bury it." Fiona shakes her head. "Maybe it wasn't as innocent as he made it out to be, telling Jake about my powers."

My mouth falls open. "You think he did it on purpose?"

"Not before, but now? I don't know." Fiona meets my eyes, the rage replaced by desperation. "Why wasn't Canter with you? Why are you here at all?"

I explain about the free Reps, the prison, and my confrontation with Jake Melfin. My hands start shaking as the words spill from my lips, like I'm reliving it all again. I sit on the ground, and Fiona sinks opposite me, then drops her head into her hands.

"I'm sorry you were caught up in all this," the gray-haired man murmurs. "All of you. We'll do our best to make your lives here as fulfilling and happy as possible." He extends his hand to me. "I'm Charlie Foden. Fiona and I reside in the region near the northeastern shore."

"Charlie's the elected leader of their community," Ava explains, coming to join us. "He'll make sure you're well taken care of."

"We can't stay here," I insist. "We've got to get home. Jake Melfin—"

Fiona snarls. "Let Jake destroy the Settlements. They're all descended from the ones who were content to leave the Botans here to die. Maybe it's time they paid for their ancestors' decision."

"My parents are still out there," I protest. This red-haired woman, boiling with fury and vengeance, is so different than I imagined.

Ava settles next to me. "We're a family here, too. You'll see. I can promise you'll find more acceptance among us than you ever found out there."

I hate to admit it, but she might be right about that. Even so . . . "I can't give up on them or my friends so easily."

"Oh, don't worry about that." Fiona looks into the sky. "I *will* find a way to get Canter."

Charlie nods toward Bernard. "And what about you? Are you a Botan, too, or were you just caught up in Jake Melfin's schemes?"

"A little of both," Bernard says, stepping closer. "I'm a Rep. Well, I was. I'm not really sure what I am now."

I stand and take his hand. "You're Bernard."

"A Rep." Fiona studies his face, recognition lighting her eyes. "Named Bernard?"

CHAPTER FIVE

CANTER

I LOUNGE AT MY WORKSTATION FIDDLING WITH THE pendant around my neck, eyes glued to the time. The teacher drones on and on about primary electrical parameters, and I swallow down a wave of nausea. Not only have I known all this since I was about five, but learning about electricity is as painful as it is dull.

I rub at the back of my neck, my fingers tracing the long-healed wound from where the guards injected the magic-suppressing chip. We'd just landed on Venus when they boarded and swarmed us. Dad howled something about it not being a part of the deal, but a man with a gleaming badge smirked and said the deal had been updated and if we gave them any trouble, it wouldn't be the last change.

I've pretty much accepted that my dad is one of the worst humans in the galaxy. At least top five. To his credit, he didn't cooperate, and neither did Lila or I. In the end, it didn't matter. They pinned us to the shuttle wall, then jabbed needles into our necks.

It took three guards to take Dad down. They crushed him to the floor, stabbing the needle into the crease between his throat and shoulder. And then the minuscule implants flowed into our bloodstreams. Lila tracked hers briefly before it overwhelmed her magic and her powers vanished.

By the time they hauled us off the shuttle, none of us had any desire to fight. And no more reason to. My mother is gone. My best friend is gone. Bernie—Bernard—is gone, *again*. And my magic, Botan and Elector, is gone, too.

When we arrived at the Venusian apartment block, my dad turned to me, his eyes red-rimmed. "Canter, I'm sorry."

It was the last thing he said to me. I wasn't sure what he was sorry for. Maybe all of it. Maybe none of it.

The doors opened, and I followed Lila inside without looking back. Dad might have called my name. Maybe he even tried to follow me. I didn't care. I still don't care. I haven't seen or heard from him since.

I glance back up at the teacher, then catch eyes with Lila, who's sitting, back straight, behind her desk like a model student. Yet the screen in front of her is blank. No notes. No texts. Just an empty dashboard.

I feel like I have a lot in common with that screen.

Her gaze is hollow, glassy. Her eyes are rarely dry these days. She's haunted by the same ghosts as me.

My temples throb, and I drop the pendant to rub them. The movement breaks Lila's trance. Her chin turns toward me, and for a moment it's the old Lila scanning me for all possible ailments, running through her protocols for mending them. But then she winces.

When I flick my gaze to the door and she nods, I click the button on my workstation to request a visit to the bathroom. The teacher's eyes drift to the alert on her screen. She reaches out and presses a button, then goes back to her lecture. A light on my control panel glows green and I slide out of my seat, grabbing my backpack, and head toward the door. She doesn't question why I'm taking my bag with me.

It might just be me, but the teachers at this non-Creer school don't seem to care all that much about attendance or performance like the teachers at S.L.A.M., or even at V.A.M.A. The Venusian school was more laid-back in a lot of ways, but they still were invested in our progress. The vibe's different here.

I turn a corner and wait. A minute later, Lila appears, her own bag slung over her shoulder.

"I still can't believe they let two students leave at the same time," she says, falling into step beside me. "Ms. Goble would never have allowed that."

"Thank your lucky stars they do," I mutter. "We'd be stuck listening to that lecture."

Lila sweeps her curly hair off her forehead. "Electrical Studies must be torture for you. My Mending Principles class is miserable."

I nod but don't say anything, trying to ignore the ache rippling across my skull like fireworks. A teacher turns into the corridor and we both freeze. "Act like you're supposed to be here," I whisper.

"And like you know where you're going," Lila adds, then bites her lip. "Never go to the same place twice."

My throat goes tight. Myra's rules for cutting class. Still accurate, but now risky to recall. When I think of Myra, the last thing I can be is calm.

The teacher passes us by, and we both exhale loudly before hurrying off to the Junk Room. I don't know what it is officially, but that's what Lila and I named it when we discovered it a few days ago. Random bits of machinery, tools, and actual trash are heaped in bins. Maybe they're emptied periodically. We haven't been here long enough to find out.

Lila hops up on a counter and starts sifting through the piles for parts that might be useful.

I hoist myself up next to her, shifting my bag onto my lap, and gingerly remove a mangled heap of metal from inside, then carefully place it beside me. The lump re-forms in my throat as I take in the burnt wires and cracked metal hull that were once Bin-ro.

At the bottom of my bag, I pull out the fuses and panels we scavenged from this room yesterday—everything we thought could potentially help in repairing our robot friend.

"We'll have him back together in no time," Lila says, her voice falsely cheerful. Even she knows fixing Bin-ro will be near impossible. And without my Elector magic? We may as well give up.

But I can't.

I start sifting through the nearest pile of scraps. "Nothing in this galaxy will stop us."

"What even is that thing?" a small voice asks.

I jump, nearly dropping the motor I was inspecting. Lila catches the edge of the counter before she can topple off.

A young boy steps out from behind one of the bins stacked in the corner. It's the same kid we met on the apartment building roof.

"What, are you spying on us?" I snap.

"No!" the boy protests. "I was here first. Maybe *you're* spying on me."

"Why would we spy on a little kid?"

"Maybe you're trying to steal my inventions." He twists some sort of contraption behind his back. "And I'm not little."

"We're not trying to steal anything," Lila says soothingly. "You just startled us. Shouldn't you be in class?"

"Shouldn't you?"

Fair point.

"Hey! Can I help?" The kid's eyes gleam. "That looks like a tricky project."

"Not a chance. Go find somewhere else to work."

The boy's not even looking at us anymore. He's studying Bin-ro. "I think I saw a microcontroller that would fit your robot." He points to a pile of parts on a different counter. "It was over there."

"Oh, really? Thanks. We'll check." Lila beams at him.

I grit my teeth. I don't know how she can be so nice all the time, especially after everything that's happened. I used to like that about her, but lately it gets under my skin.

"Want to see what I'm working on?" the boy asks eagerly.

"Sure," Lila says.

"Nope," I snap at the same time, and she has the nerve to frown at me. We're supposed to be fixing Bin-ro, not babysitting.

I'm about to remind her of that when she asks the kid, "What's your name?" as she hops off the counter.

"Eli." He turns, then displays a mangled contraption. "This is my stun launcher."

Lila frowns. "Why would you need that?"

"Why wouldn't you?" Eli replies with a laugh before

diving into a detailed explanation of the device's capabilities and the parts he used to assemble it.

Lila nods along, amused.

Meanwhile, I close my eyes, trying to control my temper and quiet my pounding headache long enough to tell the kid to scram so Lila and I can get back to work. I won't be distracted from my mission this time, no matter how hopeless it is. Maybe if I'd been more focused before, things would have turned out differently. I wouldn't be here. I'd be at V.A.M.A. with Myra. Or back at S.L.A.M. Or—

A voice bleeds through the door from the hall outside, and the hairs on my arms stand up. Has my headache rattled my brain? Made me hallucinate?

Lila whips around to face me, her eyes wide. "It can't be. That's impossible."

Without a word, I tuck Bin-ro back in my bag, then tiptoe toward the door and crack it open.

A woman with short, dark hair stands with her back to me. Wires wrap around her wrists, sparking electricity.

CHAPTER SIX

MYRA

FIONA RISES, THEN WALKS A SLOW CIRCLE AROUND Bernard. "Saturn's rings," she whispers. "Bernie, it really is you."

Bernard shifts uncomfortably under her gaze, and Hannah glances anxiously between us. I open my mouth to explain that even though he has the same DNA as Bernie, Bernard is his own person, but Ava speaks before I can.

"You know him?" she asks.

"Yes. Well, no," Fiona says, slumping back to the ground. "But you sure look like him. A bit younger, obviously, but there was only one Bernie. Just like there's only one you."

Bernard's eyes light up, and I breathe a sigh of relief. "Bernard is pretty great, too," I say.

She turns toward me. "Sandra tells me you were very

close with him. I'm sorry about what happened. I really am. I never thought . . ." She shakes her head.

"Sometimes I wish I'd never brought Bernie back into the garden," I whisper.

Fiona laughs, and it makes me jump. "Like you could have stopped him." Her eyes are soft, and for a moment, she looks like the woman in the photo Canter kept in his room. "I'm sure he grunted and moaned about it, but once he knew you'd found the garden, you wouldn't have been able to keep him away. He loved that place as much as I did. Maybe more."

I give her a small smile. "He worked his own magic there."

"That's true," she says, the light leaving her eyes.

"How did you meet him?" I ask after a moment, but she doesn't answer. "Did he stumble into the garden, or did you tell him?" She's silent, staring ahead, like I'm a ghost, or maybe she is.

Charlie clears his throat. "You mentioned something about Botan magic?"

Bernard glances at Fiona, then returns his attention to Charlie. "It's sort of a new discovery. I don't have any training or anything."

"Not yet," Ava says, gently elbowing him.

"You will soon," I add, forcing myself to look away from the woman slumped beside me. "Now that you've got your magic back, I mean."

"But how?" Charlie asks. "Aren't all Reps blocked from using their Creer powers?"

Hannah fills them in on the device Ms. Curie perfected and how she tested it on Bernard.

Fiona still doesn't react, but Charlie's brow furrows. "That was very brave, and even riskier."

"Not much to lose," Bernard says with a shrug.

"That's not true," I counter. "We could've lost you."

"And then *we* wouldn't have had the pleasure of meeting you," Charlie adds.

For a moment, the warmth returns to Fiona's eyes. "Don't let your circumstances decide your value."

Bernard flushes as he nods, then finds the ground suddenly fascinating.

"Hopefully, lots more Reps have recently found their circumstances changing," I say, looking up at the sapphire sky. With any luck, Perennial's group was able to restore magic to all the Reps, and now they're causing lots and lots of trouble.

"We can ask during the next communication window," Charlie offers. "In the meantime, you can both practice using your magic."

I glance hopefully at Fiona. "I'd love to hear about how you built the moongarden."

She doesn't answer.

"I'm sure there's lots you could teach me," I add. "And Bernard."

"It might be good to have someone who understands their background training them," Charlie says gently.

"Anyone here could teach them to grow a rose," Fiona murmurs. "All I'm good for is making thorns."

Charlie frowns. "That's not true. You're a very talented—"

"The only person I'm interested in teaching is my son," she snaps.

"We'll find another way," Charlie insists. "The next time we speak to your friend."

"I didn't realize there were still satellites around the Old World," Hannah says. "How did Indra, I mean Sandra—Ms. Curie . . ."

A wave of annoyance washes over me. "How did she do it?"

"I'm curious about that, too," Ava says. "Do all the regions know you can communicate with the Settlements?"

"Most of the leaders do," Charlie explains. "The ones we're connected with on the plant network, anyway. There are hundreds of old satellites still orbiting the Old World from before the evacuation."

I raise my eyebrows.

"They were all long forgotten," he continues. "But

Sandra located ones that still had the trace of a charge and used her Elector powers to propel the viable satellites through the atmosphere. Eventually, one landed in a neighboring region, and she commandeered the radio waves."

"I only understood about half of that, and it's pretty impressive," Hannah says, gaping.

"I'm less impressed, seeing as Ms. Curie didn't bother to tell Canter." Heat flashes through my cheeks as I remember his desperate schemes to contact his mother when he thought she was being held on Mercury. All that time, his old Elector teacher was chatting with her here.

"Don't blame Sandra," Fiona says softly. "I forbade her from telling him. There was no way for her to get me off planet, and even if she did, if the Governing Councils—or at least the members who knew I was here—had caught wind of our plan, there'd have been blowback for me and my family. I was sure of it. But once I found out everything Robert had done . . ." She shakes her head. "The plan changed."

I'm not entirely convinced of Ms. Curie's innocence, but I can see that Fiona will never blame her friend, so I move on. "Why do we have to wait to contact her?"

"Communication's only possible during certain periods of the Old World's orbit. Sandra always calls to check in as soon as we're in range, and that will be in—" She raises an eyebrow at Charlie.

"A few days. We can use the time to return to our region, where the satellite's stored. There are some matters we should go over in the meantime." He exchanges dark looks with Fiona and Ava. "There's more you need to know about life here."

"I'm dying to know about the technology you've developed to get by," Hannah says eagerly. "How do we even get to your region? Do you have transports?"

"Not the kind you're used to, but we manage." Charlie rubs his head. "Fiona tells me Canter's trained as an Elector. If we can get him here, he could really help those who have a trace of electrical magic."

"And with the electrical storms," Ava says quietly. Charlie nods gravely.

There's something they're not saying. I open my mouth to ask what they mean when a clap of thunder booms in the distance.

The adults whirl around, eyes trained on the sky.

"Impossible," Charlie mutters. Dark clouds bloom on the horizon.

"It's just a storm," Hannah says, studying the adults and then the sky. "I thought the Old World had tons of different weather patterns."

A flash of lightning is followed by another crack of thunder, this time much closer. I've only ever seen storms on Venus, and those rolled in quick, but these clouds seem to be approaching far faster than should be possible. A moment ago, they were barely visible, and now they're nearly upon us.

"They must have tracked us here!" Charlie barks, gripping Hannah's arm. "We need to get the kids to shelter and round up the others."

"Who tracked you here?" Bernard asks as the adults herd us toward one of the tree houses. Avon bursts outside, heading in the opposite direction, and Ava sprints after him, vines twisting around their arms and hands like vipers.

"Gather the others!" Charlie calls after them. "They'll be here any moment."

"*Who's* here?" I demand. Fiona grabs my wrist in one hand and Bernard's arm in the other, hauling us toward the shelter. "What's happening?"

"Let me go!" Hannah shouts as Charlie drags her forward. "Whatever this is, we can help. We can fight."

Charlie grimaces. "Not them."

"Not *who*?" I ask again, digging in my heels. Vines burst from the ground, wrapping around my ankles, holding me in place. I cross my arms as a bolt of lightning slices down, opening a small crater in the earth a dozen yards away. "Is this some sort of magic? How is that even possible?"

Charlie shoves Hannah and Bernard inside a building. Fiona waves a hand, and the vines around my ankle wither and retract. A branch from the tree swoops down, shoving me toward the door. I grab hold of it, clinging to the rough bark so it can't shake me off. Behind Fiona, balls of ice as big as my fist hurtle down, accompanied by more crashing thunder. "Tell us what's going on!"

"When the rest of humanity fled for the off-planet Settlements, the Botans weren't the only Creer left behind."

"What are you talking about?" I fight the tree, which is still trying to sweep me inside. "What other Creer?"

The branch snaps, and I tumble backward as more limbs and leaves swoop down, filling the entry and sealing us in.

CHAPTER SEVEN
CANTER

"WHAT IS SHE DOING HERE?" I HISS AFTER EASING THE door shut again.

"I don't know," Lila whispers back. "Nothing good."

Eli stands on tiptoe, trying to see out the frosted glass. "Who is it?"

"Shh!" I snap. "She'll hear you."

"They're walking away," he argues, pressing his ear to the door. "Is she a teacher?"

"Not here," Lila says, then frowns. "I'm not sure where she teaches, actually."

"Hannah's school," I remind her.

"Why don't we like her?" Eli asks, opening the door and peering down the hall.

"Will you slow your jets?" I say, once more easing the door closed. "And leave that alone."

"She's . . . bad. *Very* bad," Lila tries to explain, though I'm not sure why she's bothering.

Eli's eyes widen. "Want me to pay her back?"

I glower at him. "What do you mean? Why would you do that?"

"Because we're friends, and no one messes with my friends."

I huff a laugh. "We're not friends, kid." Lila elbows me, but I ignore her.

Eli's unfazed. "Then how about because it'll be fun? C'mon!" Before I can stop him, he opens the door and darts into the hall, his sonic propeller, or stun launcher, or whatever it is, slung over his shoulder. "I've been wanting to test out this thing for ages."

Lila looks at me, chewing her lip. "We should warn him that Ms. Curie's an Elector. If he tries to use that thing on her, she'll fry it right out of his hands."

The kid's turning out to be a real pain in the booster, but I really don't want him on the receiving end of Ms. Curie's wrath.

I'd much prefer she was on the receiving end of mine.

I sigh. "It probably won't work, anyway. He hasn't got any magic, remember?"

"Then it'll be even worse. But don't tell him that. If he's anything like my little brother, it will just make him want to prove us wrong. We're better off trying to distract him."

When I don't move, Lila plants her hands on her hips. "Besides, if we follow Curie, maybe we'll figure out what she's doing here."

I know better than to argue with Lila when she's got that look in her eye, so I sling the bag with Bin-ro onto my back and follow her out the door. We hurry down the hall, though it doesn't take long to locate Eli.

The kid's crouched outside a doorway, bright light from the opening forming a yellow square on the ground at his toes, his launcher balanced on his shoulder.

"Eli, come on," Lila whisper-yells, motioning him toward us. "Why don't you show us some of your other inventions?"

"Wait till you see her face when it hits," Eli says, his cheeks flushed. "It'll make her fuzzy at first. We've got to be gone when she comes to."

"Don't do it," I whisper. "She's an Elector. She'll trace it back to you in two nanoseconds. *If* it even works."

Lila steps on my foot as Eli's expression turns stony. "It *does* work."

"Let's not worry about—"

"I'll show you!" Eli hisses, dropping his chin to look through the device's sights. "Three, two, one, blast-ON."

A *whoosh* bursts from the launcher, and the lights inside the room flicker. The square on the ground wobbles and dances. A shriek breaks the silence, followed by a curse and a thump. Eli whoops, dropping to a knee and punching the air, before bounding up and racing by us. "C'mon! We've gotta get out of here."

I take off sprinting, Lila right behind me.

"We should go back to class," she pants.

"Good idea." Eli ducks around a corner. "See you guys later. This was interstellar!"

Lila and I turn down another corridor and skid to a stop outside our classroom. We hadn't planned on returning.

"Will she notice we've been gone almost the whole period?" Lila asks.

"Or that we're coming back at the exact same time?" Noise in the adjoining hall makes me start, a quick *thump-thump* of footsteps. "She's coming!"

I grab the handle just as the bell rings, then jump back as a stream of students pours through the door. Lila and I disappear into the wave as Ms. Curie, hair standing on end like branches reaching toward the sky, appears in the corridor. Her head swivels, searching, until her dark eyes latch onto mine.

"Canter!" she shouts, pushing kids out of the way. "I need to talk to you."

"I thought you wanted a tour of the school before deciding on our offer," a harried woman with thick gray hair calls. I vaguely remember meeting her on my first day here. She's the director or assistant director. Something like that. It was all kind of a fog. It still is. "If you want to speak to a student about transferring, or whatever it is you're interested in, you'll need to ask his guardian."

"Canter, please!" Ms. Curie ignores the woman, pushing through the crowd until she's right in front of me. "I need to explain."

"Explain it to Myra." My face is hot as my hands tense into fists. "Tell it to Bernard or Hannah or Bin-ro."

"Wait!" Ms. Curie reaches for me, but I dart away.

"Really!" the administration woman huffs. "The boy clearly doesn't want to speak with you, and without permission—"

I don't wait to hear the rest.

Later that night, Lila and I lounge on the roof, discussing Ms. Curie's sudden appearance. Unfortunately, we're not the only ones.

"So what's the story?" Eli asks, plopping down next to us, still cradling his stun launcher. "Why do we hate her?"

I lean my head back against the wall and close my eyes. "Will you promise to leave us alone if we tell you?"

"Sure, I promise," he chirps.

I raise my eyebrows. "Seriously?"

"Yes!" Eli grins. "But you should also know that I'm a liar."

I groan.

"Oh, tell him," Lila says, barely able to get out the words, she's laughing so hard. "What does it matter, anyway?"

I sigh loudly.

"At least tell him the short, little-kid version."

He glowers. "Little kids don't invent interstellar stun launchers. Give me the real version."

"She used to be our teacher," I say flatly. "And she was my mom's best friend. But she betrayed her, betrayed us, betrayed our friends . . ." I rub at my neck, as if trying to loosen something that's choking me.

"Bad things happened," Lila finishes.

"To who?" Eli asks, eyes wide.

"All of them," I say. "All of us."

"Ms. Curie deserves way worse than a stun launch," Eli finally replies, frowning.

"How'd you get that to work, anyway?" I ask, relieved to change the subject. "I thought she would've traced it to you."

"I scramble the signal so it doesn't go right to the target," Eli explains, flipping open a panel. "The wave of energy homes in on the mark, but it takes a roundabout route, so it can't be traced."

"How'd you manipulate the sensors like that?" I ask, leaning over to look at the device's innards. A complicated circuit panel gleams back at me.

Eli shrugs. "I just fiddled with it until it did what I wanted."

"Yeah, but *how*," I press. "That's really complicated electrical programming."

"It wasn't *that* hard," says Eli, rolling his eyes.

I furrow my brow. "Are you sure you don't have a Creer?"

"Nope!" he says proudly.

"Don't you want one?" Lila asks. "It seems like you should be talented enough to develop Tekkie powers, or even Elector."

"And then I'd have to let magic have all the fun?" Eli scoffs. "No thanks." He studies us. "Do you wish you had Creers?"

Lila and I exchange a glance. *How much should we reveal?* But really, who's he going to tell? Who'd even believe him?

"We did have Creers," I say quietly.

"I was a Mender," Lila offers. "Well, a Mender student, anyway. Canter was an . . . Elector." I smile and she winks.

Eli's mouth falls open, though he quickly snaps it shut. "What happened?"

"A bad man took our magic away," I say.

"Does he work with that lady from school?"

"It turns out she works *for* him," Lila replies. "We didn't know."

"I didn't realize people could take away magic," Eli says quietly.

Lila sighs. "The Governing Council has been doing it to Reps for centuries."

Not just the Reps, I almost add, but bite my tongue.

Eli's head snaps up. "I've always wondered why Reps don't have magic."

"Most people don't think about Reps at all," I say, eyeing him with new curiosity.

He glowers. "I do. Most of my friends are Reps. I'd rather hang out with them than the kids in my class. Carmen works here in the apartment building's maintenance department. Well, she used to. I haven't seen her in a while. Or the Reps that work at the school. It's like they all just vanished."

Lila's eyes widen. Could Perennial's team have succeeded in flipping the switch? Have the Reps abandoned their posts because they found their magic?

Eli looks back and forth between us. "What aren't you saying?"

Lila and I hold a silent conversation. Or, more accurately, a silent argument. In the end, after lots of glares, huffs, eye rolls, and sighs, Lila's victorious. She quickly tells Eli about what happened with the Reps last year.

When she finishes, he leans back against the wall, staring up at the stars.

"Why do we even have Reps, anyway? Why can't people just do whatever jobs they want?"

"I think it started because there were jobs people didn't want to do," Lila says slowly. "Those became the jobs Reps were designated when they signed on to the program."

Eli shakes his head. "That's not true! Carmen liked her job. She used to say she was fighting an ongoing war with the building's main generator. It breaks a lot, but she always fixes it. Sometimes she'd let me help her wage her battle—that's what she called it—and we would defeat it together."

I take a deep breath. "But not everyone—"

"And Eleanor, in the cafeteria at school, always told me that the best part of her day was coming up with the ingredients for the students' lunch. She said she had her own cooking magic."

A chill runs through me, followed quickly by burning rage as I remember someone else with cooking magic, but Eli plows on.

"I bet lots of people would still want those jobs, magic or not. It's not fair to force them."

"We agree with you," Lila says, putting a hand on his shoulder. "That's what Perennial was trying to change. But to get there, she needed to free their magic, if they have any."

"If they *want* any," he corrects.

I still don't understand why someone wouldn't want magic, but it's not worth arguing about. "Even if they don't," I say, "the Governing Council shouldn't be able to take someone's magic away."

"So, was this bad guy who took your magic on the Governing Council?" Eli asks.

"He was," Lila answers. "He's not anymore, but he still has a lot of power. Too much power."

"He runs the galaxy's food supply company," I explain.

"He's in charge of MFI?" Eli frowns. "I used to help Eleanor unpack the boxes from them sometimes. Ever since they changed the food, she hasn't needed me as often. Before she disappeared, I mean."

"Jake Melfin's good at making people disappear," I whisper.

Lightning flickers in the distance. A storm approaching.

Lila shoots me a warning glare, then nods at the clouds. "I don't think I'll ever get used to the storms here. They're so beautiful. We don't have any weather on the Moon."

"That's not true," Eli argues. "The Moon has solar winds. You just can't feel them like wind here."

The kid keeps talking, but I'm barely listening as another flash lights the night, reflecting on the water and illuminating the rows and rows of clouds rolling like upside-down hills across the sky. I close my eyes, willing myself to feel the pulse of energy in the air. But there's nothing.

Eli leans forward, waving his hand in front of my face.

"Hello! Venus to Canter. What do you mean Jake Melfin can make people disappear?"

Lila bites her lip. "Canter just meant he doesn't feel like himself without his magic."

"If we find this group, they'll know how to get you your magic back, too, right?" Eli asks, his hair ruffling in the sudden breeze.

Lila gives him a small, sad smile. "That's the idea. We've got to find them first."

"And do it without Melfin also finding them. Or realizing what we're up to."

Eli shrugs. "He already took your magic. What else could he do?"

Lila and I are both silent, but I'm sure we're thinking the same thing. The black-covered book. The list of names and the Creer that Lila quickly read out. Or, more accurately, *Creers*.

"Plenty," I say, thunder booming overhead as rain starts to fall.

CHAPTER EIGHT

MYRA

"WHAT'S GOING ON?" HANNAH DEMANDS AS I TURN to face them. "Can you get us out of here?"

I place my hands on the inner walls of the tree trunk, calling my magic to me. Nothing happens. "Fiona must have done something to keep us from getting out."

"Why?" Bernard asks. "What's happening?"

"We're under attack." I pound my hands on the unresponsive wood. It might as well be made of metal.

"By who?" Hannah asks.

"She said the Botans weren't the only Creers left behind when everyone evacuated."

Hannah's mouth falls open.

I turn to Bernard. "Do you remember any other Creers when your original was on the Old World?"

He squeezes his eyes shut, searching his memory.

"Is it magic related to water?" Hannah asks as rain roars outside.

"It's not just water." As if proving my point, the room suddenly blazes with light, then dims, and an instant later a boom shakes the floor. "It's a storm."

"Meteorons." Bernard's eyes fly open. "They controlled the weather."

A chill runs through me. "And they're still here."

Shouts echo outside, cutting through blasts, bangs, and booms of thunder so frequent, they sound like a giant's beating heart.

"It doesn't seem like the two groups get along," says Hannah.

"We've got to get out of here. We could help." I refocus my efforts on the wall.

"If your Botan magic won't work, maybe we can use my gardening skills," Bernard suggests. He heads to the kitchen, opens a drawer, and pulls out a handful of knives, then hands us each one.

Hannah's skeptical as she accepts hers. "What are these for?"

"Pruning," he says, his eyes glinting.

We scale the walls, using furniture and then the natural footholds in the wood until we reach the roof. Bernard points out good places where we might be able to carve out an exit. Branches that could be removed without endangering the tree. With the three of us working together, it doesn't take long to cut away a section large enough to squeeze through.

When we emerge into the branches, it looks like we've entered an underworld. The sky's inky black. Plumes of dust and grit swallow everything in their path. Spouts of water erupt from the dirt, blasting away everything within twenty feet.

On the ground below us, a battle rages. Emerald-and-gold mist cloaks the combatants, periodically pierced by thorny vines and sharp branches, before melting back in on itself. A blond-haired woman, possibly Ava, whirls a lasso of green over her head and snaps it around someone a few yards away. The man crashes down, and the ice he was clutching when he fell whizzes by her ear.

Fiona's amber hair cuts a red streak through the battle. She's everywhere and nowhere. Lethal-looking plants trail her. One creeps at her side, its roots digging a narrow defensive trench, its oversized bloom snapping at anything that comes within a few feet of her. I think I even see thorns like teeth lining its petals.

And though the Botans seem to be fighting well, they're still outnumbered. Charlie duels with a woman in black directly beneath us. She dodges a flower's barb-filled snap before sending a bolt of lightning at him. While Charlie darts out of the way in time, the bush beside him isn't so lucky. It bursts into flames, which spread rapidly around him, eating up the tall grass and trapping him inside. All too soon, the plant life is gone, and with it, Charlie's magic.

"We've got to help him!" I'm already shimmying down the trunk when Hannah grabs my sleeve.

"How?" she snaps. "You're barely trained, and you have about twice as much practice as me or Bernard."

"I don't care!" I yank my arm away, and we both nearly topple out of the canopy. Hannah hugs the trunk, steadying herself, while I grab onto a branch and then continue my descent.

"Myra, stop!" she yells. A pang twists in my chest as I think of Canter. He would've raced me to the bottom.

I drop to the ground, jumping when a thud sounds behind me. It's just Bernard. Hannah climbs slowly after him, glowering at me, but I'll deal with that later.

I run toward Charlie. The blue flames leap higher and higher. If I can summon some plants near him, I'm sure he can harness enough magic from them to break free. But what could reach?

I close my eyes and imagine one of my favorite trees, a weeping willow. We had one in the original moongarden, and I always loved sitting beneath its drooping branches. I let the memory fuel me, my love for the tree blooming in my chest. The ground shakes, and a thick trunk erupts beside me, its leaves propelling up to the sky, then spilling toward the ground like rain frozen midair, hovering over the ring of fire.

Startled, the woman glances my way. It's just the distraction Charlie needs. The branches surge until they've smothered the flames, and he leaps up from the charred ground, wielding a staff made of wood and greenery. Vines slither toward the woman like snakes. She shrieks and scuttles back.

But Bernard is there. A neat row of bushes sprouts up in her path, and she tumbles over them.

With another flick of his staff, Charlie has her tied up.

I turn my attention back to Fiona, who's battling two Meteorons alongside Avon. The black-clad pair hurl balls of ice, but Fiona and Avon manage to dodge them all. One of the Meteorons, a silver-haired woman, drops to the ground. A deafening crack echoes through the air, but this time it isn't from the sky. Ice consumes the earth beneath our feet, making it shake and shudder, then crack. A chasm yawns open, separating Avon from Fiona.

In no time, they've constructed a bridge of leaves. Avon races across as Fiona lifts a fist, and the grass the Meteorons stand in shoots up, swallowing them. Avon twists his wrist, and the blades braid together, forming a cage.

As Fiona catches sight of us, her eyes go wide. "Get back inside!" she shouts over the still-raging storm.

A hand claws its way through the woven grass, sparks flickering between the fingers.

"Watch out!" I scream, trying to summon whatever Botan magic might block a bolt of lightning, but I'm too late.

Thankfully, Hannah isn't. She throws out both arms, and rocks—tiny pebbles to giant boulders—fly toward Fiona, scattering dirt like snow before piling into a makeshift wall, just as the Meteoron lets her electricity fly.

The gray wall flickers, then goes dark. Fiona glances back at the grass cage, winding more blades together, and the hole vanishes.

The battle seems to be turning. Dark-clad figures run off into the forest, disappearing into the shadows. The storm clouds clear, and I realize I can see the sky again.

A small form dashes by me, not much bigger than I am, her long black hair rippling behind her like a stream. Hannah stiffens, then bursts into a sprint.

"Wait!"

Hannah's feet pound like thunder, but the girl is too far ahead. She slips into the thick foliage.

Hannah skids to a stop, panting. We both know the girl's

gone. The rising Moon reflects in Hannah's dark eyes when she turns back to me. "Did you see?" she asks, clutching her side.

"I think so. I couldn't be sure."

"I am." The shock on her face gives way to determination. "I'd know my sister anywhere. That was Meredith."

CHAPTER NINE

CANTER

THE STORM PETERS OUT AS IT ROLLS IN, UNTIL IT'S just a light mist.

"Do you think that's where the Reps from this building went?" Eli asks, jolting me out of my thoughts. "And our school? To join this Perennial person? Carmen, Eleanor, and the others?"

"It's possible," Lila says. "We know Perennial was recruiting before. Mostly from MFI factories, but her group may have expanded its reach. Or the Reps are joining on their own."

"Sounds like she's building an army," Eli says eagerly. "If you find them, you could join and get your magic back!"

"You don't need to worry about any of that," I reply quickly. "Just forget we said anything about Melfin or

Perennial or any of it. We have no way to track them down, anyway."

Eli is silent again, still gazing into the night sky. Then, all at once, he leaps to his feet.

I calculate how long it'll take me to tackle him if he makes a run for the door.

But he doesn't move. Instead, he grins at us, starlight sparkling in his eyes. "I know how to find them."

"Are you sure you know what you're doing?" I ask, lounging on the floor by the bed frame while Eli types. "There haven't been any new posts since before . . ." I swallow, trying to ignore the dull ache buzzing behind my eyes. "They're not using the same sites to coordinate meetings. Who knows if they're even having meetings anymore."

"I'm not trying to geolocate the posts," Eli explains, his hazel eyes skimming back and forth across the screen. "I'm looking for a fingerprint."

I frown. "My computer's clean. I wiped it down yesterday."

Lila laughs from the bed. "I don't think that's what he meant."

"I'm searching for a device fingerprint from the poster." His eyes meet mine over the top of the screen. "Its unique identifier."

"And what are you going to do with that?"

He looks at me as if he's not sure if I'm joking. Like it's the most obvious thing this side of the sun. "Trace it on the open network. Once I find its signal, I can do a search and see when it was last online and track them from there."

I gape at him, trying to decide if he's delusional, or thinks I am. "That's impossible."

He cocks his head to the side. "Why?"

"I've taken a few Tekkie classes," I say, sitting up straighter. "I've never heard of anyone tracking down a user on the open network using their footprint."

"Fingerprint." Eli shrugs. "I've done it before."

"Why?" Lila asks, leaning forward to peer over his shoulder.

"When the food shortages started, there was this one delivery company that still had the old food," Eli explains, focused on the screen. "Everyone was hounding the delivery shuttle, so the pilot only made deliveries late at night. As soon as anyone heard he'd made a drop, the food was gone like that!" Eli snaps. "So I tracked down his personal device's fingerprint and traced him on the network."

Lila laughs. "And got the last of the food?"

"I could see his route and figure out where he was going. I know a lot of shortcuts. He'd land, and I'd already be waiting. He used to ask me how I always knew where he'd be, and I told him it was magic." Eli stops scanning and taps a few keys. "Got them."

Lila and I slide over to sit beside him. Lines and lines of complicated computer code fill his screen. He taps a cluster of random letters and numbers. "That's them. Now I can trace it." His tongue sticks out from the corner of his mouth as he taps a few more keys, scans, taps some more, then gives a whoop. "The posts are coming from an apartment building on the River of Monet."

Lila frowns. "That's where the Rep facility is."

"It's a huge river," I remind them. "How do we get there? Aquaxi?"

Eli hops up. "I'll order one."

I'm about to argue. Tell him he can't come. It could be dangerous, and I'm still not sure why we're letting him tag along at all. I glance back at the row of characters that are apparently Perennial's fingerprint. Maybe having him around isn't the worst thing.

I pick up my backpack, my arm sagging under the weight.

"Why do you always lug that old robot around?" Eli asks.

Scratch that. The kid isn't coming. I open my mouth to tell him so, but Lila cuts me off.

"That's Bin-ro," she says, her voice wobbling. "He was the best robot friend you could ask for. The bad people broke him, but we're hoping we can fix him someday."

Eli's eyes light up. "Can I try?"

"No," I snap.

"Maybe—" Lila begins, but I shoot her a glare and she sighs. "It's kind of a personal project."

Eli shifts his weight from foot to foot, studying my bulging pack, obviously itching to start tinkering. "It's my fault he's broken," I say quietly. "If anyone's going to put him back together, it has to be me."

Lila opens her mouth to argue, but I swing the bag over my shoulder and head outside first.

We take the aquaxi to the coordinates Eli identified. Compared to the apartments I've seen on Venus—Hannah's and ours—these look like a palace. Sleek, sloped walls curve up from a raised platform that looks like it was chiseled from marble. On the higher levels, balconies with transparent floors jut out over the river. It must look like you're standing right over the water.

"These must cost a Jupiter Jackpot," Lila murmurs as we climb out of the aquaxi.

"It's definitely an upgrade," I agree.

"They're some of the nicest apartments on Venus," Eli tells us. "The only ones nicer are on the Sea of da Vinci. Your contact must be doing pretty well."

"Good," I say. "But how do we find her? Just start knocking on doors?"

"I can't trace her much closer than this," Eli replies, pulling out his computer and double-checking the reading. "She's definitely here, though."

We cross the shimmering white platform. Someone's coming through the door. Lila stops midstride. I look from her back to the door. Boiling rage simmers in my veins, and my hands immediately ball into fists. "You."

Noah holds his hands up and takes a step back. But I don't want him to surrender. Not until I make him. Not until he's begging for mercy.

"Canter, Lila. Please. Just hear me out."

"I'm not listening to a word you say," Lila says, her voice like ice underpinned with steel. Noah flinches as she walks toward him, but she just keeps going, passing through the door, which is still propped open. "C'mon," she barks.

Eli scurries after her, but I haven't moved. It's all I can do not to lunge at Noah right now. Throw him against the building or toss him into the river. After everything he's done, he deserves that and much, much more.

"Canter, come on!" Lila calls.

"She's not in there," Noah says quietly.

"What did you say?" I ask, stepping closer.

Lila freezes, her eyes like dark storm clouds. "What are you talking about?"

"Perennial. She's not here."

I blink. "How did you—"

"I changed the fingerprint in the code," Noah says in a rush. "I thought after what happened . . . I heard from . . . Well, never mind. That's not important. I knew you'd want to find her. I guessed you might go digging in the code from the meeting posts for clues, so I . . . I changed the fingerprint to match my device."

"Interstellar idea," Eli says breathlessly.

"You baited us here?" I ask, closing the distance between Noah and me like a meteor being sucked in by gravity.

"I needed to talk to you," he says, backing up another step. "I wanted to say I'm sorry."

I sneer. "Sure."

"And I want to help you with . . . with whatever you need." He studies his feet. "I work at MFI now. Maybe I could, I don't know, pass you information. Spy on the operations and Mr. Melfin."

"Like we would ever trust you," Lila says, stalking toward him. "After what you did to us. To Perennial's group. To Myra."

Noah winces, and Lila snags the collar of his shirt. "Don't do that," she says, her voice a deadly whisper. "Don't act like you cared about her. It's your fault she's . . . she's . . ." Tears slide down her cheeks as the words die in her throat.

"Don't even say her name," I finish, the fire in my blood chilling to ice.

"I didn't mean for any of it to happen," Noah pleads.

"I swear I didn't. I want to make up for it. Or try to. I know I can never—I can't ever take it back." He looks between us. "Please. Just let me try."

Lila drops his collar and turns away. "No."

I follow her back to the aquaxi. Eli trails behind us like a sad puppy. Another transport has pulled up behind ours. The door swings open and out steps another familiar face. I whirl back around to Noah.

"You rotten, slimy piece of space junk!" I'm frozen on the platform, stuck between two of the last people in the universe I want to see. "This whole thing was a trap."

"Canter, what—" Lila peers past me and freezes, the color draining from her face as Ms. Curie glides away from the second aquaxi, straight toward us.

CHAPTER TEN

MYRA

"I TOLD YOU KIDS TO STAY INSIDE." FIONA'S EYES blaze like bonfires as she stalks toward us, wiping sweat from her brow with the back of her hand. "You could have been killed!"

"You should have told us about them." I plant my hands on my hips. "They're Meteorons, aren't they?"

"There wasn't time," Charlie says, limping over. "We were going to explain on the journey home. Still, I have to admit"—he flashes us a crooked smile—"I can't really complain about you jumping into the fray."

Fiona's gaze rakes over the scorch marks on his pant leg. "What happened? We need to get you burn ointment."

"It's not urgent. Let's just say these kids got me out of the hot spot."

"My sister is with them," Hannah blurts out. "Does she have Botan *and* Meteoron magic?"

"She doesn't have either," Fiona answers, the fire in her eyes cooling to embers. "She didn't have any magic we could trace. That's why she left."

"What do you mean?" Hannah asks. "She was exiled here. She grew plants. I saw them!"

"Just because someone has a talent for plants doesn't necessarily mean they have Botan magic," Charlie says gently.

Hannah shakes her head so hard her hair swings like a pendulum. "No, that's impossible. She has magic! She was exiled for having Botan magic."

"She was exiled for *growing plants*," Fiona replies grimly. "There are people here who were sent for having seeds."

Hannah sets her jaw and crosses her arms. I know that look. She's done arguing, but she's not convinced. She's just given up on convincing you.

"So, she joined the Meteorons?" Bernard asks. "Why did she leave your group?"

"She . . . she was frustrated with us," Charlie begins. "She was determined to develop magic. We told her she could contribute to the community in other ways—but she was sure we were holding back Botan magic from her purposely. That we were refusing to teach her."

"Were you?" Hannah asks, her voice tight.

"Of course not," Fiona says. "One night, she disappeared. I assumed she'd gone to another region, though I couldn't be sure. You saw her, I take it?"

Hannah nods, her lips pressed together in a thin line.

"Why did they attack us?" I ask. "You said they tracked you here. Why?"

"The Botans and the Meteorons have been in conflict ever since the others fled for the Settlements," Charlie explains. "Old hostilities. Old blame bleeding from the past into the present."

Bernard huffs. "What does that mean?"

"The plants weren't the only reason the others left," says Fiona. "The erratic weather patterns, the shifting climate . . ."

"People blamed them for having to leave the Old World," Charlie adds quietly. "Almost as much as they blamed the Botans."

"And as far as we can tell, the battles have continued since then," Fiona says. "Both groups holding grudges."

"What do the Meteorons want?" asks Hannah.

"Our land. Our resources." Charlie shrugs. "Everything we have."

"It's been hundreds of years." I shake my head. "Wouldn't it make sense to unite? To help each other survive?"

"If it didn't happen then, when things were far, far bleaker, it certainly isn't going to happen today," Charlie says, looking tired. "The resentment runs too deep now."

"That's the most ridiculous thing I've ever heard," Hannah snaps. "Get over it already. You're all stuck here. You should figure out how to live together peacefully."

"A couple weeks ago, you thought your sister was locked away," Fiona fires back. "Maybe even dead."

Hannah eyes her suspiciously, then gives the tiniest nod.

"What would you have done if you could have confronted the person who locked her away? Killed her?"

"I'd hunt them down," Hannah whispers.

"You saw the Meteoron attacks," Charlie says, his voice grave. "It's not uncommon for our battles to end with injuries, death. . . ." He looks us each in the eye. "You try convincing our people to shake hands and forgive them. And I promise you, they don't want our forgiveness. They want our blood."

I can't help but wonder why that is. Why the Meteorons hate the Botans so much. They can't be completely innocent in all this. But I don't ask.

The adults aren't interested in fielding more of our questions, anyway. We're shepherded back to our tree, with its new window in the roof. They don't comment on the addition.

We're ordered to sleep. Bernard drifts off almost instantly, but Hannah is restless. I can hear her tossing and turning.

"Hey."

"Yeah?" she says softly.

"Where did Meredith get the seeds?"

Hannah's so quiet, I think she must have fallen asleep. "Remember our neighbor, Ms. Claudette?"

I nod, even though Hannah can't see me. "The old lady with the dog?"

"Yeah. She invited Meredith over for tea one day. It was around when she took her Creer test—she was upset she didn't have any magic indicators. Meredith didn't tell me what they talked about, but she came home with the green box."

I sit up. "Was Ms. Claudette a Botan?"

"I don't know," Hannah says. "Meredith didn't do anything with the seeds for a long time. I didn't even know she had them until years later, when she decided to see if she could get them to grow." Hannah pauses. "You know the rest."

I don't say anything else, and neither does Hannah. After a few minutes, her breathing is as soft and even as Bernard's.

I lie back and stare at the ceiling, through the hole we carved, and up into the small square of night sky. By chance, the Moon is just visible through the opening, glowing silvery white next to a swarm of twinkling stars. I gaze up at my old home—the one I never thought I would miss in a million light-years—and wonder what my parents are doing. They must think I'm dead. Dust. Star vapor. I think back to my last confrontation with Jake Melfin. How he threatened my parents. Hinted he'd take their Creers from them.

I shudder, pulling the blanket up to my chin.

He can't, I tell myself. My father's on the Governing Council. My mother's a prominent teacher at Lunar University. People would notice if their magic suddenly disappeared. It would be suspicious, and Melfin wouldn't want that. No, he was just trying to torment me.

Unfortunately, it's working.

The next morning, we set off for the Coastal Region. Without trained Tekkies or Electors to build transportation systems, I expect to be walking, but the Botans have rigged up an alternative, a contraption that looks like two couches strapped to oversized wheels.

Hannah raises an eyebrow. "What the meteor is that? Is there even a motor?"

"It's a PPV. A plant-powered vehicle," Charlie says with a wink. "Hop on."

After a brief but surprisingly sad goodbye with Avon

and Ava, we settle ourselves onto the cushions in the back row. Charlie and Fiona take the front. And then we wait.

"Uh, do we need to get out and push?" I ask.

Charlie laughs. "No, but you can add your magic to get us there faster if you want," he says, flicking his fingers.

At the same time, Fiona gives a low whistle, and the wheels start turning slowly.

Hannah, Bernard, and I lean over the sides, trying to spot what's propelling us forward, but there's nothing. And then I notice the movement, or maybe I sense the magic in the air, or both.

The grass ripples behind us, like the wake behind a boat. At first, I think it must be the ground cover being compressed by the wheels and then springing up again, but when I look closer, the grass seems to be moving before the wheels touch it, tucking down and springing back up.

We accelerate—I'm sure of it. Eventually, we meet a stream, and before I can ask how we'll maneuver over it, the plants show me. Just like the cage Fiona built around the Meteorons, the grasses stretch into the weeds, which weave together to form a thick bridge. The car rolls over and continues on.

When the sun is directly overhead, Charlie raises his hand, the cart slows to a stop, and we all jump out to stretch our legs and eat some of the nuts growing on nearby trees. Fiona wanders deeper into the grove and

I follow, awed as she waves her hand and fruits in a riot of color burst from the tangle of branches. She plucks a fluorescent-green apple and takes a bite.

"I used to love the apple trees in the moongarden," I say, moving closer. She doesn't startle or even turn toward me. "Those were all different shades of red, though. There weren't any like these."

"Didn't have seeds for that variety," she says. "And I didn't know how to evolve the seeds with my Botan magic back then."

My eyes widen. "You can modify seeds with magic? How? That would be—"

She turns, her blue eyes cold as she studies me. "I thought I already told you that I'm no teacher."

I take a step back. "Sorry, I . . ." I have no idea what I'm sorry for or what I could have done to make her look at me this way.

She sighs, and some of the anger leaches away, but not all of it. "I came out here to be alone."

My stomach swoops and I retreat another step. "I didn't know."

"Clearly."

"I just . . . I wanted to get to know you," I blurt out. "I've thought about you so much. Ever since I found your pendant—"

"What pendant?"

"I found your old pendant in the moongarden," I say quickly. "That's how I figured out it was your garden."

Her gaze drifts to the sky. "I left it there the day I found out the Governing Council knew about me. Sandra came to tell me they were on their way, and I rushed out to find Robert." Her eyes flutter shut.

"So that was the last time you were there?"

She nods, her eyes still closed.

"How did Ms. Curie know?"

When Fiona meets my gaze again, her eyes are colder than the core of Neptune. "Not only do I have to deal with Charlie's incessant chattering while we travel, but apparently I also have to endure your endless questions when we stop?"

"I thought Charlie was your friend."

She laughs bitterly as she stalks past me. "I haven't had a friend since I left the Moon."

Hours later, the sun's beginning to set, sending streaks across the sky like paint. The cart slowly rolls to a stop, and we start to make camp.

"We'll reach the coast by tomorrow," Charlie says. "Get some sleep. We leave at first light."

He joins Fiona in putting up their tents. I turn to ours, ready to crawl inside and sleep, when I sense movement from the corner of my eye. The sun's below the trees and the sky's quickly fading to gray. The woods alongside us are already pitch-black, but something's moving along the tree line. Bernard sees it, too. He nudges me and nods toward the shadows, one of which has stepped out from behind a dead trunk.

"Hannah," I whisper. She turns and follows my gaze.

Meredith stands at the edge of the forest. She beckons to us once, then disappears into the darkness.

CHAPTER ELEVEN

CANTER

"WHAT?" NOAH'S HEAD SWIVELS BETWEEN US AND the second aquaxi, his gaze raking over Ms. Curie. "I didn't do anything. I don't even know who that is!"

"Sure you don't." I lunge forward, my right hand balling into a fist. He winces as I haul my arm back, but I don't swing. I can't.

Lila clutches my wrist. "Wait, Canter," she says. "Look."

If it were anyone but Lila, I would rip my arm away. I turn and follow where she's pointing. Ms. Curie's not alone. My mouth falls open as Ms. Goble climbs out of the aquaxi, and then Myra's mother.

"Mrs. Hodger?" Lila takes in the trio, her eyes wide. "Ms. Goble, what are you—how did you find us?"

"She tracked us," I say. Only a talented Elector could

have pulled it off. "You planted a transmitter on me at the school, didn't you?"

Ms. Curie beams like I just answered a question correctly in class, and it makes me want to summon all the electricity in the universe and send it crashing into her. My hands shake with magic that won't come. "Clever, as always, Mr. Weathers," she says, her dark hair falling across darker eyes. "I knew it would be difficult to speak to you, even if the school administration was agreeable, so I had a contingency plan." She nods at my feet.

I look down and immediately zero in on it, a speck of metal glinting from the top of my shoe. Without a word, I lean over and pluck it off, placing it carefully on the ground, and then grind it into dust with my heel. "I think you're going to find that it's still difficult," I growl.

"Canter, we need you to listen," Ms. Goble says, her voice stern but her eyes kind. "We have news to—"

"So you're working with her, too," I cut in. "Old friends reunited."

"We were never at odds," Ms. Curie says evenly.

"Oh, I get it. You've been coordinating with your old pal Melfin all along." I jut my chin toward Noah, who's still hovering at the edge of the group, unsure what to say or do. "Maybe you even work for MFI, like him."

Ms. Goble frowns. "That's not—"

"I don't care what it is!" I'm yelling even though I know I shouldn't be. Really, why should I care? I don't have anything left to lose. "I just know I don't want anything to do with you," I say, glaring at Ms. Curie. "Or you," I add, pivoting to face Ms. Goble. "Not if you're helping her."

"And what about me?" Mrs. Hodger asks quietly.

"Why are you with them?" Lila asks, her voice soft, disbelief etched across her features. "How can you be helping them? After what she did . . . after what happened to . . ." Tears glint in her eyes. I reach out and squeeze her arm.

"That's what we wanted to talk to you about," Mrs. Hodger says. "Please. Five minutes. That's all I ask. For me. For Myra. I promise, you won't regret it."

I turn to Lila and see the same questions that are ricocheting around my mind reflected on her face. "We can't say no," she whispers.

My silence is enough of an answer. Ms. Goble lets out a sigh of relief.

Mrs. Hodger smiles. "We'll make it quick." Her eyes flick to the unfamiliar faces behind us. "Can we trust . . ." she asks, gesturing to the others.

"No," I bark, pointing at Noah. His face falls. "He's fine, I guess," I add, patting Eli on the shoulder. The way the kid swells with pride, you'd have thought I'd declared him Emperor of the Universe.

Noah looks like he wants to argue again, but he slinks

away instead. I wait until the apartment building's entry shuts behind him before turning back to the adults. "Five minutes."

What feels like hours later, I sink to the ground, dropping my head into my hands. "So you're telling me that Myra, Hannah, and Bernard are alive . . . My mother's alive, and they're all living happily ever after on the Old World."

"I don't know about happily ever after," Ms. Curie says. "And we haven't been able to confirm that the shuttle landed intact. But assuming everything went smoothly, yes, that's all true."

If someone had told me yesterday that I'd find out everyone I'd thought was dead and gone—space dust—was actually alive, I'd have done cartwheels. I'd have whooped louder than if I'd won a million hoverball championships. Relief and joy would have flooded through me and carried me away like zero gravity.

Right now, I just feel sick.

I lurch to my feet, hurtle toward the aquaxis, and heave into the water.

Lila's there in an instant, patting my back as I wipe my mouth, and then my eyes.

The rest of the group edges toward me, like I might be contagious.

Lila simmers with anger when she breaks the silence.

"The entire goal was for Canter to be exiled? You wanted *him* to be on that shuttle."

"It was only supposed to be Canter and me," Ms. Curie protests. "It's what Fiona wanted, and I would have thought it was what he wanted as well."

She's not wrong. Would I have chosen exile if it meant seeing my mom again? Maybe. It's hard to say now. Hard to rewind the events of the last few weeks—months. My life's taken too many twists and turns to unravel them all.

"You should have told me," I say to Ms. Curie, my voice low. "You should have given me the option."

"You might be right." Shame flashes in her eyes for the first time. "It's too late to consider *what-ifs*. All we have is *what do we do next*."

"You approve of all this?" Lila asks Ms. Goble, then turns to Mrs. Hodger. "And you?"

"I don't know about *approve*," Ms. Goble replies, "but the gravity is out of the enclosure, and there's no going back. Only forward."

"And moving forward means getting my daughter back," Mrs. Hodger adds, clenching her hands into fists at her sides. "That's all I care about. Maybe someday I'll have the luxury of reflecting on how we could have done things differently, but now my only focus is Myra."

I swallow, forcing down another wave of nausea. "What's the plan? How do we get to them?"

"The next communication window is in a couple days," Ms. Curie explains. "First we need to make sure everyone arrived safely. Then we can figure out our next move."

"How often can we communicate with them?" Lila asks.

"It depends on the time of year," Ms. Curie says. "Generally, at least once a month."

Eli frowns. "Why don't you just bounce the signal off the other unused satellites? The charge could activate the lingering battery power enough to transmit a signal." He rattles off some formulas and theories, and Ms. Curie raises her eyebrows, studying the kid through narrowed eyes.

"Can they repair the shuttle they landed in?" Lila asks. "Between you and Canter, I bet you could give them enough instructions to do it."

"And me!" Eli pipes up.

"Their shuttle was pretty fried," Ms. Curie says. "The warden's crew directed it from the ground. But"—her expression glazes as an idea forms—"if we could crash a working shuttle on the surface, so long as it's not too heavily damaged, that might work."

"How would we keep it from being completely useless?" I ask.

Ms. Curie shrugs. "Crash it into the ocean. Your mother's community is on the coast. They could retrieve it and possibly repair it."

"Okay, say that works," I reply. "Where would we get a

shuttle to crash in the first place? And how could we send one that far off course? Nothing flies to the Old World."

"MFI food shuttles from Venus fly past on their way to the Moon," Lila muses. "I bet it wouldn't take much to get one near the Old World's atmosphere."

Ms. Goble shuts her eyes, and misty numbers stream from her temple.

"That could work," Mrs. Hodger says, grimacing as she studies the formulas drifting through the air. "The calculations aren't astronomical. If they were, I wouldn't be able to . . ." She sighs, and it's only then I realize I haven't seen any hazy numbers drifting from her, and I know she's suffered the same fate as us. Her sadness melts away, replaced by determination. "We could do it."

"We still need a shuttle," Ms. Goble reminds us. "Commandeering one from MFI will be no small feat."

I glance toward the apartment building, and the door Noah disappeared through, then curse under my breath. "I might know someone who can help."

CHAPTER TWELVE

MYRA

AS SOON AS I STEP INTO THE FOREST, I WONDER IF this was a mistake. There's no sign of Meredith, though the shadows seem to bend and stretch around me, like something alive.

I call on my magic. My fingers, then hands, then arms tingle, warmth flooding through me, and the trees glow like jewels. I can feel them beside me, their leaves and branches stretching out, protecting me, their roots reaching through the dirt deep below my feet, grounding me. I take a breath and hurry after Hannah.

Bernard trails behind us, uneasy.

"Reach for the trees," I whisper. "You'll feel better when you're connected to them."

He takes a breath, and his posture relaxes slightly as he keeps pace.

By now, Hannah's so far ahead, I can hardly see her. "Slow down," I hiss. For a moment, the thought of being lost in the woods makes me stumble, but knowing the plants will guide me home quickly chases away any fear.

I don't know if they can chase away everything that haunts these woods, though.

Up ahead, Hannah stops and scans the surroundings, giving Bernard and me enough time to catch up to her.

"Where'd she go?" I ask.

"She's here," Hannah says, squinting through the trees.

"Is she leading us somewhere?" Bernard asks. "Why doesn't she just come out?"

Hannah frowns. "She must want us away from the camp."

A twig snaps behind us, and we all jump, then turn as one. There, standing between a forked tree and a wilting lilac bush, is Meredith.

A noise, half shriek, half sob, escapes Hannah's chest before she races around the tree. Meredith hugs her sister tightly, burying her face in Hannah's hair.

Bernard and I walk slowly toward them, reluctant to intrude on the reunion but eager to hear whatever Meredith has to say. After a minute, the sisters break apart, both wiping their eyes and grinning. I haven't seen that spark in Hannah's eyes in ages. It's like the clouds clearing to showcase a star-filled sky.

Meredith turns to face me. Without thinking, I take a step forward and clasp my hands together, as if praying at a Worship Center. "I'm so sorry," I whisper. "I never meant for any of this to happen. I didn't think Hannah was telling the truth when she said you had seeds. I'd never have—I wouldn't have ever . . ." The words evaporate like rain on Mercury.

"I don't blame you, Myra," Meredith says, placing a hand on my shoulder. "Being sent here was the best thing that ever happened to me."

Hannah's mouth falls open. "What do you mean?"

"I'm a non-Creer," Meredith says, her voice strong. "I've fought against that idea my entire life. It took meeting the Meteorons for me to realize that it doesn't matter. I don't need magic to have value."

"I—I thought you had plant magic," Hannah stammers. "I heard them muttering about Botan powers when they hurried you off to Mercury. And you got that plant to grow."

"Luck," Meredith answers with a shrug. "Maybe a smidge of talent. But no magic. When I was sent here and found out Botans are still alive . . . I thought my magic would bloom. It never did, and the Botans don't care about anyone who isn't exactly like them."

"That's not true!" I protest.

"Oh, really?" Meredith raises an eyebrow. "And you know this how?"

"They told us they didn't know how to help people with other kinds of magic. They don't have anyone to teach them. But that doesn't mean—"

"They didn't mention helping non-Creers, though, did they?" Meredith waits for me to answer, and when I don't, she nods knowingly. "That's because they think as highly of them down here as they do up there." She waves absently at the stars overhead. "Which is not at all. You're right, though. They respect others with magic, even if they can't help train them. But no spark of magic and you're as worthless as an untrained Rep."

Bernard flinches.

"Reps aren't worthless," I growl.

"I know that. Not everyone does." Meredith glances at Bernard as if seeing him for the first time. "So, what's your story?"

"I'm Bernard," he says, without hesitating. "Former Rep, originally a gardener, but now a newfound Botan."

Meredith's mouth falls open. "A Rep with magic?"

Lava flows through my veins. "He's *Bernard*."

She nods slowly.

"Reps' magic is blocked," Bernard explains. "But a group's found ways around it."

"And they've released Rep magic for everyone?" she asks.

Bernard nods. "We hope so."

"Good." Meredith gives a sharp nod. "Great, actually. It's about time there was a reckoning."

"What are you doing with the Meteorons?" Hannah asks.

"They're much more forward-thinking than the Botans." Meredith's mouth twists into a sneer. "They welcome all to their cause."

Bernard tilts his head. "Which is?"

"The Botans have dominated this planet since everyone else left. Some say they did it on purpose, turned the plants toxic so they could drive everyone away and keep Earth for themselves."

"That's not true!" I snap.

"How do you know, Myra?" Hannah asks carefully.

"Did you know they discovered the *cure* as soon as everyone else evacuated?" Meredith interrupts. "Wasn't that convenient."

"It wasn't convenient." Heat blooms in my neck and cheeks. "It was a miracle. You'd be dead by now if they hadn't. All the Meteorons would, so the Botans must have shared the cure."

"That's beside the point." Meredith turns to Hannah. "It's clear these two are already aligned with the Petal Pushers. But you're no Botan, right?"

Hannah hesitates, then shakes her head. "Tekkie. But I'm not trained."

Meredith beams. "They don't care about that. They'll still help you as best they can. Teach you what they know. Unlike the *Botans*." Her eyes glitter like ice in moonlight. "Come back with me. We could be together again. Share a house. Bicker. Laugh. Be sisters."

Hannah glances over at me. "But what about—"

"We're family," Meredith presses. "She's your friend. Or *was*. Doesn't seem like she was good at even that."

"People make mistakes," I grit out.

"With me, she can have family again."

"What about your parents?" I counter. "The Botans are going to help us get home."

"They promised you that?"

I bite my lip. They didn't really.

Meredith rolls her eyes. "Exactly. And even if they could, they wouldn't. Just like before."

Hannah raises her eyebrows. "Before?"

"What are you talking about?" Bernard asks.

"When the conditions here were deteriorating, the Botans could have told the others it wasn't the Meteorons' fault," Meredith insists. "It was the plants that drove everyone away."

"And the weather," I spit back. "The natural disasters."

"My history texts said it was a combination," Hannah interjects, "but it was the plants that tipped things over."

"The Botans could've taken the blame. It was their fault."

"That's a stretch, Mer," Hannah says, her voice wavering.

"The storms killed people, too," Bernard argues. "And there was famine. And floods. And wildfires. I remember," he says, his blue eyes flashing. "I was there."

"They could've moved inland!" Meredith is raging now, as if she personally suffered the abandonment of hundreds of years ago. "They could have found solutions to the climate problems, but people couldn't breathe the air."

Bernard's cheeks flush red. "That was generations ago. The people involved have been dead for centuries."

"And plants have been banned from the Settlements all that time, but the Settlements have figured out how to deal with storms just fine."

"That's not fair," Bernard argues. "Storms on the Old World are very different from the ones in the Settlements."

"The dust storms on Mars, the solar storms sweeping the galaxy, they all have catastrophic potential." She sneers at Bernard. "Looks like the apple doesn't fall far from the tree. The Botans wouldn't help the Meteorons back then, and they won't help them now."

"Okay, well, what do the Meteorons want?" Hannah asks, glancing between Bernard and her sister.

"In the beginning, they wanted remorse. Now they just want revenge."

CHAPTER THIRTEEN

CANTER

I GO DOOR TO DOOR, KNOCK, WAIT, APOLOGIZE, and move on to the next. I'm on the third floor before a panel slides open, revealing a shocked and slightly disheveled Noah.

"Canter, what—"

I hold up a hand. "How can you prove that we can trust you?"

Noah considers for a few moments before waving me inside.

I hesitate, shifting my heavy backpack, before following him. His apartment's spacious, but only because there's almost no furniture. A small couch rests against one wall, an even smaller table in front of it. Besides a putty lounger in the corner, there's nothing else.

"Do you live here with your parents?" I ask, looking around.

"They come around from time to time," he says, dropping into the lounger and gesturing toward the sofa. "They're mostly traveling."

"For work?" I ask, still standing.

He shrugs. "They used to, but now they're retired."

The phrase makes me flinch. I fight back the memories it triggers.

"They won't be around today. Or this week, for that matter." Noah sits back, but his posture is stiff, rigid. "Have you changed your mind? About letting me help?"

"How are you going to prove that you won't run to Jake Melfin the moment I leave?"

"I can't ever prove to you that you can trust me," Noah says quietly. "I know that. But there must be something you need that I can provide. Otherwise, you wouldn't be here."

I nod. "So what do we do?"

"You won't ever trust me," Noah repeats, "but maybe I can give you something to hold over me. A consequence or—"

"Collateral?"

"Exactly." Noah leans forward, opens a drawer in the table, and pulls out a small device. A recorder. He tosses it to me. "Here."

I catch it, turning it over in my hands. "Is there some kind of confession stored on here?"

"No," Noah says. "But there could be."

I raise my eyebrows.

"I'll record one," he explains. "I'll say everything that happened on Mercury on camera. How MFI's food codes are broken and Melfin covered it up. How he's stealing the magic of his enemies. And using My—er—and how he's using the garden at V.A.M.A. for himself and—"

I almost drop the recorder. "What?"

Noah twists his hands together. "Oh, right. You probably wouldn't know about that."

"Explain."

He tells me how Melfin took over the garden. How he's using it to feed himself, and anyone he needs to manipulate or impress or blackmail. Rage boils through me, and I wish Noah hadn't told me. If it was going to be difficult working with him before, it'll be near impossible now.

"Forget this," I say, tossing the recorder at him.

"Canter, wait!" He leaps up and blocks my way. "I'll say everything I just told you on camera, and more."

"More?"

Noah fidgets. "MFI's expanding."

"I know. We already heard they're opening a new factory." I grimace. "I don't see why, though. Wouldn't they need less space, producing imitation food?"

"It's not just food anymore. They're taking over other industries. Or planning to."

"What do you mean?"

"Paints, dyes, textiles. Even some building materials. Concrete. Plastics. Everything Chemic magic produces, they want in their factories."

My throat is dry when I try to swallow. "The Governing Councils won't allow that."

Noah snorts. "Half of them are already on Melfin's payroll. And the other half will be soon, or they'll find their magic suddenly disappearing."

"Even if you did confess all that on video, what good would it do? If I release it to the media, Melfin will just squash the story. Blow it off, like he did when the food cloning news first broke."

"Probably, but he'll still make it his personal mission to ruin me."

"And?"

"And there's your leverage."

We stare at each other for a few seconds. When I don't say anything, Noah sighs. "Let's just do this, and then you can tell me how I can help."

We record the confession, I send it to my messenger, and then I fill him in on what we need.

Noah paces, deep in thought. "It'll be tricky. I don't usually work in the factories."

"So where *do* you work?" I ask.

He doesn't meet my eyes. "There's a small facility near V.A.M.A. The fruits and vegetables from the garden don't keep that long. Melfin likes me to stay close by so the food I produce is fresh, or in case he needs me to prepare a meal for a meeting . . ."

He must notice my white knuckles and flushed face, because he hyperjumps to a different subject.

"I'm sure I can come up with a reason why I need to go there." Noah considers for another few minutes, then snaps his fingers. "We've been talking about doing deliveries for off-planet partners. I can tell him I want to review the shipping procedures and packing materials to figure out how I can best preserve the food for shipment. And then I can find a shuttle headed to the Lunar Settlement and . . ." He glances at me. "Then what? I'm no Elector, and I definitely don't know enough Elector theory to hijack a shuttle."

I'm no Elector, either. Not anymore. But I know the principles backward and forward. "Can you get me in with you?"

He starts pacing again. "Probably?"

"That doesn't sound too confident."

"Because I'm not confident, but—" He pauses. "It's not like Melfin would accompany me. And no one else is going to recognize you. I don't see why you couldn't just come with me."

"So, you're in? You can do it?"

He looks me in the eye for what I think might be the first time today. Maybe ever. "I'm in. And I *will* do it."

CHAPTER FOURTEEN

MYRA

First Month, 2450

FORTUNATELY, HANNAH DIDN'T GO WITH MEREDITH.

Unfortunately, she hasn't ruled it out, either.

The next morning, we ride in almost complete silence, passing remnants of houses clustered together in neat rows covered in creeping ivy and tangles of daisies and dandelions—an Old World neighborhood, overtaken by the wild garden covering the majority of the planet.

Patches of concrete lie broken and crumbling under grass, and as we pass over an ancient, moss-covered bridge, I spy half-collapsed buildings stretching toward the sky in the distance like heaps of knocked-over toy blocks, their edges sharp against the mounds of honeysuckle, yew, and juniper surrounding them. How much of the deterioration is from years of unchecked growth, and how much is the result of battles between the people left here?

"It's amazing, isn't it?" I ask Hannah. "The power the plants have."

She doesn't answer.

"You're not seriously considering staying here with Meredith, are you?" I finally blurt out.

Hannah whirls around, eyes big like I read her mind. Like it wasn't completely obvious what she's been thinking about all day.

"We've got to focus on getting home," I remind her. "And you should be trying to figure out how to convince her to come with us."

"How do you know I'm not?" she asks, then presses her lips together.

"Because that face is *not* your scheming face. It's your thinking-it-over face."

"What does my scheming face look like?" Hannah asks, snorting.

"Like this." I look down, a sly grin pulling at one corner of my mouth, before I tuck the end of my ponytail between my lips and chew on the strands.

Hannah breaks out in a fit of giggles. Even Bernard chuckles. "I do *not* do that."

"Yes, you do. Especially when you're up to something," I say matter-of-factly. "But your expression the last three hours is the same one you had when Jaxon Peters asked you to go with him to see a vid-stream."

She slaps my arm. "Now I *know* you're lying. I never even considered going with him."

"Nope, you did. And you looked exactly like you do now."

She sighs and slumps back in her seat. "We can agree to disagree about Jaxon," she says, "but I *was* thinking about Meredith. Even if we find a way off planet, what then? We go into hiding? Stress about Melfin finding us for the rest of our lives? No thanks."

"It doesn't have to be that way," Bernard says. "If we can get off planet, so can the other Botans. And if they want, the Meteorons, too. In fact," he adds, leaning forward, "that would be a great olive branch to extend to them from the Botans."

I frown. "Why do they want olives?"

He chuckles. "It's an old expression. It means it could be a way for the Botans to make up for whatever crimes the Meteorons think they committed."

I adjust my glasses. "That's not a bad idea."

Hannah sits up straighter. "And then Meredith would come. It could work!"

I glance toward Charlie and Fiona, seated in the row in front of ours. "We should tell them."

"You should probably wait for the right moment," Bernard suggests. "Don't just yell it across the field."

I snap my mouth shut, blushing, like I wasn't about to do just that. "They're probably still a little upset about the ambush. It'd be better to let things cool down a bit."

"They still might say no," Hannah warns, glancing sideways. "Especially if Meredith is right about them."

"The Botans saved us from being poisoned and from the Meteorons' storms. How are they the villains after one conversation with your sister?"

Hannah rolls her eyes. "She's been here a lot longer than we have. She knows more about the politics of this place than you do." Irritation rushes through me. "Or any of us," she adds quickly before I can snap at her. "Still, maybe she'd come around if the Botans offered to bring some Meteorons off planet with them."

"First we have to figure out how we're getting off planet," Bernard reminds us.

I settle back in my seat. "Let's start brainstorming. Throw out every idea you've got, no matter how wild it is."

Hannah raises an eyebrow. "Shouldn't we think for a bit and come up with something good instead of wasting our time on ideas that probably won't work?"

I shrug. "Sometimes a wacky idea leads to a good one. That's what Canter, Lila, and I would normally do, and it worked for us."

Hannah flinches, then silently stares off into the

distance. Bernard and I bounce ideas back and forth, but she doesn't even glance our way, clearly committed to fully vetting all of her plans before sharing them.

Or maybe she's not thinking of leaving at all.

Later, hours after the sun's crossed the pale blue sky and started to sink back toward the horizon, we arrive at Fiona and Charlie's coastal settlement. I notice the change in the air first. It's heavy and salty, with a hint of something slightly foul, but still pleasantly earthy.

The plants shift, too. The thick forests and lush grass give way to a more muted color palette, as if everything's been coated in a thin layer of taupe dust. The grass is taller and dryer, and the leaves cluster in hardy bunches at the tops of the trees. We crest a hill, and for the first time, I see the ocean.

In some ways, it reminds me of Venus, but in others, it couldn't be more different. On the Morning Star, the sky always had a golden haze, more orange than blue. Here, it's hard to tell where the sky ends and the water begins. If you swam out far enough, maybe you'd fly off into the clouds.

The sand is a stark gash between the green, willowy grass and the deep blue ocean. It's as if someone took a giant eraser and stripped away all color, leaving a beige smudge in between.

The transport turns, and I hop out, stumbling through

the sand, which reminds me of moving through moondust. My feet sink and slide with each step, but unlike the chilled Lunar gravel, this sand is warm. I bend down and scoop up a handful, letting it trickle through my fingers. I expect it to be chalky like on the Moon, but the grains are gritty like microscopic pebbles. I hold my palm up to my eyes, marveling at the variety of colors—umber and copper and gold and tan, even flecks of green that might be glass or some kind of jewel. A treasure that's almost too small to see.

Hannah flops down beside me and leans back, sweeping her arms and legs to create a Hannah-sized trench. Charlie laughs as he and Fiona approach us, watching us take it all in.

Bernard hovers at the layer of wet sand between us and the ocean, watching the waves bring the water closer and closer to his feet. A surge ripples over his shoes and he smiles, turning back to grin at us.

As I join him, I notice the setting sun makes the wet sand glisten like grated gold.

"I never saw the ocean when I lived here," Bernard murmurs when I reach his side. "I was farther inland, in the center of the continent, and my original never came here."

"You saw the sea on Venus," I remind him.

"It was nothing like this."

"Water is water," I say, staring out at the line where

the sky and ocean meet. "But there's something about the waterways on Venus being man-made, and this ocean being here all along before there were even people. It feels different, even if it doesn't look different."

"It looks different," Bernard says. "To me, anyway. I think just knowing how far this ocean stretches—you know it covers most of the planet—makes it seem bigger and stronger. Like nothing could ever conquer it."

I can understand what he means. Waves crest far out toward the horizon, foam spraying in a streak that seems to span the whole beach. A minute later, the ripples create smaller waves that lap over our feet. I know people had boats and water transports that could ride out over them, out into open water, but standing here watching the rise and fall, it seems desperately reckless, like if the waves decided not to let you pass, you'd find yourself stranded on the ocean floor.

Fiona calls to us, and Bernard and I trot back to join her and the others.

"I'd like to take Hannah to meet some of the folks in our settlement," Charlie says, pointing to a nearby hill. "It's in the valley, just past there. We've got some kids who we think have Tekkie tendencies, but we haven't really been able to offer much."

Hannah twists her black hair between her fingers. "I told you. I'm not a trained Tekkie."

"But you've had years more theory than we could ever give them," stresses Charlie. "Maybe by sharing with them, you can coax out more of your own magic."

Hannah shrugs like she's still not convinced, but I see the pride sparkling in her eyes. "I'll give it a try."

"Great." Charlie grins back, motioning her to follow him. "And while they're doing that," he adds, "Fiona can get started with you two."

Bernard and I exchange a hopeful glance. "With what?" I ask.

"Your magic!" he calls over his shoulder before disappearing over the hill.

Eagerness surges through me like a wave as I turn back to Fiona, but she's halfway across the beach, headed in the opposite direction.

I call her name, but she doesn't look back.

CHAPTER FIFTEEN

CANTER

BACK OUTSIDE, I FIND LILA AND ELI PERCHED ON THE hood of the aquaxi, talking to the adults.

"Well?" Mrs. Hodger asks as soon as I'm within earshot.

"He says he can do it," I tell her, setting my bag down. A tiny bit of the tension eases from her shoulders. "He's going to get me into their factory, and I'll hijack the shuttle."

"But how will you, you know . . . ?" Lila asks softly, watching Eli as he tinkers with some small contraption he must have had in his pocket.

Ms. Curie purses her lips. "Melfin didn't steal Canter's brain when he took his Creer. If one of my students can't infiltrate the system of a simple commercial shuttle without the help of magic, then I'm a terrible instructor. And I happen to know that I'm excellent at what I do. Canter will be fine."

Despite my complicated emotions, I can't help feeling a rush of gratitude.

"But it would be even easier if we had our magic back," Lila insists, hope flickering in her brown eyes. "You worked on Perennial's device. Can't you make another one?"

Ms. Curie shakes her head. "I'm a talented Elector, but I'm no Tekkie. I didn't build the device. Just fine-tuned its charge. Our best bet for restoring your magic is locating Perennial's group."

"Have you had any leads?" Mrs. Hodger asks eagerly.

Ms. Goble places a hand on her shoulder. "Nothing substantial enough to trace. All we know is that after they successfully deactivated the Reps' magic-suppressing chips, they evaded capture and disappeared."

"I'm sure they'll be lying low for the foreseeable future," Ms. Curie adds.

"If they deactivated the chips, why do ours still work?" Lila asks, rubbing at her arm. I'm not sure if she's drawn to her Inscriptions or if she thinks the chip might still be lurking there. Or both. Or neither.

"Those were activated afterward," Ms. Goble says gently. "They use a different frequency. The same one they're using as they capture Reps to reactivate their chips."

My heart pounds in my chest in time with the throbbing in my head. "We've got to stop them. Stop Melfin."

Mrs. Hodger shrugs away from Ms. Goble. "Our first priority is getting my daughter back."

"And my mother," I add, my voice harsher than I intend. "And Hannah, and Bernard, and any other Botans who want to leave. As many as we can fit on that shuttle. But then what? Even if we get them off planet, they'd have to go into hiding. The Governing Councils will just hunt them down again. Send them back, or worse." I shift my gaze from adult to adult. "What happens next? This can't keep going on the way it has."

"It won't." Ms. Curie's eyes flash, and for a moment I see my own rage reflected there.

"What do you mean?" Lila asks, then inhales sharply. "Eli! Don't touch that!"

I follow her gaze, then reach down and snatch my backpack from his lap. The remains of Bin-ro are halfway out of the bag and nearly tumble to the ground. I quickly settle the robot back inside. "What do you think you're doing?"

"I can fix him!" Eli insists. "I noticed his processor is still mostly intact. A little fried, but I could—"

"No, you can't!" I know I'm overreacting—no actual harm was done—but I can't stop myself. "No one asked you. You don't even have magic! You've *never* had magic! If I can't fix him, then you definitely can't."

Eli opens his mouth and closes it, his cheeks pink and his eyes glassy.

Regret rushes through me. "I'm sorry I—"

He pushes past me and into the aquaxi and the door whizzes shut behind him.

I wish a wave would come and wash me into the sea.

After a few awkward moments, Lila clears her throat. "So, what happens after we rescue Myra, Fiona, and the others?"

Ms. Curie tears her gaze away from the transport. "We fight."

"Who's we?" Mrs. Hodger asks. "Half of us don't have magic to fight with."

Ms. Goble clicks her tongue. "Magic isn't everything."

"Easy for you to say, Val," Mrs. Hodger snaps.

Ms. Goble shrugs, unfazed. "So many people never had magic, like that clever boy." She nods toward where Eli disappeared, and my cheeks warm.

"Isn't that the point?" Ms. Curie adds. "The nonmagical have always outnumbered those with Creers, but somehow we've managed to position ourselves at the top of the pyramid."

Mrs. Hodger sniffs. "Because we're the most skilled. It's not unjust. It's just reality."

"But it doesn't mean people with Creers have more talent," Ms. Goble argues.

"Or that they're more valuable," Lila adds. "I can't imagine a Creer who could do what my dad does. He's building structures right into the ice on Neptune. What magic can do that?"

"Tekkies, for one," Mrs. Hodger says.

Lila shakes her head. "They designed it, but it's my dad's team that's actually building it. Sure, some Tekkies help. But the really intricate things need to be done by hand. My dad says you have to feel the materials to properly maneuver them, and that magic can get in the way."

"That's not proven theory," Mrs. Hodger snaps. "But we're getting off track. How did we get onto this subject, anyway? I thought we were talking about what to do about Melfin."

"Which is exactly what we were discussing," Ms. Curie says. "And you've just proven my point perfectly, Claire."

Mrs. Hodger raises her eyebrows, clearly torn between being pleased at scoring the winning point in the argument and wondering if it was for the side she wanted to claim victory for. "Care to elaborate?"

"Your attitude toward non-Creers is exactly the same as most people with magic."

"I never—"

"And I would wager a Jupiter Jackpot the non-Creers are tired of it," Ms. Curie continues. "Most of them, anyway. The same goes for the Reps, especially since getting their magic back. The media is hardly discussing it, thanks to the Governing Councils I'm sure, but most have left their posts. Broken their contracts and disappeared."

"To join Perennial?" I ask.

"Hopefully." She exchanges a smile with Ms. Goble.

"And so," Mrs. Hodger says slowly, "you're thinking of gathering an army?"

Ms. Curie shrugs. "Seems like one is already assembling."

"To fight the Creers of the galaxy?" Mrs. Hodger sputters.

"I'm sure some with Creers will join us," Ms. Curie replies. "People with families who've been stripped of their magic, or those who never had any to begin with. Or maybe just folks who feel like the system has been unjust for too long, despite their privilege."

Mrs. Hodger seems to wilt. She stares off at the horizon. "Myra kept the truth about her magic from me for so long. She was afraid of how Joe and I would react. But if she'd told us, we would have done anything to support her. Found her the best non-Creer school. Helped her pick the best path she could have hoped for without magic." A tear streaks down her cheek, and she absentmindedly swipes it away. "I told her I was disappointed she didn't tell us. Hurt, even. But maybe she was right not to." More tears fall. She doesn't bother wiping these. "I was disappointed she didn't tell me, but I was also disappointed that—" She shakes her head and sinks to the ground. "What a horrible mother I am."

Ms. Goble steps toward her, but Ms. Curie is closer. She sinks beside Mrs. Hodger and pats her knee. "Parents are people, too. They make mistakes, just like anyone."

Mrs. Hodger wipes her face on her sleeve. "Nothing would make me love Myra less. *Nothing*. But maybe I did put too much value in magic. Maybe I still do."

"The great thing about life is that every day, every moment, is a new opportunity," Ms. Curie says, her hand still on Mrs. Hodger's knee. "To change. To make different decisions. Better ones. Or to start over completely, guided by what we've learned from the past."

Mrs. Hodger nods. "So," she says, pushing to her feet. "We rally the Reps, the non-Creers, and the Creers who have more sense than me." She flashes us a watery smile. "And then we confront Melfin and his allies."

"Don't forget the Botans," I add. "Melfin won't want to face them after everything he's done."

Ms. Curie smiles broadly. "That's more true than you know."

"What do you mean?" Lila asks.

"Melfin has lots of secrets," Ms. Curie says. "And I know them all."

CHAPTER SIXTEEN

MYRA

THE SUN HOVERS SO CLOSE TO THE HORIZON, IT looks like it's sinking into the water. The light reflecting off the surface is like a pedestal rippling toward us. More colors than you'd find in a bouquet of wildflowers stream across the sky, mirroring the garden we've created in the sand.

All around us plants are blooming. Lilies and raspberries and lupines and dogwood trees and bayberries. Some in neat rows. Some growing haphazardly, tangling together. All of it beautiful.

"Well done," Charlie calls, crossing the beach. "Did you kids do all this on your own?"

"We haven't seen Fiona since you left," I say, crossing my arms.

Charlie sighs. "I was afraid that would happen."

"What's wrong with her?" Bernard asks, vines winding after him like friendly pet snakes. "Is it because Canter isn't here?"

Charlie shakes his head. "In the weeks leading up to the shuttle's arrival, she was like a new person. Funny. Cheerful. Engaged. Even her magic was blooming in a way I'd never seen before."

I hesitate. "What was she like before that?"

"Fiona mostly keeps to herself," Charlie says, his callused hand rubbing against gray stubble. "She rarely uses her Botan abilities."

"I would've thought her magic would be so much more powerful here," I say, sweeping my arms in an arc. "It's been so much easier to practice my Creer since we arrived. I feel like I almost don't even need someone to show me how. It just—"

"Happens," Bernard finishes, smiling as his vines coil around his leg, wrap around his torso, and settle across his shoulders. "I can feel the magic in the air. It's everywhere."

"I'm glad." Charlie grins. "Though hopefully we can still teach you a thing or two." He flicks his fingers and the row of hedges I created just before he arrived suddenly doubles. And then again and again until there's an entire army of shrubs.

My eyes widen. "How'd you do that?"

"Once you've got one blooming, the prospects are endless," he says. "Each plant has the potential to create the next."

Bernard brushes his hand over the top of the bayberry nearest him. "So, you just summon the seed from the first plant, grow that one to maturity, call the seed it produces to form the next, and on and on."

"Until forever," Charlie finishes. "Plants can be infinite."

"Immortality," I whisper, thinking of a conversation I had with Bernie what seems like a lifetime ago.

"Plants have sophisticated methods of telling each other things, warning one another. Humans give off nonverbal cues, too. The plants pick up on far more than we actually say to them."

"So, they understand us?" I ask. "When we talk."

"Oh, yes." Charlie chuckles. "They even appreciate our art. Music, especially. Scientists, hundreds of years ago, believed it had to do with the vibrations, but we know now that it's so much more."

Without thinking, I mime playing the trombone, like I learned back on V.A.M.A., pulling the slider back and forth, buzzing imaginary notes into the mouthpiece. "They can hear the music."

He smiles, watching me. "They enjoy it. Plant growth is stimulated by music. We've done lots of studies, and have even found that our magic is amplified by music. It inspires us to create our own art—through the plants, through our magic."

"So how do I control my Botan magic?" I ask. "I know it's tied to my emotions, but it's always been really inconsistent for me. Before I came here, anyway."

"The plants give us what we need. It's a partnership. When you're feeling heightened emotions—grief, anger, fear—the plants respond because they're responding to you. But it doesn't have to be that way. Watch." Charlie glances around at the garden that's sprouted up around us and points to a patch of daisies at his feet. He bends and touches them gently, like someone might take the hand of a toddler, and all at once, the flowers stream upward, taller and taller, until they're towering over us. A few more seconds and they're as tall as trees.

"A big reaction," he says, sweeping his arm to follow the still-growing daisies, "but without any big emotions."

"How'd you do it?" Bernard asks, awe lacing his voice.

"I asked them to. I love those daisies. I've always loved daisies. They're cheerful and bright and simply looking at them brings me joy. I appreciate them, and I told them so. In exchange, they agreed to do as I asked."

I frown. "So they could decide not to? If you're asking, that means they might not obey."

"And sometimes they don't." His eyes grow stormy. "Our history makes that very clear."

"You mean, when they became toxic," I ask, and he nods.

"In the past, hardly anyone valued what the plants had to offer. People forgot how important they were. How lucky we are to have them. How we're partners on this planet, allies with nature, even with every breath we take." He pauses, shaking his head. "People stopped caring. The plants fought back, but people forget we poisoned them first."

I stare at the blossoms far above me, their white petals framed by the stars of the darkening sky. I've known for a long time that what happened was humanity's fault, but this is the first time I've felt sorry about it.

"I wonder if they were lonely," Bernard says quietly, still watching the flowers. "When everyone left."

"Not everyone," Charlie reminds him. "The Botans have always stood by flora. That's why they were able to find a cure. Once the plants saw that there were still those who loved them, in spite of the battle between humans and the environment, they forgave us. And we forgave them." He smiles. "It's been a partnership ever since. That's the real secret to Botan magic. We work *together* with the plants. We help them to grow, and in exchange, they help us flourish."

Finally, it all makes sense. I had all the pieces before, but not how they fit together. I kneel, sinking my hands into the sand. The ground vibrates and honeysuckle vines drape over the beach, winding over trees and hedges, forming a tapestry across the night sky. Two strands wrap around me, lifting me into the air as if I'm on a swing. I twist and twirl as the flowers bloom in my hair and between my fingers, their sweet aroma mixing with the salty air as I glide across the sky, my feet kicking up toward the silvery Moon.

Far below, Bernard lifts his arm, and a rope of honeysuckle wraps around it, launching him upward. As he flies toward me, more vines bloom, twining together to form a bridge. He dances across it, starlight sparkling in his eyes. We soar together, like little kids on a playground.

Who-knows-how-long later, exhausted and exhilarated, we climb the vine ladders back to the ground.

"Looks like you've sprouted some new techniques," Charlie says with a grin. "But it's getting late, and I should show you where you'll be staying. You can get back to this tomorrow if you like."

"Sounds interstellar," I chirp as he leads us across the sand.

A few minutes later, we stop in front of a cluster of tree houses like the ones in Ava and Avon's community. People are still milling around outside. I spot Hannah in the center of a group of kids.

"Hi," I call, hurrying over to join them. "Charlie's going to show us where we're staying."

"Oh, okay." She glances at me, then at the teenagers, but doesn't move.

"I can come back later if you want," I say. "I'll go check it out. I'll show you when you're ready."

"No, it's fine." She relaxes slightly, but her jaw still seems tight. "I was just finishing a story. I'll catch up in a nanosec."

"Sure." I back away, and trip over my feet. The Old World kids snicker.

Hannah smirks, and a wave of anger washes over me. Before I can say anything, she laughs, and a real grin spreads across her face. "Don't mind Myra. She's still getting used to the gravity levels here."

I relax and mime taking big steps, as if a giant asteroid's pressing me down. The teens laugh even harder.

Charlie and Bernard are waiting outside a large tree house. The trunk grows straight for several feet, then splits into two large sections, reaching far into the sky. Branches covered in wide, yellowish leaves block the doorway.

"This is it," Charlie says with a sweep of his arm. The leaves rustle and part, clearing the way for us.

"What am I supposed to do when I need to get inside?" Hannah asks from behind me.

"If you nudge them, they'll move," Charlie assures her. "They respond to touch, too."

She nods but doesn't look pleased as she pushes past us. Bernard and I say a quick good night to Charlie, then follow her.

The interior is similar to where I first woke up after the Botans swarmed us with the medicine. There are a few windows carved into the walls, and furniture's scattered around the living area. The trunks I saw diverging outside form a V-shaped staircase leading to rooms on a second level.

After Bernard goes upstairs to explore, I turn to Hannah. "Did you happen to see Fiona?"

She nods. "She stormed by when I was working with the Tekkie kids. She disappeared inside the dark tree away from the other houses."

I cross to the door and peer outside. On the very edge of the loop of homes sits a small, gnarled tree house. "Is that even big enough for someone to live in?"

Hannah shrugs. "Maybe she doesn't need a lot of space."

"I'm going to go see if she's still there. Do you wanna come?"

"If she wanted company, she probably wouldn't have left."

That would never have stopped me or Canter or Lila. "Maybe we need to convince her she wants visitors."

Hannah sighs. "She probably won't even answer the door."

"She will if I keep knocking."

"Won't that just annoy her more?"

I swallow down my own frustration. "That's kind of the whole poin— Oh, never mind. Are you coming or not?"

"Not," Hannah says. "Actually, I wanted to tell you about teaching the others Tekkie theory. One of the kids even assembled a staircase from a pile of branches. It was galactic!"

"I'll be right back, I swear." I'm already halfway out the door when I see her face fall. "I really do want to hear all about it. As soon as I'm back!"

Hannah looks a little brighter, but as my magic directs the branches back into place, I catch the smile slipping away.

I'll make this quick.

I cross the village and hover outside the twisted tree. At first, I wonder if it's dead. The bark is a dry pewter gray, darkening to an inky black at the top. The leaves are sparce and colorless. If I squint, the structure looks more like a funnel of smoke than a tree. I take a breath and knock.

She doesn't answer.

I lean toward the tangle of branches blocking the doorway. "Hello? Fiona?"

The tree shudders and the branches creak as they curl away, their joints knotted and gnarled like an old woman's fingers. A flash of red makes me jump as Fiona appears in the doorway.

"Are you lost?" she asks, her gaze steely.

"N-no," I stammer, peering around her, but all I can see are shadows. "I just wanted to see if you were okay."

She raises her eyebrows. "*If I'm okay?* I've lived here for years. Shouldn't you be the one who isn't okay?"

I swallow. "Well, you disappeared from the beach."

"I'm no teacher. Not anymore. Charlie knows that."

"Then why—"

"Because he's hoping I'll change my mind. As if it's something I decided—like I just woke up one day and chose to be difficult."

"Charlie seems nice," I say slowly.

"Oh, he's incredibly nice." She leans against the doorframe and sweeps amber hair out of her icy eyes. "Kind, compassionate. An eternal optimist. That's why he's the best leader this region's had for years."

I can't decide if she's being serious or sarcastic. "Do you think I could come in for a minute?"

"Why?" But before I can answer, she sighs. "Oh, fine. But just for a minute. Do you want tea?"

"Sure?"

She jerks her head toward her living space before retreating into the shadows. I hurry after her before she can change her mind.

Inside is darker than the night outside. "How do you see in here?"

"Your eyes adjust," she says. Clanking and rattling echoes in the darkness. "Tap that spidery-looking plant next to you."

I squint and locate a hanging pot with long, leafy tendrils dangling from it. I lay my palm over it, unsure what I'm supposed to be doing, but the plant seems to know. It glows.

"They're bioluminescent," she calls back to me.

"It's like it heard me ask for light," I marvel. "Charlie said the plants can understand us."

"Of course they can," Fiona replies, emerging with a chipped cup full of steaming liquid. I take a cautious sniff and a sweet fragrance tickles my nose. "Sometimes they know what I need before I think to ask for it," she says, turning and picking up her own cup.

"How?"

"I always thought of them as guardians, sentinels to time," she says, watching as I drink. The tea is sweet and musty, like honey and lavender. "To history. They've seen everything since the very beginning. They must know everything. I wonder sometimes what they must think of us. I've asked them."

"Did they answer?"

She takes a sip and shakes her head. "I think they know

better." When she smiles, she looks years younger. "They're wise, remember?"

"Bernie told me once that plants had true immortality."

She laughs softly, and the light from the glowing plant makes her hair sparkle like copper. "He told me that once, too."

"But how do they do it?" I ask. "Is there science behind the communication? Or is it pure magic?"

"There's data showing that the plants talk with one another through their roots, even through electricity." Her eyes cloud, her features frozen, and I know what she's thinking.

Canter.

He's supposed to be here, not us.

"I'm sorry," I whisper. "I know you should be teaching this to Canter, not me."

I expect her to explode. Tell me to get out. But she just deflates.

"I don't know that I could teach him any better." She puts her cup down and crosses her arms. "All my magic seems to be capable of doing is causing destruction. Even here. Just like I ruined our lives out there."

"Canter would never have discovered who he was without that garden," I say softly. "He wouldn't have known about his Botan powers. We'd never have been friends, or found Bernie . . ." My throat feels tight. "You did your best. You tried. And when you try—"

"—you never know what magic you can create," Fiona finishes, looking at me for what feels like the first time.

But like a flower closing in on itself at dusk, the moment passes, her glow fades, and she stares off silently into space.

She doesn't need to kick me out. I know it's time to leave. I thank her for the tea and head back across the village. She doesn't say goodbye.

As I walk slowly back to our tree house, a ghost trails me. Several ghosts.

What's happened to Canter and Lila? Are they taking care of each other? Are they plotting against MFI, trying to avenge us? Or has Jake Melfin squashed our little mutiny the way he tried to snuff out Perennial and her associates' rebellion?

I hope he's failed, but I've been through too much, seen too much pain and destruction and been betrayed too often, to believe that's likely. I know better now. Things don't always work out the way they should. The galaxy isn't fair.

But I'll set right what I can. I'll get off this planet and back into the fray.

And when I do, I won't be fighting fair, either.

CHAPTER SEVENTEEN

CANTER

MS. CURIE WOULDN'T ELABORATE. SHE SAID THAT once she figured out what to do, she'd share all she knew about Jake Melfin, and no amount of prodding, even from Mrs. Hodger, would change her mind. In the end, we all went our separate ways with plans to reunite once the communication window with the Old World reopens.

Back in the aquaxi, I try to get Eli to talk to me. I even offer to help him with whatever he's got going on the roof. He stares silently out the window. When we dock back at our apartment building, he jumps out and disappears.

Lila looks at me, disappointment lining her face. "You need to apologize."

"I did!"

"No, you tried to bribe him. That's not the same."

I sigh. "All right. I'll find him later and say I'm sorry. Satisfied?"

She just rolls her eyes. With a groan, I drop my head and follow her inside. Her parents are in the kitchen.

"Where have you two been all day?" Mrs. Crumpler asks, looking up from the pot she's stirring on the stove. "I haven't seen you since this morning."

"We, er . . ." Lila looks to me for help.

I smirk. Lila's a terrible liar. Out of our trio, she's the absolute worst. I'm second best, and by far, Myra is— The smile falls from my face like a meteor crashing through atmosphere. "We went to, uh . . ."

Lila gapes at me as I stumble to piece together a story. Memories are flashing through my mind: empty cells, angry words, out-of-control plants, unchecked magic. Everything rockets through so fast, my brain aches. I grab my head, squeezing my eyes shut.

"We went to the Mending Center," Lila says quickly. "Canter's been having headaches, so we decided to get him checked out."

"Really?" Mrs. Crumpler says, hurrying over. She lays a hand on my forehead, the other hovering above my head . . . until she slowly lowers it to her side. "You don't feel warm, but unfortunately . . . unfortunately there isn't much else I can do." A veil of frustration falls over her eyes, but she quickly blinks it away. "What did the Menders say?"

"What did they say?" Lila asks, glancing at me, but I can barely see. The lights suddenly seem painfully bright. "The wait was too long, and Canter felt better, so we decided to come home."

Mrs. Crumpler frowns, placing her hand against my cheek. It's cool against my skin, her touch gentle. What I'd imagine someone might call motherly.

But I don't know if that's accurate. I might never know.

"Well, maybe you should lie down," she suggests. "Just in case. It's probably a migraine. Did you eat enough today?"

I nod, but the movement makes the ache in my temples vibrate like a plucked violin string. "I think I'll just go to bed." I head to my room, trying to ignore Lila's silent questions.

As I lie on my borrowed bed in the apartment where I'm a guest on a planet where I'm a prisoner, I'm not sure what *is* exactly wrong . . . except all of it. What keeps floating to the top, though, is Myra. And close behind her, Eli.

The words I yelled at Myra on Mercury echo in my head, but what I can't stop seeing is the look on Eli's face as he ran to the aquaxi.

I stay in my room for hours, long after the hushed voices and muffled movement fade away and the rest of the house settles in for sleep. Sometime after midnight, I hear Lila's dad come home from work and listen to him bustling quietly around the apartment before he, too, turns in. Then everything is once again silent.

When I can't take it anymore, I slip my backpack over my shoulders and creep out of my room, out of the apartment, and up the stairs. I wedge open the door to the roof, and as the fresh air washes over me, I take a deep breath, and then another. It feels like the first time I've actually filled my lungs with oxygen since coming back from Noah's apartment.

A sudden crash on the other side of the roof makes me jump. There's another loud bang, and then another. "What the . . ."

I tiptoe around the perimeter of the roof, peering around the edge to the other side. Eli stands over a heap of machinery, a heavy-looking tool in his hand. Tears stream down his face as he smashes into the pile over and over again.

"Eli! What are you doing?" I rush across the roof as he whips around, wiping his face on his shirt.

"Getting rid of this," he growls.

My heart plummets like it's been sucked into a black hole. "Because of what I said?"

He doesn't answer, and I don't need him to. I approach the mangled machine and kneel, studying it.

"A fluoroscopy reductor and an irradiator. And that's a light amplifier over here," I say, pointing at the bits and pieces I can still recognize. "Why would a fluoroscopy reductor and an irradiator be paired together? Wouldn't they interfere with each other?"

"Only if they're wired that way," Eli says with a sniff. "When you have them set up opposite each other, they have a balancing effect."

I nod. "Clever. So what does this whole thing do?"

Eli doesn't sit, but he does drop the wrench. "It's an atomic transmitter. It scrambles the molecular structure of small objects and sends them to a device that reassembles them."

My eyebrows shoot up. "You're joking. And you actually got it to work?"

He shrugs. "Not every time. There was a glitch that sometimes made it turn off midcycle, but I nearly had it sorted out before . . ."

I look back down at the dented metal and shredded wires. "Before I said what I said?"

He nods, sniffling. "Who would want something invented by a non-Creer anyway?"

"Who wouldn't want something like this? It's even more impressive that you built it without magic."

"Magic doesn't make you smart," Eli says, his cheeks flushing almost as red as his hair. "It would just get in the way."

"What do you mean?"

"I like to use my hands to put things together." He squats beside me and points at a smashed circuit breaker.

"It took me three tries to get that assembly right, and I was shocked twice, but that helped me figure out how to pair those two parts together." He taps the irradiator. "If I had used Creer powers to magic it together, I probably wouldn't have gotten the idea to pair it with the reductor. And then the whole thing wouldn't work."

I sit with his words for a minute. "I never considered that. I thought magic made things easier. Better. But you're right. Maybe there're all sorts of ways to invent something."

"Have you ever tried? Without magic?"

I shake my head. "I guess I'd better learn how, though. Doesn't look like I'll be getting my Creer back anytime soon."

"What was the device that lady was talking about? The one she didn't invent, but adjusted?"

I describe the magic-restoring machine Perennial's group created. What it did, how it worked, and what it looked like when it did what it was supposed to. I can see the wheels and gears turning in his mind.

"That doesn't sound that complicated," he says when I'm finished. "The trick's getting the sensors right, and you said your teacher fixed that."

"Well, if you figure out how to build one, I'll be your first customer."

He actually cracks a smile. "Even though I'm a non-Creer?"

"*Especially* because you're a non-Creer," I say. "If you can make stuff like this"—I nod toward the broken machine—"I trust your instincts more than I trust most people's magic."

Eli looks sadly at the pile of parts and sighs. "It's going to take forever to put that back together."

I'm quiet for a minute. Then I slip my bag off my shoulders and put it in my lap. "It might take even longer."

"Why?"

"I have another project I need sooner. I needed it yesterday, but without my magic, I can't . . ." My eyes sting and I squeeze them shut. "It's beyond what I can do right now. But I need it. I need him back." I ease blackened, silent Bin-ro out of my backpack and pass him to Eli.

He takes him carefully as if I just handed him a Jupiter Jackpot. And Bin-ro's not that. He's worth a hundred Jupiter Jackpots.

"What happened to him?" Eli whispers, cradling the robot in his arms as his eyes pore over every fried wire and circuit.

I tell him the short version.

"So, this Melfin guy is basically the worst," Eli says, eyes still on Bin-ro.

"The absolute worst. But there're a lot of others almost as bad."

"Like the warden."

And like my father.

"I want to help you," Eli says. "I want to help you get back at them."

I smile for what feels like the first time in a cosmic year. "Fix Bin-ro for me, and you can help with whatever you want."

Eli grins back. "Deal." His gaze shifts to his own smashed invention. "On one condition."

I raise my eyebrows.

"While I work on him, you have to work on that."

My stomach swoops. "I told you. I can't. Not without magic."

He shrugs. "Doesn't magic come from being smart? Studying and tests and all that?" I nod. "Then go back to what you had first."

I know Eli will still try to repair Bin-ro if I don't agree. There's no way he'd say no. I scan the mangled machinery, not knowing where to even start. But I owe him and I can't refuse. Even if I want to.

"You've got a deal."

CHAPTER EIGHTEEN
MYRA

THE NEXT DAY, CHARLIE TAKES BERNARD AND ME ON a tour. He even convinces Fiona to come. Hannah decides to hang back in the village. There's a group of kids who have taken to following her around everywhere, begging for more Tekkie theory, but she doesn't seem to mind. Teaching them what she knows about magic has brought back a spark to her eyes. And, more importantly, it's left her with less time to think about her sister's offer.

Our trip to the edge of the Coastal Region isn't just for sightseeing. We're scouting for Meteoron camps, making sure none have been set up nearby recently. Apparently, the Meteorons creep in on the Botan settlements from time to time to steal supplies, plan attacks, or just spy.

"Why don't you wipe out all the plants in their camps?" I ask as we walk a path leading away from the ocean.

"Then they wouldn't have any food, and they'd have to come to you to make some sort of agreement."

"History doesn't suggest that starving the enemy fosters goodwill," Charlie says with a patient smile. "Besides, would you want to kill all the plants in an entire region?"

I shudder.

Fiona adds, "If we were going to go that route, the Meteorons could send a wave of storms our way, drown our plants, burn them, and then where would we be?"

"*Everyone* would starve," says Bernard.

"Exactly," Charlie says. "Over the past few centuries, we've had varying levels of peace with the Meteorons. They've never been allies, but there've been times when we tolerated each other. Tensions have escalated lately."

"The population's grown," Fiona says. "There are more exiles. More people than ever with other Creers."

"And they all want to use their magic," I conclude.

"Discontentment leads to frustration, which leads to conflict," Charlie explains. "We don't have anyone to take it out on except one another."

"So why don't you meet and figure it out?" Bernard asks. "You're not enemies. Not really. Maybe working together, you could make a plan to get off world. I'm sure there are plenty of people without Botan magic who'd want a chance to see the rest of the galaxy."

"Botans, too," Charlie says. "Some of us, at least. The

idea has been raised over the years. The current Meteoron leader, Ophelia, and I have even exchanged communications. It would be nice to be able to access technology we can't replicate here. Connect with lost generations of family. Even bringing our plant magic to help the rest of humanity has its appeal. It seems they need it, and us, badly. But any progress with the Meteorons always seems to fizzle out before we get anything accomplished."

"There is no way off planet, anyway," Fiona grumbles. "And even if we did manage to escape, then what? The galaxy would never accept us."

"Even more reason to unite," I argue. "If you could find a way into the Settlements, the more of you there are—Botans and Meteorons—the less chance there is they could reject you. Especially now."

"It doesn't matter," Charlie says. "There's no way off. We have to make the best of what we're given."

"And protect *that* from the Meteorons," Fiona adds darkly. "See."

She points ahead, and I crest the hill, shivering. The higher I go, the colder it gets, until it feels like I'm standing in a refrigeration unit. At the top, I gasp. The rolling green ends suddenly at a blackened gash. Charred earth stretches like a desert as far as the eye can see.

"Why would they do this?" Bernard asks.

Charlie's mouth forms a thin line. "To limit our territory. It stretches on for miles. There's a thick layer of ice under the ash. It's impossible to get plants to grow in an environment like this, so it makes traveling difficult for Botans."

"Why would they burn the ground *and* freeze it?" I ask. "Isn't destroying it once enough?"

"Fire doesn't always destroy," Fiona explains, bending down and holding out her hand. Seeds stream into it from the nearby forest. She hands them to me. "Lodgepole pine trees, banksia flowers, and eucalyptus. All plants whose seeds are activated by heat. Fire actually helps them grow. It's how the land naturally regenerates after a wildfire."

Charlie winks, and I tuck the seeds into my pocket. "See. Told you that you could teach."

"Anyway," she says, frowning. "That's why the Meteorons coat the earth in ice after they scorch it. There's only one path left that connects us to the region you landed in. That'll be their next target."

"Where are the Meteorons based?" Bernard asks.

"We'll show you," Charlie says. "But we need to be careful. They'll have scouts patrolling."

We backtrack, hugging the coastline, and make our way around the charred earth. Charlie and Bernard walk together, lost in conversation about the Old World centuries ago. Fiona and I are left to trail behind. She's quiet as she stares out over the ocean. But I realize she's not looking at the water. Her gaze is focused too high, settled on the pearly-white Moon barely visible in the day sky.

"I didn't think you could see the Moon unless it was night," I say, and she starts.

"It depends on the time of day, the time of year, how clear the sky is. I always loved days when I could see it, back when I knew Canter was living on the Lunar Settlement. I'd look up and wonder what he was doing. Was he at school? Playing with his friends? Reading?"

I laugh. "Probably not reading. More likely playing a holo-game. Or hoverball."

Her head whips around. "What's he like? Sandra told me a little, but it's not the same through text, and she only knew him as a teacher. What was he like as a friend? As a kid? What can you—" She takes a breath, mussing her red hair, leaving tangles behind.

"Canter does that, too," I say softly. "When he's nervous or frustrated or excited, he runs his hands through his hair."

Tears glisten in her lashes. "He used to do that when he was little. He'd pull at it until it stood straight up like he'd electrocuted himself." She wipes her eyes, smiling sadly. "What else does he do?"

"He can't ever get up in the morning. He loves his sleep." She laughs, her eyes as bright as starlight. "I wish he loved it when he was little. He didn't sleep through the night until he was . . . Actually, I don't know when. He never did. Not when I knew him."

"Well, he definitely does now. Um, he's really good at hoverball. Like the best on the JV team at S.L.A.M., but don't tell him I said that. I'll deny it."

She smiles. "What else?"

"He's funny and smart. He invented reflector paper to evade the curfew trackers."

Her eyebrows shoot up, and I remind myself that as his mother, she might not approve of Canter breaking school rules, but a moment later she's grinning.

"That's my son! He gets that from me. Robert would never step a toe out of line. But some rules are meant to be bent, am I right?"

"He's . . . he's a good friend," I say quietly. "A *great* friend. When I first met him, I thought he was stuck-up and arrogant. A bully. But he's not. Not at all. He's funny and clever and he cares about people, especially his friends."

Now it's me blinking, trying to clear away tears before they can escape.

Fiona puts a hand on my arm. "You must be a good friend, if you're so close to him. Sandra told me you're his best friend. I'm sure he misses you, too."

I sniff. "I do miss him. More than I'd ever admit to him, honestly. But it's not just that."

She brushes a strand of hair behind my ear the way my mother would. "What happened?"

I take a breath. "We had a fight at the prison just before everything went wrong. A bad fight. We said awful things."

"It happens to the best of friends," Fiona says gently.

"I don't know," I whisper. "I think he might have meant the things he said."

"Did you mean whatever you said to him?"

"Yes and no." I pick painfully through the conversation. "Everything maybe had a seed of truth in it, but I was trying hard not to get so upset. I didn't want to say anything I'd regret."

"And what about him?"

"He was . . . angrier than I was. I'd already been stewing over what was bothering me for a while, but he was reacting to something difficult he'd just found out, so it wouldn't be fair to be upset with him for what he said."

"We're all in charge of our own emotions and reactions." Fiona leans closer. "You can't apologize for him. He has to do that for himself."

I'm quiet awhile. "Did you ever have a fight with Ms. Curie? Or Ms. Goble?"

"Of course! There's a saying that those you're closest to are the ones who can hurt you the most, and the ones *you* can hurt the most. You know each other well enough to know what buttons to push, and it stings that much more when they push yours. It's normal, but never fun." She smooths her hair back down. I get the feeling that even on her best days, it's never really tame. "But Myra, it's what you do *after* that counts. The friends who can say *I'm sorry*, and mean it, are the ones worth keeping."

"I hope I get the chance," I whisper.

"You will."

Bernard and Charlie are already waiting in a grove of trees. Charlie holds a finger to his lips, and I creep forward, peering through the branches. I can just make out a small clearing a hundred yards or so away. Small houses built from chopped-down trees are clustered in a circle. A fence draped with netting forms a bull's-eye in the center. Small sprouts, likely for some sort of green bean plants, and tomato bushes fill the space. A garden.

"The Meteoron settlement," Fiona whispers. She points to a petite, white-haired woman leaving the garden and heading into the largest house in the settlement. "That's Ophelia."

Dozens of people move about the tiny village, but we're too far away to see any of their faces. We watch for a few more minutes before Charlie taps me on the shoulder and leads us away.

"They have a garden," I say when we can talk safely. "How? They don't have Botan magic."

"Plants don't *need* Botan magic to grow here," Fiona

reminds me. "Their crops don't flourish the way they might if we were tending them, but they grow well enough to feed the others."

"And supply wood for their houses," Bernard adds, grimacing.

A sick feeling twists through my stomach. "Do they really need to chop down the trees?"

"The Meteorons can't make the forest adapt the way we can," explains Charlie. "But they've learned some basic gardening skills to survive."

"Like the antidote," Bernard says. "Isn't that complicated magic, though?"

Charlie shrugs. "The ingredients are easy enough to find."

"What do you use?" I ask.

Fiona scans the ground. "One of the ingredients most closely resembles chamomile. Oh, there!" She kneels, cupping a tiny flower with white petals. The stalks are tall and thin, shaped almost like lavender, but the flowers are silvery, like the Moon still glowing overhead. She gently plucks a stalk, rubs her fingers together over the sprout, and two new blooms grow in its place. Then she hands the flower to me. "We grind it down, soak it in boiled water, and allow it to brew for a few weeks with some other routine herbs and fungi."

"And that's it?" Bernard asks, shaking his head. "That's all humanity needed to survive?"

"The solution *is* simple," Charlie says, "but it took time and patience to find it. We'd stopped listening to nature long before it turned on us. I imagine even the Botans had lost some of their connection to the plants. Once everyone else had gone and we were left with no choice but to figure out a solution or die, that was when this little guy made itself known." He smiles fondly at the plant like it's a treasured niece or nephew. "Who can guess how long it was growing here, literally right under our noses, before people took the time to notice."

I lift the flower to my face and breathe in its aroma. It's very faint, but sweet and earthy. "Thank you," I whisper, then lean down, placing it back on the ground. I lay my hand over it and feel warmth rush from my heart to my hand. Light trickles between my closed fingers, and when I lift my palm, the plant grows from the sandy soil. "What's it called?" I ask, rising and brushing dirt off my pants.

"We call it the aurora flower," says Fiona. "*Aurora* means dawn in an ancient language. A new beginning."

"Like what you all have," Charlie adds, leading the way. "I know you never expected to end up here, but I hope you're starting to see that you have a real future with us. One that you could never have out there."

I know he's right, but the idea of being trapped here, marooned, with so much still uncertain in the Settlements makes me feel like I'm drowning. Still, I don't argue. After we make contact with Ms. Curie, and Lila and Canter realize we're here, we'll come up with a plan.

We always do.

As we approach the Botan settlement, we hear tense voices echoing in the distance. A young man rushes to meet us.

"What's wrong?" Charlie demands.

"The satellite. It's ruined."

"What do you mean *ruined*?" Fiona barks. "That's impossible."

"It was the Meteorons," he says. "They attacked it."

CHAPTER NINETEEN

CANTER

A SOFT KNOCK ON MY DOOR STIRS ME FROM THE light sleep I fell into sometime after dawn. "Canter," Mr. Crumpler's voice calls, a note of worry in his voice. "Could you come out for a minute?"

"I won't be late for school, I swear."

"There's no school today."

I crack my eyes open, searching for my digital calendar glowing on my desk. He's right. "Is everything—"

"Your father is here to see you."

I sit up, any haze of sleep replaced by rage. "I don't want to see him."

"I don't think you've really got a choice, kiddo," Mr. Crumpler says.

He's right, even though I hate that it's true. I rack my brain for an excuse to blow him off.

"He says he just wants to talk."

"Sure he does," I mutter.

"What's that?"

"I'll be right out." I swing my legs down, preparing myself for the conversation ahead. For a moment, I remember sitting on a bench outside my father's office, reflector paper in my bag and seeds in Myra's pocket. A wave of sickness washes over me.

She's alive. Myra is alive. She has to be.

I repeat the words until I can force myself to swallow and stand, hurtling toward the door before I change my mind, or before my stomach decides to become less cooperative.

Mr. Crumpler's waiting outside, looking worried as he runs his hands over his balding head. "I'm sorry about this, Canter."

"I'm sorry about all the trouble."

"No trouble here," he says with a weak smile. "I'm headed to work. Mrs. Crumpler's already gone. Lila and Landon are still sleeping, but if you want privacy, I can take them with me."

I shake my head. "This should be quick."

Mr. Crumpler looks as unsure as I feel. "All right, kiddo. He's in the living room. I'll see you later." He pauses, like he wants to say more, but claps a hand on my shoulder and gives it a tight squeeze before heading out the front door.

I wish I could follow him. Instead, I take a breath and turn into the living room.

I hardly recognize the man standing there. My father's formerly dark-blond hair is mostly gray, matched by silver stubble along his jaw. It's like he's aged years in weeks.

He relaxes when he sees me, some of the tension leaving his shoulders. We stare at each other for a few long moments, neither of us saying anything.

His silence makes the anger simmering in my belly flare into a bonfire. "What do you want?" I finally snap.

My father's eyes flick to the closed doors behind me. "Let's take a walk," he says.

I cross my arms. "It's just Lila and her brother, and they're sleeping. Besides, I'm not going anywhere with you."

My father frowns. "I'm asking right now, Canter. Don't make me have to tell you. If I do—if you force me to go into that mode—you might not be returning here."

I take a step toward him. "Now you're threatening me?"

"It's not a threat if it's true." He sighs. "Look, I've let you stay here without argument. I get it, son. I do. But I'm not having this conversation here. Don't make this more difficult than it has to be."

More difficult. More *difficult*? Like he has any idea what my last few weeks have been like. *Difficult* would be a vacation. An oasis in a Martian desert. I'm about to tell him so—tell him where he can take a walk to—when a whisper of reason sneaks in.

He's right.

"I'm coming back here."

He sighs. "I'm not going to force you to come home if you want to stay."

"I don't have a home." This time, he winces. I bend and grab my shoes, shove my feet into them, and stalk out the door.

I walk briskly down the path in front of the Crumplers' apartment building. There are a few on this island, and I assume my father wants to do a loop, but when I turn right at an intersection, he stops.

"This way," he says, gesturing to the left. "I live in that building."

I balk. "I'm not going there."

"I'm not having this conversation with you in the open."

"Then we should have stayed where we were!"

My father's eyes narrow. "The sooner you hear me out, the sooner you can go back." He doesn't pause to see if I'll follow, and I know I'm stuck. I sigh and trudge after him.

He leads me into a building just as dilapidated as the Crumplers', then scans his hand on a nondescript entry and heads inside.

All the furniture is hard, cold, and uninviting. A stiff couch is positioned against a smudged, faded wall with a bulky, chipped table in front of it. A simple hardbacked chair rests against the opposite wall. There's nothing else. My father gestures toward the couch, but I cross my arms and keep my feet planted.

"Look, Canter," he says, sighing as he sits on the couch and places his hands on his knees. "I know you're angry with me, and you have a right to be, but now that you've had some time to cool down, I need to explain what's actually happened."

"Cool down?" Can he possibly think that after a few weeks, I'm suddenly over the fact that he let my best friend be murdered, or so he thought, anyway? That he had my other friend—my mentor—sent to his death? That he lied to me my entire life about what happened to my mother?

"I didn't say you've moved on and are leading a perfectly happy and contented life. I meant that the initial blinding rage and grief have subsided, and you're now able to process new information with some degree of reason."

"Wrong. I don't just flip a switch and turn off my emotions. I'm not you."

When he flinches, a surge of pride rushes through me.

"You'll see someday," he says quietly. "When you have children, you'll understand that sometimes you need to bury the things that hurt you most in order to carry on for someone else. To make sure both your lives aren't an endless parade of agony. It doesn't mean I switched anything off. I'm not a robot, though sometimes I wish it were as simple as flipping a switch."

I blink. I've never heard him speak this way.

"I'm deeply sorry about what happened to your friends. More than I can put into words. I tried everything I could think of to negotiate their release. *Everything*. Melfin wouldn't hear it, and neither would the warden. The most I could finagle was you and Lila. The others were already in too deep."

I open my mouth to argue, but he raises a hand. "We can go back and forth on this, Canter, but it's the truth. Debating it won't change anything. They're gone. I'm sorry, but they're gone." He swallows. "Just like your mother."

For a wild moment, I consider telling him he's wrong, but I quickly come to my senses and ask the question that's been burning in my mind ever since that day on Mercury. "Did you know she was exiled?"

He shakes his head, pain flashing in his eyes. "I had no idea. I wasn't allowed to communicate with her. They wouldn't even let me conduct an annual wellness inquiry, given the nature of her conviction. I never suspected . . ." He swallows again. "It used to give me comfort, knowing she was there. That she was safe, if not free. I could never have imagined the galaxy without her in it."

"Then why did you turn her in?" I ask, my voice rising again. "Why'd you out her to your buddy Melfin?"

My father frowns. "What are you talking about?"

"I read it in the log at the prison." My face is hot and my palms are sweating. "It said she was secured on information provided by her husband."

My father rubs his face. He looks even older. "It's not how it sounds."

"How can it be anything else? *You* did this to her. It's your fault."

"I know it's my fault! But not the way you think."

"Then how—"

"*That's what I'm trying to tell you!*"

His outburst steals the words from my mouth.

"I did tell Jake that your mother had seeds. He was my best friend and poised to take over at MFI when his father retired. Your mother's garden was in full bloom by then, and it was getting difficult to contain, along with her abilities. I was afraid bouquets would be bursting from her pockets before long if I didn't do something. I thought if Jake agreed to help—if as head of the largest food production company in the galaxy, he supported her abilities and agreed to use her garden as a cloning source, it would solve everything. We could live a normal life. *She* could live a normal life. Use her magic. She'd be free. So I told him that your mom had plants, and that she'd discovered she had Botan magic."

"And he ran right to the Council," I blurt out.

My father shakes his head. "No. He was intrigued. Or seemed to be, anyway. I didn't tell him about the garden, thankfully. Who knows what would have happened—" He shakes his head. "But I told him enough. MFI was already having troubles with the food cloning formulas. Nothing like what's happened recently, but enough that Jake was interested in an alternate source. So much so that he wanted to tell his father about your mom." My father sighs and rubs his face. "I told Jake not to. Begged him. But he insisted everything would be fine. Fiona would be able to go public with her magic even sooner. We didn't need to wait for him to take over."

"And you agreed? You really thought everything would work out?"

"He was my *best friend*," my father says, his voice full of pain. "And your mother, she'd started bringing you with her to the garden. I didn't want her to. You were so young. What if you talked about the plants to someone? You seemed drawn to them, and I worried . . ." He looks me in the eye for the first time. "I was worried your mother wasn't the only one with Botan magic."

We're both quiet as I try to see the story through my father's eyes. It's hard to imagine how I'd feel about my own kid, my own partner, or to know what I'd risk to protect them. But I have a best friend. Or had, anyway. And I would have trusted her to do what was right. I would have trusted Myra with anything.

"You know the rest. Jake told his father, and Mr. Melfin Senior insisted on turning your mom over to the Council. At least that's what Jake told me. Who knows what really happened."

I shift from foot to foot, with no idea how to respond. After a moment, I cross the room and sit carefully on the hard couch. Not near my father. On the other end. But it's something.

"I understand if you still hate me," he whispers. "And if you want to stay with the Crumplers, that's fine. I just wanted you to know the whole story."

"You've been lying to me my entire life," I say, though the fight's gone out of my words. "Why should I believe you're telling the truth now?"

He shrugs. "I have no idea. But it is the truth."

An awkward silence fills the room. I'm about to tell him I have to go when a knock at the door makes us both jump. "Rob!" a familiar voice booms. "Let me in. I need to talk to you."

Jake Melfin. I'd know that voice anywhere.

My father looks at me, at the door, then back at me. "Hide."

CHAPTER TWENTY

MYRA

WE RUSH TO THE CENTER OF THE VILLAGE, WHERE people are clustered around a heap of metal and wires and parts, intermixed with glistening crystals.

"Are those jewels?" I ask, pointing at clear shards of glass.

Fiona is silent, staring at the mess, but Charlie shakes his head. "It's ice. Hail. But how would they even know to send a storm here?"

"It blew in not long after you left," the man who greeted us explains. "We think . . . they must have known you'd be away."

"They have eyes here." Charlie scans the buildings around us. "We'll have to be more careful."

"But what do we do about this?" Bernard asks, gesturing to the mangled metal.

I meet Fiona's gaze. She doesn't say anything, and I can't,

either. If I try, I'm not sure what will come out. A scream? A cry? A curse? Maybe all three.

"I can fix it," a voice says behind me. Hannah is standing with her hands clasped in front of her. "I think I can, anyway. I could try."

With each backpedaled word, she grips her hands tighter and tighter.

"The communications window is tomorrow," Charlie says. "You'd need replacement parts."

"Didn't you say there were other shuttles?" Bernard offers. "We could scavenge from them."

Charlie doesn't look convinced. He turns to Fiona, but she's still staring silently at the broken machine. He takes a deep breath and addresses Hannah. "Anything you need, any extra hands, we're at your disposal. All of us."

She gives a firm nod. "I'd better get started, then."

"Please, Hannah," I say softly. I know I shouldn't put more pressure on her. I know that's not fair. But I can't stop myself. If she can't fix the satellite by tomorrow, we'll have to wait another month. And if she can't . . . "You have to fix it."

"She can," Bernard says, kneeling in front of the debris. He picks out chunks of ice and flings them away. "I don't know much about building or fixing, but I'm pretty sure water and electronics don't mix."

Hannah gives him a small smile. "That's a good place to

start." While Bernard removes the melting bits of hail, she sits down and starts sorting through the mess.

"We'll begin checking the other shuttles. See what can be salvaged," Charlie says. The other adults head off with him. All except Fiona. I can't move, either.

"Do you remember when we broke your mom's favorite coffee brewer because we tried to use it to make hot chocolate?" Hannah asks after a few minutes.

I blink. "What? Oh, yeah. She loved that thing because it calculated the liquid down to the milliliter and she could compute exactly how much caffeine she was getting every day."

"And we stuck a block of chocolate in it, thinking it would melt, and it clogged up all the mechanisms?"

I nod, still staring at Hannah's hands as they sift through the dented metal. "I remember. But what—"

"Did we get in trouble?"

I think back, though it's hard to focus on anything besides what's in front of me. "No," I finally say. "We fixed it before she got home."

"*I* fixed it before she got home," Hannah corrects, holding a small cylinder up to her eye, sighing, and tossing it on the pile of discarded parts. "Do you remember what you did to help while I worked?"

"I . . . I didn't help at all. I went and played a hologame."

"Exactly. I told you to because all you were doing was staring at me while I tinkered, and it was stressing me out." She pauses and gives me a pointed look.

"Oh." I actually crack a smile. "Okay, fine. I'll go. If it'll help."

"It will," she says gently. "And take her with you. It's ten times worse when an adult does it."

Fiona doesn't seem to have heard our conversation. I take her elbow. "We should let them work."

She jumps but follows me away.

"So," I say, trying to distract myself as much as her. "Did you know my parents growing up?"

"What?" she asks, blinking.

"Joe Hodger?" I remind her. "Claire Bedford?"

"Oh, right. Yes. I didn't know them well. They were in a different circle."

"It was just you, Ms. Curie, and Ms. Goble, right?"

"And Robert and Jake," she adds, scowling.

"Ms. Curie said she stole the seeds she gave you from Melfin," I remember suddenly. "But where did *he* get them?"

"They'd been in his family for years."

My eyes widen. "How do you know?"

"I'll show you."

Fiona leads me toward her small tree house and pushes through the front door. In the full light of day, it's not nearly as creepy. Inside are as many plants and flowers as there are outdoors, weaving through cracks in the wood, hanging from the ceiling, climbing up from the floor. A chair assembled from two large rocks, secured with vines, sits in front of a small stone table. Moss covers the seat and back of the chair, making it look comfy. She heads to the far wall, reaches inside a knot in the wood, and pulls out something small and green.

When she returns and hands it to me, I gasp. I've seen this box before, in Hannah's apartment what feels like a century ago. It's just like the one Meredith had—the one that supposedly held the seeds that got her sent here. I take it gingerly, turning it over in my hand. It's carved out of what looks like ancient, green wood, once polished to a sheen. You can still see patches of the gloss, but most of it has worn away. Where Meredith's box had a lock, this one has four strings. Just like the case holding the books in Melfin's office on Mercury.

"Do you know how to open it?" I ask.

Fiona plucks the strings. It's a different order than Melfin's other box, but the case springs open just the same. It's empty.

"The seeds are long gone," she says quietly, running her hands along the interior, which is lined in a rough fabric, except for inside the polished wooden lid. Something's engraved there. I hold it closer to my eye, squinting to make out the letters.

GM, WM, PM, JM, ZM, KM, WM, FM, BM, JM

"What do they mean?" I ask.

"It's how I know this box was in Jake's family for a long time," she says, pointing at the last pair of letters. "Jake Melfin." She slides her finger down the row. "Bradford Melfin. That's Jake's father. Frank Melfin was his grandfather." She pauses. "I think it was Walter Melfin, then Karl, and oh, I can't remember the others. I looked them all up once to be sure."

"It's his ancestors," I say. "Dating all the way back to the Old World?"

Fiona nods. "I think they must have smuggled the seeds out during the evacuation. Maybe they took them as an emergency measure in case the food cloning broke down, but that would have been exceedingly dangerous back then."

"That is what they did," I say, glowering. "Melfin told me before he shoved me on the transport. They've been repairing the food cloning codes for generations with real plants, until Ms. Curie took the seeds."

"Good," Fiona says, leaning back against the wall. "I'm glad to hear I've still caused him trouble. I wonder how they got the plants to grow. It's not impossible without

Botan magic, but it's extremely difficult. They must have done well with it, though, to keep the cloning going as long as they did."

"And now he has my garden to fill in the gaps." I dig my nails into my palm as I replay the rest of my conversation with Melfin. "It'll feed him and his buddies for the next hundred years."

"If the public only knew," Fiona says wistfully. "Not only was he using illegal plant growth to keep himself in business and push everyone else out, but now he's eating real food while the rest of the galaxy chokes down the garbage MFI's producing." She takes the box back, running her fingers over the engraving.

"How could we ever prove it, though?"

Fiona looks up at me, her eyes sparkling like sapphires. "With this."

I frown. "But it's empty. How could we prove it had seeds?"

"It's not the first box of its kind to be found. It might not look like much, but it's equipped with preservation capabilities perfect for stabilizing plant material. And with the line of initials carved into it . . ."

I'm afraid to even hope. "Would it be enough?"

She shrugs. "It's a start. But we'd have to get it off planet."

I raise an eyebrow. "We?"

"You kids did so much—risked so much—trying to get

to me," she says softly. "I can't hide here anymore, waiting. I can't depend on other people to bring my son to me." She sighs. "I was never someone who sat around, following rules that never made sense, or stood by while my friends were in trouble." Resolve washes over her features. "I hardly recognize myself anymore, but that changes now."

"You'll go with us off planet if we find a way?"

"I'm getting Canter and bringing him home." She winks. "And I'll cause Jake all sorts of trouble along the way."

New determination swirls inside me. "I'll find a way out of here."

And when I do, nothing will stop me from taking down Jake Melfin and his family once and for all.

CHAPTER TWENTY-ONE

CANTER

DAD GRABS MY ARM AND HAULS ME OFF THE COUCH and into his bedroom, and shuts the door.

I hear the entry door slide open, followed by a booming voice. "Just hear me out for one minute, Rob," Melfin says.

"Why on the Moon would I do that? My wife's gone. My son's life is ruined. All because of you."

"Some of that I can't fix, and I'm sorry. I really am." Melfin's voice is slick as oil. "But some of that I might be able to put right."

"What are you talking about?" Fury simmers in my father's voice, and if I were Melfin, I'd be backing up a step.

Footsteps like heartbeats sound against the floor. I wonder if Melfin retreated after all.

"What if I told you I could get Canter's magic back?"

There's a moment of silence, and I imagine my father

studying his former friend, looking for the trick. "What do you want, Jake?"

"You've been my best friend since we were at S.L.A.M. I just want to help."

"And what do you *want* in exchange for that help?"

Mr. Melfin sighs so loudly I can hear it through the door. "You're one of the few people in this galaxy I trust, and I know you feel I've betrayed you. I admit, I've made mistakes. But if you think about this rationally, you'll see that it isn't really fair to blame me for everything that's happened. In fact, without me, the outcomes would be worse."

"Worse?" Dad snorts. "How could things be worse?"

"Canter could be dead," Melfin says quietly, and my stomach swoops. "That's what the warden wanted. Curie, too. They thought he should have been on that shuttle to the Old World. I stopped them. You know I did."

"It was your fault he was in that situation in the first place!"

"I didn't force him to meet with that group of terrorists on Venus."

My dad laughs. "That's a little strong, don't you think? It was a group of Reps in breach of their contracts, that's all."

"You know that's not all," Melfin growls. "They're the ones who deactivated the chips suppressing Rep magic."

"Not just Rep magic, right, Jake?" Dad says, his voice dripping with venom.

"They're the reason that half the Reps have left their posts."

"I don't know much about that. I'm a little out of the loop here."

"That's why I wanted to talk to you." Melfin's voice is oily and coaxing again. "Just so we're clear, I never thought in a million light-years Canter would have had seeds on him. I called you to come get him, remember? I was after the Hodger girl. I owed her for the misery she put me through last year, and she had some things I wanted." He pauses. "Never mind all that. It's not important anymore. The bottom line is this: I want to make some of this up to you, if I can."

"So, you're offering to restore my son's Creer," Dad says slowly. "And like I already asked, what do you want in exchange?"

"Your help. MFI's expanding, and I need someone to keep an eye on operations. Someone I trust. I have more than a few enemies now, as you know."

"You mean other people you've stripped of their powers? Can't say I blame them."

"Well, Canter doesn't have to be one of them. I wish I could offer you the same, but the warden was adamant. She's agreed that since Canter's still a child, we might return his Elector magic. As long as you agree to help us."

"Oh, it's *us* now."

"Cass has been my partner for a long time. You know that." Melfin clears his throat. "That's the offer. She'll deactivate Canter's device in exchange for your help."

Footsteps thud on the other side of the door, and I can only guess that my father is pacing, thinking it over. "What would you need me to do?"

"Move to MFI headquarters on Mercury and help me manage the company," Melfin says, relief flooding his voice. "Keep an eye on the pockets of my enemies. Help me track down the rest of those rebel Reps. I hear they're still going around deactivating chips placed since they infiltrated the Venusian facility. Basically, handle MFI's operations. If you say yes, I'll see that Canter's magic is restored."

"What about the Crumplers and the Hodgers?" Dad asks. "Did they really deserve to get swept up in all this, too?"

"The Hodgers can go spark themselves," Melfin spits. "Joe Hodger got me kicked off the Lunar Council, and his daughter being what she is—or was . . ."

Heat floods through me, and it's all I can do not to burst through the door. Thankfully, my father's quicker.

"And the Crumplers? Their only crime seems to be that their daughter was in the wrong place at the wrong time."

"I may be able to do something there," Melfin says slowly. "But why do you care about them?"

"My son hates me. Maybe it'll help heal that wound."

"I'll see what I can do. So, do you agree?"

The room's silent, and I wonder if I missed Dad's answer. Maybe he nodded or shook his head.

Then I hear his voice. "I'll do it."

As soon as the door shuts, I hurry into the living room.

"Why would you agree to help him? I don't want anything from Melfin. Not even my magic."

"Don't turn down a weapon in a war, son. Even if you don't like the hand extending it. Once you have it, you can always turn it back on your enemy."

"What are you talking about?"

"Jake just offered us three valuable weapons," Dad says, smirking. "Your magic and Lila's."

"He didn't agree to that," I say, but Dad waves a hand dismissively.

"He will. He's playing a game, but I've seen it many, many times before."

I don't know how he can be so calm, but clearly he sees something I don't. "So, what's the third weapon?"

"The most powerful of the three. Information. He wants me handling MFI's operations, monitoring his enemies. . . . Just think what would happen if that intel falls into the wrong hands. Or the right ones."

The Reps. I think I'm beginning to understand. "Won't

he worry you'll turn on him, though? After everything that's happened?"

"Perhaps," Dad says, "but in his mind, the reward outweighs the risk. Jake and I have a long history, and he assumes I'm as anxious to rekindle that as he is."

"Are you?"

Dad actually rolls his eyes—something I thought I'd never see. "What you need to understand about Jake is that he's not an easy person to get along with. He's never been close to many people. Even he and his wife, well, it was more business transaction than happy marriage. And from what I've seen, his relationship with his son is strained."

Kyle Melfin's smug face flashes through my mind. "I can see why."

Dad's expression softens. "Don't be so hard on Kyle. Jake wasn't exactly a doting father."

I'm about to say *Neither were you*, but I bite my tongue. Still, I think he reads the words in my eyes.

"I know I haven't been a shining example myself," he says quietly, "and that's no one's fault but my own. But I hope you know, Canter, it was never you. It was me. I—I lost a part of myself when I lost your mother."

"When *we* lost my mother."

His shoulders slump. "You're right. And even though I truly thought I was doing what was best for her, I still felt guilty for telling Jake. For being the catalyst. Every time

I looked at you, I felt that shame. I knew it was my fault, even if what they did to her was the last thing in the galaxy I could ever have wanted. I closed myself off from everyone, including you. And I'm sorry, son. I'm so sorry for that." He drops his head into his hands. "I'm sorry for a lot of things."

Part of me wants to tell him it's okay, but I know it's not, and I can't pretend.

I sit down on the couch. "So, you're going to work for Melfin?"

Dad nods. "He'd never suspect I'd betray him and risk having your magic stripped again. In the meantime, I can pass you information."

"And what are we supposed to do with it? What's the goal?"

Dad smiles. "Take down Jake Melfin, once and for all."

Eventually, I agree. I know magic isn't everything. I know magic doesn't make me important, or any more valuable than anyone else. Eli taught me that. But my magic's part of who I am, and I want it back. I consider telling Dad my own secrets—that my mother isn't gone; that Myra might not be, either—but I decide against it, at least for now.

If information is power, I'm not sure I want to share mine quite yet.

CHAPTER TWENTY-TWO

MYRA

AS THE FIRST RAYS OF SUNLIGHT CREEP OVER THE horizon, I slip back into the center of the village. Hannah lies on her stomach, a tool in one hand, her chin resting in the other as she squints through tired, dark-rimmed eyes. Bernard is leaning against a tree a few yards away, dozing.

"How's it going?" I ask, tiptoeing closer. From the corner of my eye, I catch a flash of red. Fiona checking on the progress.

Hannah's chin slips off her palm. "Crashing comets, Myra! Don't sneak up on me like that. I'm almost done."

I gasp, but the sound's drowned out by Fiona's sharp intake of breath. "You did it? It's fixed?"

"Nearly," Hannah mutters, rubbing her eyes. "I thought we were lost in orbit until Bernard dug up a battery from one of the shuttles." She nods at his still-sleeping form.

"That was a couple of hours ago. I just need to finish closing up the console, and we'll be zooming."

Charlie emerges from a nearby tree house, yawning and stretching.

"It's fixed," Fiona announces.

"I know," he says through another yawn. "I was checking in all night. Just wanted to catch a few before the sun came up."

"It's *not* fixed," Hannah says, tongue peeking out of the side of her mouth as she gives her tool a hearty twist. She looks up and grins. "Okay, now it's fixed."

I roll my eyes. "*So* dramatic."

"Watch it," she says, shaking the tool at me. "I'm also sleep-deprived."

"So, when can we send the first message?" I ask, bouncing on my toes.

"As soon as you wake up Bernard." Hannah climbs to her feet. "He did almost as much work as I did."

My feet pound the sand as I race Fiona to Bernard's side. "Wake up!" I say, shaking him.

He jolts up. "Is it the Meteorons?"

"Oh, no," I say. "Sorry. Nothing to be alarmed about. Just excited. Hannah fixed the transmitter!"

"And Bernard," Hannah calls.

"And you," Fiona repeats, clasping his hand and pulling him up. "Saving the day as always."

He blushes, and I know he's debating whether he should take the compliment.

"What do we say to them?" I ask as Charlie bends over the newly repaired machine, where a complicated array of buttons glows hopefully.

"We've found that shorter messages tend to transmit more clearly," he says.

"I'll do it," Fiona offers. She kneels down beside me and begins to type.

CHAPTER TWENTY-THREE

CANTER

THE NEXT MORNING, MS. CURIE SHOWS UP AT THE Crumplers' apartment in an aquaxi. Lila and I cram in beside her and Mrs. Hodger, and we set off.

"Where's Ms. Goble?" I ask.

"She's at S.L.A.M.," Ms. Curie explains. "She's taken over as interim school director. I'll vid-call her later to tell her how it went."

"What about Mr. Hodger?" Lila asks. "Is he already at Ms. Curie's apartment?"

"He isn't coming," Mrs. Hodger says softly. "He said he couldn't take it. He—he didn't want to be around people if it didn't work."

Or if Myra's not there. The thought makes my temples throb. Myra's alive. I know she is. If anyone could survive on the Old World, it's her. Out of pure stubbornness.

"It'll work," I say, funneling every bit of confidence I can summon into my voice. Mrs. Hodger gives me a small smile.

It seems like forever before we arrive at Ms. Curie's building. I clamber up the steps behind the rest, not sure if I'm excited or anxious as Ms. Curie leads us to the roof. Tucked in a corner, buried under a heap of junk, is the transmitter. She sweeps the parts and pieces away, flips a switch, and it glows to life.

Ms. Curie squats down next to it. "There's already a message."

Ms. Hodger chokes out a sob, and my stomach drops as we wait.

"They're okay!"

Lila and I hurry closer, bending over the screen.

M, B, H arrived safely and are with us in the CR.

My stomach swoops, but I can't let myself believe it quite yet. "CR? What's that?"

"Coastal Region," Ms. Curie explains.

I swallow. "Is that where my mother— Is my mother . . ."

Ms. Curie doesn't answer as she bends down and types.

Is FW there now?

Yes.

The reply is so fast, I don't even have time to prepare for it. My mother's there. On the other side of a screen like this one. Typing messages to *me*. A strange queasiness bubbles in my stomach. Fear of being wrong, of losing her again. Fear of not losing her, of meeting her and not recognizing her. Or of never meeting her, after I've gotten so close. Everything twists in my mind like a tangle of vines until I have no idea how I feel.

Is CW with you?

Ms. Curie answers, but I don't catch what she types. I imagine my mother a hundred million miles away, maybe feeling the exact storm of emotions I am.

"How do we know whoever is typing is telling the truth?" I ask. "How do we know someone isn't impersonating them?"

"They gave us their initials," Mrs. Hodger says.

"Someone could have intercepted the signal." I spent years believing my mother was dead. I spent months believing she was on Mercury. I won't let myself be fooled again.

Ms. Curie leans forward.

Can you provide proof of person?

The screen is blank for a few seconds, and then a few more. My stomach aches with each moment that ticks by. But then the screen glows with a response.

Did you have to get up early for this, hotshot?

I don't even know I'm crying until Lila puts her arm around my shoulders, wiping my face with her sleeve.

"That's Myra," I choke out. Tears are sliding down Lila's cheeks, too. "They're okay."

"Now the next step, and it's more complicated. We need to get them home," Mrs. Hodger says, her eyes dry, steel in her voice. "Tell them the plan."

Ms. Curie types it out as succinctly as she can, but I'm hardly paying attention.

Myra's alive. My mother's alive. They're all alive. And we can get them home.

Me and Noah.

"Don't tell them about Noah," I say. "Myra won't like that."

Mrs. Hodger frowns. "I'm sure she won't care if—"

"She'll care. Trust me, she'll care. A lot."

"Canter's right," Lila says, meeting my eyes.

"The fewer specifics, the better, anyway," Ms. Curie says, sweeping dark hair from her face. "Is the plan still to go to the MFI factory in three days?"

I nod. "Noah said Melfin definitely won't be around. It's the perfect opportunity."

Ms. Curie types some more. "We're going to lose the signal soon. Is there anything else you want to say?"

Mrs. Hodger rattles off a message that's definitely too long to transmit, but Ms. Curie doesn't complain. I get the feeling she shortens it, though.

I feel like I should say something to my mother, something profound, but I have no idea what. And Myra . . . there's so much I want to say to her, but not anything I want read by a crowd. *Two* crowds. I opt for short and to the point.

See you soon, Mixture Myra.

One final message comes through, and I know it's not from Myra.

I'm so proud of you, Canter.

I blink, fighting against a lump in my throat, as I lean forward over the console and type the first words I've said to my mother in ten years.

CHAPTER TWENTY-FOUR

MYRA

THE SCREEN FLICKERS, displaying a new transmission.

That's all I've ever wanted.

As soon as Fiona reads Canter's message, she bursts into tears.

And then we lose the signal.

I bite my lip, fighting to keep control of my emotions. They burst out of me anyway, but not the way I expect. At first, it's a giggle, then full-on laughter. Hannah looks at me like maybe the next thing she'll have to put back together is me, but Bernard catches my eye, and soon he's losing it, too.

"Of course he'd call me that," I gasp between giggles. "Leave it to Canter to find a way to annoy me and make me miss him in basically the most dramatic moment of our lives."

"Is that a nickname he uses for you?" Fiona asks, wiping her cheeks.

"Unfortunately," I say. "It's what he started calling me when I had to pretend to be a Chemic." Back when things were simple. Except, back then, I thought they were anything but. It's amazing how much your perception can change when your circumstances shift around you. Back then, we had one secret, and we were together. We knew who the enemy was. Now we're hiding so many things I could fill a bookpod, we're millions of miles apart, and we have so many enemies, we need to rank them in order of danger and importance. Hopefully the distance will be a problem solved soon, though. "What do you think of the plan?"

"If they can ensure that the shuttle crash-lands in the water, we'll have a real shot at recovering it in workable condition," Charlie says.

"How many people will it hold?" Fiona asks. "Have you seen an MFI delivery shuttle?"

Bernard, Hannah, and I exchange a glance. "Uh, yeah," I answer. "And they can easily hold thirty. Maybe more, but it'd be tight."

Charlie rubs his chin. "That would mean we could evacuate a decent number of Botans with you, if any want to go."

"And they could probably figure out a way to come back for more," Fiona adds.

"What about the Meteorons?" Hannah asks, and my stomach drops.

Fiona huffs a laugh. "What about them?"

Hannah shifts from foot to foot. "You've never had an opportunity to leave here. Not for hundreds of years. Shouldn't you at least offer—"

Fiona's eyes narrow. "Offer a lift to the very people who tried to sabotage our only way to learn of this plan?"

Hannah wilts under Fiona's glare. "It could be a grapevine."

"Grapevine?" Charlie asks.

"She means an olive branch," Bernard explains. "And she has a point. If you ever had any hope of repairing the damage, this would be the perfect opportunity. I'm sure there were things the Botans did in the past that weren't right."

"And there's been plenty done by the Meteorons," Fiona snaps. "They aren't innocent, and we're not giving up precious space to an enemy."

Hannah twists her hair behind her ear. "But they don't have to be—"

Charlie raises a hand. "Once some of us are off planet, we can consider how to evacuate more people and discuss making an offer to the Meteorons, but now is not the time. As it is, we wouldn't be able to evacuate our whole community, and there are many, many others." He scans our faces. "This is our plan. It needs to start with us."

I know that what Charlie and Fiona say is true—and practical—but it doesn't sit right with me.

"We don't have time to debate this," Fiona says before I can argue. "We need to start preparing. Decide who'll make up the first group and who will wait for the next ship."

"You don't even know how long it will be until we can *send* another ship," I protest. "Or if we *ever* will."

"I'll stay," Charlie says. "I'm the Coastal Region leader. It should be me."

Fiona looks ready to say something but presses her lips together.

"If anyone can figure out a way to send another shuttle back, it's you," he tells her. "Besides, your family is there. You need to go."

She begrudgingly agrees. The conversation dissolves into lists of names I don't recognize, so I tune out. Hannah stares off into the woods, and I know exactly what she's thinking about. *Who* she's thinking about.

When she wanders off, I follow. She gets as far as the tree line before she even notices me tailing her.

"Stop it," she hisses, whipping around.

"You can't tell her. She'll tell the Meteorons, and then who knows what'll happen."

"I can't just leave her here. She's my sister."

"But—"

"She won't tell anyone if I make her promise not to. I'll make her swear. Meredith's never lied to me."

I take a breath. "I don't know, Hannah. . . ."

"I do." She looks over her shoulder at the woods. "I can convince her to come with us. She only joined the Meteorons because she wanted to belong. But I can take her back home. We can be a family again. There's no way she'll turn that down."

Maybe Hannah's right. I can't imagine Meredith betraying her sister. "Well, we'd better get going, then."

Hannah raises an eyebrow. "We?"

"Only one of us knows where the Meteoron camp is. Looks like I'm your guide."

She beams at me. "Thanks, Myra. I owe you."

"Just don't let this whole thing blow up like a supernova," I grumble.

"It won't," she says, happier than I've seen her in years.

We make good time, following the same path that Charlie and Fiona showed me and Bernard yesterday. I expected Hannah to be tired, since she was up all night fixing the transmitter, but it's me hurrying to keep pace with her.

We reach the stretch of charred earth, and she stumbles

to a stop. "Crashing comets," she whispers. "What happened here?"

"The Meteorons." I dig my toe into the black, ashy dirt. It crumbles like moondust. "Nothing can grow here, which makes it harder for the Botans to travel."

Hannah stares at the endless desert, her eyes as dark as the scorched earth, and I think she might turn around. I'd like to. But after a moment, she gives herself a shake and presses on.

I hold up a hand to stop her when we reach the outskirts of the Meteoron village. "We can't just walk into the center of town and start asking around." I scan the houses and people wandering among them. "We need a plan to get Meredith's attention . . . and *only* Meredith's."

Hannah nods, gears turning behind her eyes, and then she smiles slyly.

"What? You've got an idea?"

"Not a whole plan," she says carefully. "But I think I have the seed of one."

CHAPTER TWENTY-FIVE
CANTER

THAT AFTERNOON, I'M STILL REELING FROM TALKING to my mother, if you can even call it that. Really, it was just a few words typed back and forth, but somehow, they mean more to me than any conversation I've ever had.

Lila and I are in her room discussing the plan for tomorrow while Eli tinkers with Bin-ro on the floor. I try not to look. It still feels like a lightning bolt to the heart to see my robot buddy so broken. Part of me likes having him nearby, though. And that someone's trying to fix him.

"So, once you and Noah hack into the computer console, you need to head straight to V.A.M.A., and we can control the shuttle from there," Lila says, eyes glued to her messenger.

"V.A.M.A.?" My eyebrows shoot up. "That's too risky.

There'll be teachers and administrators roaming around everywhere."

Lila shakes her head. "Mrs. Hodger says Myra's dad took care of everything. We're going to set up base in the Number Whispering classroom."

"Mr. Finch knows?" I glance down at Eli, whose brow is furrowed as he extracts some singed fuses. I shudder and look away.

"Apparently." Lila frowns. "I don't know how much, though. I guess he's an old friend of Mr. Hodger, so hopefully he's trustworthy."

"I don't like it."

"Why?" Eli asks.

"Because the more people who know, the more that can go wrong."

A knock at the door makes us all swivel.

"Come in," Lila calls, and the door swings open to reveal her mother and my father standing there looking grim.

I push to my feet while Eli tucks Bin-ro in his bag like he's contraband.

"Sorry to interrupt, kids," Mrs. Crumpler says. "Mr. Weathers stopped by, and—" Her dark eyes linger on Eli. "I'm sorry, sweetie, but I think we've got to go and run an errand."

Eli nods slowly. He carefully slings his bag over his shoulder. "Okay, I'll head home."

Mrs. Crumpler pats his head as he passes her. "We'll see you soon."

When the front door clicks shut, I turn to my dad. "Errand?"

He nods. "It's time. We're going to Mercury."

"Right now?" Lila asks.

"I'm headed there now to start my . . . new position." Dad exchanges a look with Mrs. Crumpler. "Jake thought it made sense just to bring you with me."

"Is *he* going to be there?" I ask, my face getting hot.

"Yes, and you're going to need to keep your loathing in check."

"That's impossible," I snap.

"It's possible," Dad says, a wry smile creasing his face. "It just takes practice."

Like snow falling on fire, my fury cools.

We follow him outside and onto a waiting shuttle.

During the ride, my emotions jump from anger to excitement to guilt.

"Are you okay?" Lila whispers beside me.

"Not really." I don't plan on saying more, but when I look into her dark eyes filled with concern, I sigh. "I don't want favors from Melfin."

"I don't, either, but it can't hurt to have our magic back, especially with what's coming."

I glance over to where Dad and Lila's mom are deep in

conversation. "Perennial's group must be up to something. There's got to be a next phase to her plan."

"We could help. I know we could," Lila says, squeezing my elbow. "I don't want to hold anything back out of spite for Melfin."

"I feel guilty taking anything from him. For getting my magic back."

"Losing our magic wasn't punishment for what happened to Myra, Hannah, and Bernard," Lila says quietly. "It wasn't our fault, and us not having our magic won't fix anything."

"I know that."

"Do you?" Lila leans forward. "Because sometimes I wonder. I replay everything that happened in my head over and over to see where we went wrong. What we could have changed."

My eyebrows shoot up. "Really? So do I."

"And?"

I shake my head. "There's nothing. Nothing that could have stopped us from getting caught. We were already in too deep when we showed up at Perennial's meeting. But—"

"What?"

"That's not the only thing I feel guilty about," I say quietly.

"Friends fight, Canter," Lila murmurs, her grip on my elbow tightening. "One mistake doesn't erase years of being close."

"I said such awful things to her."

"People say things with more than just words, and sometimes the message is stronger than anything you could say out loud."

Tears catch on my lashes. "What are you talking about?"

"You fought to stay in that room, even though it would have outed you and earned you a spot on that shuttle beside her. You used your Botan magic to fight to stay with her."

"And she wouldn't let me," I reply bitterly. "Her and Bernard. What a time for him to find his magic."

"They were trying to protect you. Myra knew what you were risking, but she didn't want you to die just to stick by her."

I study the floor.

"She's still your friend, Canter. What happened in that prison proves it."

"I don't think I can go back there," I whisper, and Lila takes my hand.

"I don't know if I can, either, but I think our best shot is trying to together. We'll do it for Myra."

"For Myra." I *am* going to save her, and my mother, and the rest of them. As many as I can. And the first step is getting my magic back. I can pretend I don't want to murder Jake Melfin. I can do it.

For a few hours, anyway.

CHAPTER TWENTY-SIX

MYRA

HANNAH AND I WEAVE FROM TREE TO TREE, CAREFUL to only move when there's no one in our direct line of sight, or if there is, to wait until their back is turned. Soon, we're close enough to the outer ring of houses that I could toss a stone through one of the windows.

"What if we don't see her?" I ask, crouching behind the trunk of a large oak.

"Then we'll move positions until we do," Hannah hisses, peeking around the side.

I'm about to point out that a game of hide-and-seek doesn't generally work when half the participants don't know they're playing, but before I can, Hannah grabs my arm.

"She's right there!"

I ease around the trunk for a better look. Meredith's wandering between two nearby houses.

"Do it now!" Hannah whisper-yells at me.

I close my eyes and let my mind drift to the tree we're behind. The branches stretching high overhead. The roots extending deep underground, winding through the dirt, spreading out like strands of hair. My magic bubbles in my chest and tickles my toes as it reaches out to the roots, calling them. They respond instantly. I open my eyes just in time to see the grass ripple away like a wave before something like a wooden tentacle erupts out of the ground at Meredith's feet, snagging her ankle.

She only has time for a surprised yelp before it hauls her toward us. Hannah jumps out from the tree line, frantically motioning to her to keep quiet.

Meredith snaps her mouth shut, but she doesn't look happy.

"What are you two doing here?" she demands when the root deposits her in front of us before it sinks back into the ground. She rubs at her leg. "Do you know what they'll do if they find a Botan brat snooping around here?"

"Do you know what *I'd* do if they tried anything?"

"You don't always have to escalate the situation, Myra," Hannah scolds.

I gape at her. "Since when would either of us stay silent when someone threatens us?"

"I didn't threaten you," Meredith growls.

"Look." Hannah holds up her hands. "We didn't come here to argue."

"Then why did you come?" Meredith raises her eyebrows. "Did you change your mind about joining the Meteorons?"

"That's not why we're here, either." Hannah tucks the ends of her hair into her mouth. "I want you to come back with us."

Meredith's eyes flash. "I already told you. I'm not joining the Botans."

"You don't have to join them," Hannah says eagerly. "We can go home."

"Home?" Meredith blinks like she doesn't recognize the word. "This *is* my home."

"No, I mean really go home! With Mom and Dad and me."

"That's impossible."

"It's not," I say quietly. "But we can't tell you the rest unless you agr—"

"A shuttle's coming," Hannah blurts out.

"The Botans have a working shuttle?" Meredith's eyes are as wide as twin Moons.

"No, *we* do." I glare at Hannah. "Our friends are sending it."

"And the Botans are using it to get out of here," Meredith grits out, her jaw tense. "And they aren't planning on saying a word to the Meteorons, right? That's why you're here in secret."

"That's not exactly—" I swallow and elbow Hannah.

"You can't tell them," Hannah pleads. "You have to promise, Meredith. You can't tell. I swore to Myra you wouldn't when she said she'd show me the Meteoron camp."

Meredith's mouth forms a thin line as she stares past Hannah at me. "Oh, I see. You were going to head off and leave me in your stardust. Interstellar."

"No," I snap. "I just didn't think we could trust you not to tell the Meteorons. Hannah insisted you'd never lie to her."

"She's right." Meredith's voice is softer. "I've never lied to Hannah before. She's my sister. Sisters stick together."

Hannah shoots me a triumphant grin.

"That's why you should stay here with me."

Hannah's smile falls off her face like a Moon rock. "What? No. I want to go home. With you. Why would you want to stay?"

"I have a future here." Meredith glances back over her shoulder at the village. "Here, I'm a whole new person I didn't even know existed. No one cares that I don't have magic. . . . They even put me in charge of tracking a huge solar storm passing through the solar system. It's massive! No one on the Moon would trust me with something like that."

"How?" Hannah asks. "They don't have the tech."

Meredith shrugs. "They use their magic. There are a bunch of other signals if you know what to look for in nature, in the sky . . ." Her expression shifts. "They taught me as much as they could about their magic, even if I don't have any. They appreciate me. I'll never have that out there."

"But if the Botans can help grow real food in the Settlements, not that MFI junk, it could change everything," I explain. "Especially how people see magic and Creers. Who knows what the ripple effects could be?"

"Exactly. No one knows, including you. I'm not giving up my life here for the unknown."

Tears pool in Hannah's eyes as her sister pulls away. "Think it over," she begs. "They're coming in two days. If you change your mind—"

"I won't," Meredith says. "But you could. If you do, come back. Find me. You'll always be welcome here." As she walks away, she glances back, flipping her dark hair over her shoulder. I hardly recognize her.

One look at Hannah's face tells me she barely does, either.

CHAPTER TWENTY-SEVEN

CANTER

THE SHUTTLE SHUDDERS AS IT TOUCHES DOWN, and instantly I feel heat radiating from the floor and walls. After a deep breath, I clutch Lila's hand, and we follow our parents onto the landing strip.

The scenery is just as bleak as I remember. Dark, charred rock surrounded by dark, charred buildings. It's like walking through a fire pit filled with embers. I can't believe my dad's choosing to live here.

He's doing it for me, I remind myself. *To make amends. To help the cause.* I stare up at the structure looming ahead of us—the prison. If Dad can move to this place voluntarily, I can hold it together for an hour. How long could it take to deactivate our chips, anyway?

I carefully release Lila's hand, keeping my eyes locked on the back of Dad's gray-streaked hair, fighting against the surge of memories threatening to erupt like a geyser inside me.

Familiar faces greet us at the command center. Warden Vander, a severe-looking woman with thick blond hair and a wiry frame, is leaning over a console. With a wave of her hand, she dismisses the guards before crossing to Dad and Mrs. Crumpler and shaking their hands. Her gaze rakes over Lila and me, but when she turns back to Dad, I'm relieved. "As soon as Jake arrives, we can get started. Once we finish the procedure, I'll show you to your office."

Dad nods. "I'd like to get started right away."

The warden actually cracks a smile. "Jake said you would. Oh, here he is now."

Footsteps echo behind me, but I don't turn around. With a little luck, Melfin'll ignore me, just like Warden Vander did.

"Hello, Rob," a voice booms. Jake Melfin offers Dad an enthusiastic handshake. "And you must be Mrs. Crumpler."

Lila's mom nods, giving him a tight smile as she accepts his hand. I notice she drops it quickly, like it could infect her. Melfin doesn't seem to register it.

"And this must be your daughter," he says, nodding to Lila. "I remember her from the last time. . . . But we won't get into all that. Ah, and Canter!"

He steps toward me, and I clench my teeth, forcing myself to reach out a hand. But he doesn't take it. Instead, he pulls me into a hug. I go stiff, arms glued to my sides, fighting the urge to bolt away or stomp on his foot or pummel his chest.

"Good to see you, son," he says as he steps back and smiles broadly.

He reaches out to muss my hair, and I can't help myself. I jerk backward. As his smile fades, I feel my stomach drop. *Crashing comets, Canter. You only needed to hold it together for a few minutes. Don't blow it now.*

I motion toward my head. "I, um, just did my hair."

Melfin hesitates, then bursts out in a loud guffaw. "Sorry, kid. Don't want to mess with your style." He holds his hands out. "Guess they're at that age now, eh, Rob?"

Dad nods. "He *is* thirteen."

"Saturn's rings. How did they get to be teenagers? I hardly recognize Kyle these days. Can barely even have a conversation with him."

When Melfin turns, Dad catches my eye and gives the smallest thumbs-up. I sigh. Now, let's get this done and get out of here before I lose it for real.

Dad seems to be on the same page. "Should we get going with the, er, procedure? Warden Vander wanted to show me to my office."

Melfin claps Dad on the shoulder. "There's no rush. You can jump into all that tomorrow. We'll get these three squared away"—he nods at me, Lila, and her mom—"and then I thought we could all have dinner. There are some folks I'd like you to meet. Thought it would be a good intro for your new role here."

My eyes bug out, and I feel Lila brush my arm.

Dad glances sideways at me. "That sounds fine, but surely you don't need the Crumplers or Canter. They can head home."

"I insist!" Melfin says. There's an edge to his voice. "They've never had a meal like this, I can promise you that."

All at once, I know what's happening. He's going to serve us food from our garden. As punishment. As a way to show his power. And there's nothing we can do about it.

Or is there?

I open my mouth to tell him what he can do with his dinner, but Lila pipes up first, her voice as sweet as honey.

"That sounds absolutely interstellar, Mr. Melfin. I'm hungry enough to eat an asteroid."

"Yes, that would be lovely," Mrs. Crumpler says, shifting her weight. "Thank you for the invitation."

"See, Rob." Melfin chuckles. "I've always said you need to loosen up. Let them stay. We'll celebrate the occasion. Speaking of, why don't we get started."

Warden Vander nods and leaves the room. Dad's face is pale, his jaw tight, like he's struggling to keep his temper as much as I am.

Melfin seems to sense the tension in the room. "I'm

sorry I can't do anything about your, er, predicament. I did try, but the warden wouldn't budge. Maybe someday..."

"It's fine, Jake," Dad says with a tight smile that doesn't reach his eyes. "I know you tried your best."

The warden returns with a contraption that looks nothing like the one Perennial used. This device is a simple baton with a cluster of sensors on one end. "Who's first?"

"Mrs. Crumpler," I say immediately.

The warden sweeps the device from Mrs. Crumpler's head to her toes in front of her, and behind, then glances down at a small screen and nods. "It may take some time for your powers to return. It's different for everyone."

"Do you use that often?" Dad asks, his eyes narrowed on Melfin, who shifts uncomfortably.

"Sometimes new information comes to light or there was a . . . misunderstanding."

What he's trying to say is that enemies find a way to pay him off, bribe him, or give in and accept his bribe.

Dad meets my gaze, and I'd guess he's thinking the same thing. He bites his tongue, so I do, too.

The warden sweeps the wand over Lila next. She shudders as it passes over her.

"What's it feel like?" I whisper while the warden studies the screen.

"It's hard to describe, but I swear I could feel a flutter, like it opened a tap and my magic came bubbling out."

"And finally." The warden gestures for me to step forward. "Let's finish. I believe our other guests have arrived."

I struggle not to wince when she raises the baton over my head. She waves it over me once, twice. At first I don't feel anything, but as the device passes over me a third time, my arm tingles like it fell asleep. With a *whoosh*, my skin's suddenly alive with electricity. I hold my hand out and a ball of energy pulses on my palm.

"Look at that. Good as new," Melfin says, clapping me on the shoulder before jerking away. I'm not positive, but I think I shocked him.

Rubbing his right hand behind his back, Melfin gestures with his left toward the hall. "We should head over. I don't want the food getting cold."

I wave my fingers and make the light fixtures we pass dim and flicker. Beside me, Lila's curly black hair grows and shortens, weaving into a thick braid before unwinding again.

"Feels good, huh," she says.

"Like I've been holding my breath for weeks and my lungs can finally inflate again."

We walk into what must be a dining room, and I gasp. The table is laden with a feast. Freshly sliced fruits and vegetables. Pies. Roasts. Whipped potatoes and glazed carrots and elaborate pastas. After years of eating MFI's slimy processed food squares, this looks like a mirage. A dream.

Or a nightmare. I know where every speck of this food

came from. I grew some of it with Myra. The sight of it makes me sick.

"Looks great, doesn't it?" Melfin says, surveying our stunned expressions and misinterpreting them. Or maybe not. "I should introduce the person responsible for this bounty, or one of them, anyway." Maybe I'm imagining it, but I think he throws me a wink before he steps into an adjoining room and calls, "Come on out and say hello."

The nausea is back, followed quickly by rage, as Noah steps inside the dining room.

"Meet my new head chef, Noah Morris," Melfin announces, patting him on the shoulder. "I scouted him from V.A.M.A. Hey, maybe you kids know him."

I don't trust what might come out of my mouth, so I don't answer. Thankfully, Lila pulls herself together.

"I think we've met once or twice," she says coolly.

Noah suddenly doesn't look so good himself. "I'd better check on the dessert," he says, backstepping toward the door.

"Good, good," Melfin replies. "Don't forget, I need you to do a repeat of this at my Lunar office next week. Did you sort out the delivery?"

Noah nods, catching my eye for the briefest moment, before answering. "I'm going to the MFI factory tomorrow to work out the details."

Melfin smiles broadly. "Exactly why I like you, kid. Always on top of things."

Once Noah's gone, Melfin gestures for us to sit. Not long after, two men and a woman arrive. One of the men and the woman—maybe his wife?—look thrilled to be here, but the other man looks terrified.

Plates are passed around. I avoid taking anything until Lila nudges me.

"You have to at least pretend to eat," she whispers.

I sigh and take a scoop of the pasta, then swirl it around on my plate. And that's when I see them. Grapes. I scoop one onto my fork and hold it up, inspecting it, and then let it fall. I know this fruit. Myra tried to get its vines to trip me the last time we went to the garden. She even had it wind up my back, flopping a cluster of grapes onto my forehead.

"You wouldn't think it would work," Melfin booms, leaning over the table. "Grapes and pasta. But Noah has a way of roasting them that makes for an incredible combination. Kid's a genius with his culinary powers. Who knew a Chemic could work that kind of magic with food."

"It must grow on you," I say, shoving the plate away. "Is there a bathroom nearby?"

Melfin hesitates. "Straight down the hall. Take your first left."

Lila catches my eye, and I know she sees right through my story. I'd prefer exploring with her, but it would look too suspicious.

I zip down the hall, turning into the first corridor on

my left and straight past the bathroom. Electricity flows into my fingertips as I pause at each doorway, listening for movement. If it's silent on the other side, I spark the door panel and peek inside, but all I find are deserted offices, supply rooms, and another bathroom.

A level down, the halls are lined with prison cells. I recognize the complicated locking mechanisms from the last time I was here. This isn't the same hallway, but my stomach tenses when I remember opening the door to my mother's empty cell.

Voices echo behind me, coming closer, so I hurry up a flight of stairs, emerging across from the command center. The guards are back, clustered around the console. One points at the screen. I tiptoe closer, careful to stay out of sight.

"Mr. Melfin told Vander he had this under control," one of them says.

"He's a businessman, not a general. What does he know about crushing uprisings?"

Uprisings?

"It's a little much to call it an uprising," the first guard says. "It's a few raids."

"Regardless," the woman says, "I'd better report it."

"I'll go with you." I have just enough time to duck behind a wall before they clomp out of the command center.

I peek around the corner again. The remaining guard is engrossed in the screen. The other two are almost halfway down the hallway. I dance from foot to foot. *What would Myra do?*

I follow them.

"They're gathering supplies," the woman says as I creep behind them. "Can't you tell by the locations? Food, then weapons."

"What did they take from the Council's armory?" the man asks. He turns his head, and I duck into a doorway, pressing myself against it. I wait a handful of heartbeats, listening for their footsteps, and then tiptoe back into the hall.

"Pulse generators, stun canisters, Mender supplies." I barely hear the woman's words as they turn another corner, and I hurry to catch up. "But that's not all they're after."

"What do you mean? What else did they take?"

"People."

I pause, peering carefully around a corner to make sure they're still moving down the corridor. They're not. They've stopped a few feet away. Careful not to make any sudden movements and catch their eye, I ease back, pressing myself against the wall.

"I accessed the MFI personnel files before and after the raid," the woman whispers. Her colleague gasps. "Perks of working security on the weekends. I'm glad I did, because absences are up fifty-four percent."

"So?" I can practically see the guy shrugging. "Maybe they're sick."

"Half the staff at once? No way. They're being recruited."

"A bunch of non-Creers and Reps. Good luck to them."

"Reps that have their magic back," the woman says so softly I have to strain to make out her words. "And non-Creers with enough weapons and goods to supply an army."

"Sounds like your friends have been busy," someone whispers in my ear, and I jump. Kyle Melfin stands behind me, an arrogant smirk plastered on his face. "Shouldn't you be in the other room eating your fancy dinner?"

I run my hands through my hair, catching footsteps echoing in the connecting hall. The guards are finally heading away from us. "I, uh, got turned around trying to find the bathroom. How come you're not there? Your dad doesn't like to bring you out in public?" I cross my arms. "Can't say I blame him."

Kyle winces. I think I hit a nerve.

"More like those things are so painfully boring." He looks me up and down. "Came to beg for your powers back?"

Heat flares in my cheeks. "Already got them, no begging required. How about I test them on you?"

"Careful," Kyle scolds. "My dad can take them away again just as easily. Don't forget who you owe."

"Yeah, *my* dad," I snap. "Because *MFI* needed his help. I guess I can't blame him. It's not like the great Jake Melfin can count on his son for anything, powers or not."

Kyle opens his mouth and then shuts it. "Better head back before they wonder where you've gotten to. My dad doesn't appreciate snooping."

"I can see why," I call, heading back to the dining room. "Seems like he's got all sorts of dinners and deals planned. What's he serving for the next course? Cake? Contracts? A one-way all-expenses-paid trip to the Old World?"

The blood drains from Kyle's face, but he doesn't say anything else as I disappear inside.

No one seems to notice when I slip back into my seat. Kyle makes an appearance a little while later while Noah's serving dessert.

"Kyle," his father booms. "Bet you're surprised to see your old classmates here."

Kyle slouches in his chair, ignoring the heaping platters of food. "Not really," he says, and his father raises his eyebrows. My stomach lurches as I wait for Kyle to drop the bomb and out me. "I ran into Canter in the bathroom." His expression is unreadable as he meets my eyes across the table.

The rest of the night passes uneventfully, and finally, the Crumplers and I are boarding the shuttle back to Venus.

Lila and her mom head inside the craft just as Dad exits the building, lingering on the landing pad. The monstrous prison looms behind him.

"Are you sure you want to stay here?" I blurt out.

"It's not that I want to," he says, putting a hand on my shoulder. For once, I don't shrug it off. "But I can be useful here. We'll never be safe as long as Jake holds this much power. Nobody will. No one deserves what he's put us through, and if I can stop him from destroying another family, I need to do that."

He's right. It's time for me to leave, but I can't make my feet move toward the shuttle.

"I'm sorry, Canter," Dad says suddenly, his voice breaking. "I'm sorry for everything. I should have told you the truth about your mother. I shouldn't have shut you out. Every decision I've made since telling Jake about your mother's magic all those years ago feels like the wrong one now, and every time I try to make a new choice, I just dig the hole deeper." He rubs his eyes, and I gape at him. I've never seen my father cry. "I'm sure it seems impossible to believe that I had good intentions. I never meant for us to end up like this. I may never be able to fix everything I've destroyed, but I'll find a way to make up as much as I can to you."

"Dad . . ." I want to tell him that it's okay. That I forgive him. Or at least that I want to *try to* forgive him. But those words won't come. "Not everything is as broken as you think."

He frowns. "What do you mean?"

"I . . . I can't say yet. I don't know for sure, and I don't want to say more until I do, but maybe we *can* fix some things. I . . . I want you to know that I'm going to try, too."

"I don't really understand," he says slowly, "but I trust you. And I hope you know, if you need help, I'll do everything I can to support you. Just—just be careful, son. Please. That's all I ask. You're all . . ."

He doesn't finish, and I'm glad because that means I won't be tempted to correct him. Not yet.

Instead, I surprise us both. I hug him.

His arms wrap tightly around me, clutching so hard my ribs hurt. But I don't complain. I'm pretty sure his sides must be aching, too.

And just like that, we break apart, both wiping our eyes.

"Be careful," he says as I head for the shuttle. "And Canter?"

I turn, looking down at him.

"If she were here, your mother would be so proud of you." He lifts his chin. "Just like I am."

CHAPTER TWENTY-EIGHT

MYRA

WHEN WE ARRIVE BACK AT THE COASTAL REGION, Hannah hurries to the tree house, and I let her go. I know her well enough to understand when she wants to be alone. After our meeting with Meredith, I don't blame her.

Once Hannah disappears inside, I head toward the ocean. But when I reach the top of the hill overlooking the beach, I skid to a stop. Across the sand, old damaged shuttles are lined up in a row like a graveyard. I scramble down the hill, trailing my fingers through the tall wispy grasses, and wildflowers sprout behind me like a zigzagging rainbow that continues blooming even when I reach the sand.

I stop beside the first shuttle, ours, then continue from one to the next. There are at least a dozen clustered together, just out of reach of the breaking cobalt waves. Each ship seems slightly older than the last, like the Botans arranged them according to when they crashed. At the very end is an ancient-looking ship that looks like it's been sliced in half.

"We had your shuttle hauled here this morning," Charlie says, stepping out from behind one of the ships. "Impressive, aren't they?"

"Are they all from exiles? There are so many."

He nods. "These are just the ones from our region over the last, oh, I don't know, fifty or so years? This was Fiona's," he says, leading me to one of the first in the row. "It arrived about a decade ago."

I run my hands over the dented hull, warped like the sun melted it over the years.

"And this is the last one to arrive before yours." It's in worse shape than most—cracked panels, exposed wires, and blackened metal. "It crashed a year ago."

"This must have been Meredith's, then," I say softly, surveying the damage. "Do the exiles always survive?"

"As long as I can remember."

"But the ships are in such bad shape."

"They didn't exactly start out in pristine condition," Charlie reminds me. "Who'd waste a new shuttle on a one-way mission?"

"They're like a museum exhibit, all lined up like this."

"We thought if we arranged them newest to oldest it would be easier to assess what their technological capabilities are. Or were. From there, we'll be able to figure which parts we can salvage so that when the shuttle from your friends arrives, we can begin repairs right away."

"Why is the timing important?" I ask.

He cocks an eyebrow. "Not anxious to leave?"

"I am!" As soon as the words leave my lips, I can sense the lie in them. I'm eager to get back to Canter, Lila, and my parents, and I definitely want to start making Melfin's life messier than a meteor shower, but at the same time . . . I look back over my shoulder at the wilderness behind me. Mangroves and geraniums and sea grass and yucca leaves. It will be hard to go back to the barren solar system after being around all this.

Or maybe not. Maybe with Fiona and the other Botans, we can transform the galaxy, plot gardens among the stars. I smile at the thought, then kneel down and draw a large circle in the sand. In the center, a blanket of sea campion springs up, the white flowers glowing against the pale beige sand. On the back of my hand, I trace a new Inscription of the same flower, its wide petals curling up and around my fingers.

"We'll miss you here," Charlie says, moving back down the line of shuttles. "You've got a connection with the plants that's not quite like anyone else's magic. Must be all the time you've spent coaxing them to grow in less hospitable environments. Your talent's remarkable."

I feel my cheeks go pink, but Charlie's too far away to see.

After a while, I head back up the beach and to the tree houses. Fiona is perched on a bowed branch. Bernard leans against the trunk.

"You left early this morning," Fiona says as I join them. "I saw you and Hannah walking through the village just after sunrise."

"We, er, wanted to explore a little," I say, fighting the urge to twist my hands together. I shove them in my pockets and shrug. "Since we're leaving soon, we want to soak in as much of the Old World wilderness as we can."

"Have they chosen the people who are coming with us yet?" Bernard asks.

Fiona picks up a pile of fabric in her lap, then a thin sliver of metal with a string trailing from it. "We'll have a community meeting to discuss and decide."

I raise my eyebrows. "Everyone?"

"It's how we do things here." She turns her face up to the sky, where the Moon's visible again. "We don't have Councils that decide everything for us. Just Charlie, who's elected, and he mostly handles the day-to-day affairs and breaks a tie if there's a disagreement, which is rare."

"That would be hard to manage large-scale," Bernard muses. "It'd be too much to bring everyone together to vote on every major decision in a population as big as in the Settlements."

Fiona shrugs. "I don't know about that. If it were up to me, I'd like the opportunity to have a say in the matters that affect me."

"Isn't the Council system similar, though?" asks Bernard. "Just on a larger scale?"

"In theory." She looks back to the fabric, sliding the needle through it. Up and down and up again, pulling the thread tighter and tighter. "But it also opens the door to corruption. Terms are too long. Those elected become too powerful. The general public can't be troubled to notice, and when they do it's only a handful actually paying attention. Even then, they can't be bothered to do anything about what concerns them. As long as their daily lives carry on with relative ease, it's amazing what they'll ignore." She sighs. "I was guilty of that, too. But not anymore. I could never go back."

"We *are* going back, though," I remind her. "Literally, straight back. Tomorrow."

Fiona smiles. "Yes, yes. I know. But not to pick up where we left off."

I grin. "We're going to cause all sorts of trouble."

"You bet your blossoms we are." Fiona's gaze drifts back up to the sky.

Beside her, Bernard trails his fingers down the bark of the tree. Specks of moss appear, growing into an emerald trail matching the path of his touch. For a second, it looks like the moss has grown across his hand, intricate chartreuse lines weaving together on his skin.

I inhale sharply. "Bernard! Look! You've got a Botan Inscription."

He looks down at his hand, then beams, holding it out for Fiona and me to see. Delicate, looping lines form the outline of an oak leaf on his palm. "It's not the first one, though. This was." He pulls up his sleeve, and I gasp at the cheery yellow sunflower etched on his forearm.

"It's prettier than a Martian sunset," I whisper over the lump in my throat. "When did you get it?"

"I noticed it when we first arrived here. I think it was from—"

"Mercury," I finish, flinching.

Fiona sees. "Friendships get more complicated as you get older," she says gently, tugging the thread tight. Something dark and shiny is tucked between the fabric and the string. "Everyone makes mistakes. Says things they don't mean."

"Canter doesn't seem to be holding a grudge, Mixture Myra," Bernard adds, nudging my shoulder.

"But maybe she is," Fiona says, looking at me pointedly. "And that would be okay. Just because one friend is sorry doesn't mean the other has to accept the apology, especially not before it's actually given. From what you've shared, it sounds like Canter said some pretty hurtful things. Forgiveness is earned, not claimed."

I study her, wondering if she's seriously siding with me over her son.

She laughs. "Don't look at me like that. I'm sure Canter makes as many mistakes as the next kid. Maybe more, considering his parents' record." A cloud crosses her face. "It doesn't mean I love him any less."

"Your childhood friend group seems pretty intact," Bernard remarks. "What's the secret?"

"Laughter, loyalty, and the ability to say *I'm sorry* and accept an *I'm sorry* in return," she answers without hesitating. "That doesn't mean we didn't have our fallings-out. Just that we figured out how to weather them." Her eyes fog as memories play across them. "Wait until you kids get older, or start dating. That's when you'll face the real challenge." She grins. "When it comes to testing friendships, galactic conspiracies have nothing on teenage drama."

"You mean you and Director Weathers?" Bernard asks. "Ms. Curie and Ms. Goble were upset when you started dating?"

"Sandra was. Val understood, I think, though I'm sure it annoyed her when I blew them off to spend time with Robert."

"You blew off your best friends for a *date*?" My mouth falls open. "Why didn't you just reschedule?"

"You make it sound so simple," she says with a sigh. "And I guess it is, but it doesn't *feel* that way when you're young and in the middle of your first love."

I crinkle my nose. "No thanks. Sounds like a lot of work."

She winks. "You might change your mind someday."

"Doubtful."

"Anyway." Fiona bites the thread, severing it. She strings a new, longer piece through the needle. "Sandra was really offended by all the time I was spending with Robert. I think that's part of why she gave me the seeds. So we'd have something to share again. Just the two of us."

"But I thought Director Weathers helped you start the garden?"

"I didn't say it worked," Fiona says with a sigh. "Sandra was part of it, too. Just not as much as she'd probably hoped."

"She must have been really upset," Bernard says.

"Sandra was furious at first, but she got over it."

"What made her understand?" Bernard asks.

"I don't know that she did, really. She was just too distracted to care anymore. By Jake."

Bernard and I exchange a look, then both gape at Fiona. I swallow hard. "Are you saying . . . that Ms. Curie *dated* Jake Melfin?"

"Don't look so shocked. All sorts of people pair up that you'd never expect."

"But *Jake Melfin?*" I grimace.

"He wasn't quite the way he is now," Fiona says. "Though looking back, I can see the seeds of the corruption in him. And besides, their relationship didn't last long. They were very close when they were together. Maybe even closer than Sandra was with me and Val at the time."

"But you were her best friends?" I say, grimacing. "That's impossible."

"Relationships can be different." She shrugs, picking up another dark fleck—a seed—and tucking it into the fabric.

"What are you doing?" I ask, nodding toward her project. Leaning closer, I notice rows and rows of little nooks.

"There aren't exactly a lot of plants where we're going." She tugs the thread tight around the ebony seed, attaching it to the fabric. "We're going to have to carry seeds with us, and we're going to need more than what we can hold in our pockets."

I shudder, remembering another place Lila had found to hide our seed stash. Stitching them into clothing is a much better idea.

"What happened that broke them up?" Bernard asks. "Curie and Melfin."

"I think it was Jake's father. He didn't approve. Sandra isn't from a very well-known Creer family, and he was very focused on Jake spending time with other Chemics. The foundation of all the Creers, he would say."

I sigh. "My parents used to say that, too. About Number Whispering."

"People like to project their own importance," Fiona replies. "Sometimes because they truly believe it, and other times to cover for their own weaknesses or insecurities. Knowing your parents, I think they fell into the former category, but the Melfins . . ." She shakes her head. "Definitely insecure and terrified."

Overhead, a vine shoots through the air, then erupts into an explosion of flowers, the blossoms splaying out like a firework.

"What's that?" Bernard asks, holding his hands out to catch the petals fluttering around us like confetti.

"It's meeting time," Fiona says, hopping off her branch. "We'd better go and see who'll be joining us."

CHAPTER TWENTY-NINE

CANTER

THE NEXT DAY, I CLIMB INTO AN AQUAXI, SLIDING IN beside Noah, and am instantly reminded of the first time I met him, sitting awkwardly in the front of the transport with Myra and Lila in the back as we made our way to Hannah's apartment.

Was that the moment it all began to go wrong? Was there any way to stop it? Or are we in a wild curve of an otherwise correct path?

"Ready for this?" Noah asks, tapping our destination into the computer.

"I'm ready to get Myra off that rock. And the other Botans, too."

"I really never meant for this to happen to her," Noah says quietly as the aquaxi slides smoothly through the water.

I don't answer. Out the window, familiar-looking fish stream by, bright and puffy like hoverballs, and just as colorful.

"I know you don't believe me, and I don't blame you, but I had to say it all the same."

I force my gaze away from the fish, focusing on the deep bags beneath his dark, troubled eyes. He looks like he hasn't slept in months. He looks older than he did a month or two ago. Years older. "I never liked you."

Noah blinks.

"But," I continue, "at least initially, I think I was a little jealous. Myra is my best friend, and even though I sort of— I didn't really . . ."

"Mean to ditch her?"

A spark of irritation flares in my chest.

"That came out harsher than I meant."

I shrug. "All I'm saying is, maybe I wasn't fair to you at first. Or maybe I had your card all along. Either way." I look him dead in the eye. "If you help me to fix this—if we can get Myra back—I don't care about the past."

Noah nods, then turns back to the console. "Almost there."

The aquaxi starts to ascend, and as it does, a structure like an upside-down mountain emerges in the distance. The support systems are so extensive, the factory itself must be massive. "It's like an island."

Noah nods. "It's MFI's largest transportation hub in the galaxy. For now, anyway. Melfin's always talking about expanding. He's sort of obsessed with it."

"Why?"

"I don't know." Noah rubs his chin. "It's like nothing is ever enough for him. Not big enough, important enough, successful enough. He's always talking about *infinite growth*, whatever that means."

"I know what it means: greed."

As the aquaxi breaches the surface, I see the physical manifestation of the word: *greed* in concrete form. The structure's walls stretch up so high, I'm surprised the amber-and-gold clouds floating overhead don't bump into them.

"Why does he need this much space?" I ask, climbing out of the transport. Noah's right behind me. "Don't the slime squares make packing and shipping easier?"

"It's a staging center for his new products. I overheard him talking about it during one of his dinner meetings. They're using this facility to produce all the new products."

"Are the others any better than the imitation food?"

He grimaces. "They might be worse. There have been rumors . . ."

I pause halfway along the path. "What kind of rumors?"

"That the compounds Melfin's using to make the dyes are mildly toxic."

"What does that mean?"

"Like, not enough to make you sick immediately, but no one knows what will happen after extended exposure."

I shake my head and continue toward the building. "How's the garden?"

Noah winces. "It's flourishing."

"What do you mean?" I ask, whipping around. "It must be picked clean without Botan magic to take care of it."

"It's even bigger than how Myra left it."

Maybe it's lingering magic?

At the factory entrance, Noah scans his palm on the door sensor. Inside, the floor's bustling. Carts, robots, and workers stream in all directions. It reminds me of one of the V.A.M.A. choreographed dances. Rows and rows of shelves form a network of aisles, and at the far end, I can glimpse what must be a fleet of delivery ships.

Noah walks in like he owns the place.

Always look like you know where you're going.

I follow him, trying to project a mix of confidence and purpose, topped by a dash of boredom. No one gives me a second look. They're all focused on Noah: answering his questions, guiding him to this product or that shipping container. Slowly—maybe too slowly—we inch toward the fleet of ships.

Noah manages to shoo everyone away, and by the time I can reach out and touch one of the ship's hulls, we're completely alone.

"How'd you get them to leave us alone?" I ask. "Magic?"

"No," he says, flashing me a crooked grin. "Strategic synergy."

"I don't even want to know what that is." I sigh, trailing my fingers along the wings and frames. "I can't wait to hack into one of these."

"Let's see which are scheduled to fly closest to where we need to end up." Noah pauses next to one, taps something into its console, then sighs and moves on to the next. He does this half a dozen times before turning back to me, his face bright like he discovered buried treasure. "This is the one!"

"How can you tell?"

"It has scheduled deliveries on the Moon, and then Mercury. Based on the current orbits, it'll pass within two hundred thousand miles of the Old World."

I rub my hands through my hair. "It shouldn't need much of an adjustment to send it off course. Just a nudge."

"Exactly. And this is one of the unmanned ones. It runs on autopilot. Do you have the device?"

I reach into my pocket and pull out the infiltration attachment. "Cover me," I say, heading up the ramp into the shuttle.

I probably should have asked Noah to make sure the crew were done before waltzing into the cockpit.

"What are you doing?" a girl not much older than me

demands, immediately noticing I'm not wearing a factory uniform.

"Do you even work here?" her partner asks. He could be twenty or forty. Regardless, he looks annoyed.

"No," I say, puffing out my chest. "But I'm here with Mr. Melfin's personal chef. We're using a shuttle like this one to make deliveries for his business meetings. High-profile guests. And we need to make sure it's up to his standards."

Their eyes bulge. "Jake Melfin's personal deliveries?"

I nod. "How long will it take for this thing to make a run from Venus to the Moon?"

"Not long," the girl says. "You won't even need much refrigeration."

"Perfect." I glance around, then drift toward the console. "What's the possible temperature variance for the hold? Some of the ingredients are pretty delicate." I tap the screen, swiping through various system checks.

The man rattles off temperature ranges for the main hold and various storage containers. "Would that work?" he asks nervously.

I tap my hand on the console again, praying they don't see the glint of metal between my fingertips, then flip open the casing.

"What in the orbit?" the man asks, lunging at me.

I push his hands away. "Do you mind? I'm doing a systems check."

"A what?"

I roll my eyes. "I'm making sure all the connections are sound. The last time someone guaranteed me refrigeration capabilities, the entire system overheated midway through transit and ruined the entire delivery."

But what's that got to do with the console?" the girl asks.

I sigh. "That's what controls all the systems, *including* refrigeration. I need to check that everything is connected properly. Unless you want to be personally responsible if anything goes wrong?"

She shakes her head, and I return my attention to the console, probing the wiring. "How cold did you say the freezer compartment can get?"

The girl repeats the stats, and I click the console shut. "That should work, but I'll have to double-check the specifications for the fruit sorbets Mr. Melfin's ordered."

"We could test them," the man says eagerly. "Do a trial run."

I widen my eyes. "That's an interstellar idea! What'd you say your name was?"

"Rashford." His eyes gleam.

"If it works, I'll tell Mr. Melfin it was your idea." The man swells even more.

Infiltration device dropped, I try to extract myself from the cockpit, but the workers want to show me every single feature of their ship. I humor them for a minute, then excuse myself, muttering something about a meeting.

Noah's pacing at the foot of the ramp. "Well?" he asks as I trot down to meet him.

"Let's get out of here. We've got a shuttle to steal."

CHAPTER THIRTY

MYRA

A CROWD FORMS IN FRONT OF THE SALVAGED shuttles as people stream from the village to the beach. Branches erupt from the sand, seats for the meeting.

Bernard, Fiona, and I settle near the front section while Charlie stands before the assembly, the largest ship looming behind, as he explains about the incoming shuttle.

"We've never had an opportunity like this before. Most of us descend from the original Botans abandoned here when the rest of humanity fled. Some are more recent friends, cast off by the Settlement governments, banished to die here, or so they thought. Many of us may have reasons to leave, reasons to stay, and there may be far more who opt to go than can fit on this initial shuttle."

Murmurs ripple through the crowd, but I can't gauge the mood.

"We're lucky to have all sorts of talents in our community." He pauses, steeling himself. "And we'll sort out exactly who will be on this first shuttle as fairly as we can. But one rule I am setting in place is that all on this trip must be Botans."

From the corner of my eye, I see a head flick up. *Hannah.* She's with some of the kids she's been training.

Charlie notices her, too, and holds his hands up. "With exceptions made for those who arrived most recently and are responsible for this shuttle's arrival."

Hannah catches my eye as she relaxes, her expression unreadable.

"Why are only the Botans allowed to leave?" a young man calls from Hannah's group. "Wouldn't it make more sense for those of us with other Creers to go first, since we don't have the same opportunities to learn or use our magic here?"

"That's very logical, and I sympathize with your point," Charlie replies. "However, we know that the first to successfully leave this planet will be in grave danger from the Governing Councils. That's why only those with full Creer training will be allowed on the first mission. We're also aware that there's a food crisis in the Settlements—that may mean the sudden appearance of Botans will be met with less hostility. It presents a unique opportunity for us to reestablish ourselves as a credible Creer while helping the Settlements."

"Why would we want to help them?" an older woman demands. "They cast us away like space junk. Maybe we should let them starve."

"I understand that view, too, but we'll achieve no long-term good from vengeance."

"Nothing wrong with short-term good," the woman says with a huff. A few people chuckle.

"Many of you are familiar with the food production company, MFI," Charlie continues. "They were formed before the evacuation and have only gained power since then. The leader of the company, Jake Melfin, is a well-known persecutor of Botans. Most of our recent residents were exiled here by him. The longer these food cloning issues go on, the more powerful he becomes. And I don't know about the rest of you"—Charlie's eyes glint—"but I'd like to strip every ounce of that power away. The Botans can do that."

Quiet chatter erupts again, but this time the tone is unmistakable: eager and determined, without a hint of resentment.

Charlie surveys the crowd. "One of the aims of the first group will be to send another shuttle back as soon as possible. Though let me be clear: no one has to go anywhere."

"Will you be on the first mission, Charlie?" someone calls.

He shakes his head and smiles. "This place is my home. I can't imagine ever leaving." He scans the group. "Still, I don't begrudge anyone who makes a different choice. If you're interested in being on the first shuttle, please come forward now."

Lots of people do, but many others remain seated. Charlie stands in the middle of a circle, engaged in a lively discussion with the eager volunteers. Too many to fit on the first shuttle for sure, yet Charlie listens to them all.

"Here," Fiona says, nudging something into my hand. It's the small emerald-green box. "Take this."

"Why?"

The glints of green reflect in her sky-blue-colored eyes. "Keep it as a reminder that in nature, there are good plants and bad ones. The invasive ones, the dangerous ones, *the weeds*, need to be ripped out at the root. They can't be left to infect the rest."

I nod and slide the box into my pocket "I won't forget."

"Looks like it's settled," Fiona says, jutting her chin at the group behind Charlie. The circle surrounding him has shrunk to about twenty. A handful of others drift away looking disappointed.

"I'm surprised there wasn't more fighting," Bernard says.

Fiona shrugs. "That's not how things are done here."

He surveys the crowd around him. "Then I don't see why so many people even want to leave."

"You don't have to go back, you know," Fiona tells him. "You could stay here with Charlie, and the others."

"The other Botans," he says softly.

"Like you."

He nods slowly but doesn't answer.

Panic grips my chest, and it's all I can do not to seize his hand so he'll have to come with me. But I wouldn't do that to Bernard. If anyone deserves to decide their own fate, it's him.

"I think I need to go," he finally says, and I breathe a sigh of relief. "I want to help make sure no Rep has their magic taken from them ever again."

Fiona smiles. "That's wonderful, but think bigger. Maybe there shouldn't even be such a thing as Reps."

"That'll never happen," he says, bitterness tingeing his voice. "The whole system is built on Reps. Who would do the work?"

She shrugs. "Who cares. If it needs to be done, the galaxy can figure it out. Rip down the whole system and start over."

"She's right," I add carefully. "The Botans started over here, and I don't see any Reps around."

I look pointedly at him, and he laughs. "I like the way you two think." He watches the crowd disperse. "I'm going on the shuttle, but that doesn't mean I won't come back here someday."

"Once we're done causing trouble," I say, elbowing him.

"What will you do after?" he asks.

I look up into the sky. The Moon isn't visible, and clouds are rolling in to obscure the sun. "I don't know. I haven't really thought about it. Maybe I'll come back, too. How about you, Fiona?"

She doesn't answer, but her eyes are also focused on the sky, which is darkening faster than seems possible.

"Is a storm blowing in off the ocean?" Bernard asks, following her gaze as a flash of lightning cuts across the horizon.

"Oh no," I whisper at the same time Fiona grabs our arms.

"Run!"

CHAPTER THIRTY-ONE

CANTER

NOAH GOES BACK TO HIS APARTMENT. I DON'T TRUST him enough to let him help with this next step, though I did say I'd update him on how it turns out. What I didn't say was that the update depends on *how* it turns out.

I take an aquaxi to V.A.M.A., meeting Lila on the dock. I shudder as I take in the gleaming, interlocking spheres that make up the school building. The platform is deserted, so different from the first time I arrived here. We hurry into the school and to the Number Whispering classroom. The halls are quiet, and thankfully we don't meet anyone we know.

Mr. Finch isn't in his room. Maybe he took his class elsewhere so we can access the equipment we need. Ms. Curie and Mrs. Hodger are huddled over a complicated-looking console.

"Is that the ship?" I ask, pointing at a blinking dot making its way across the screen.

Ms. Curie nods. "You're just in time. It launched from the factory ten minutes ago."

I rub my hands together. "When should we take control?"

"Not until it's closer to the Old World's orbit," Ms. Curie says. "We don't want to show our hand too early. They could try to regain control from the factory."

"We need to make it look like an accidental malfunction," Mrs. Hodger explains.

I sigh. This is going to feel like the longest however-many minutes of my life.

Mrs. Hodger gives me a tight smile. "I want Myra back with us, but we have to do it right or this will all have been for nothing."

While we wait, I distract myself by channeling the electricity in the devices, adjusting the voltages up and down, but not enough to affect functionality. It still doesn't take long for Ms. Curie to notice.

"Your magic returned quickly," she says proudly. "It took weeks for some of the others."

"Have you been in touch with Perennial's group?" Lila asks.

"Not directly. And what little communication I've had has only been recent. It took Perennial a while to trust that it wasn't me who tipped off the Council."

That was Noah. Anxiety surges through me. Were we wrong to trust him?

"One mistake doesn't equal the full value of a person," Ms. Curie says softly. I look up and see her studying me.

"How much does one betrayal subtract from trustworthiness?"

"I think we need to see the other variables in the equation to figure that one out," Mrs. Hodger adds gently. "He might surprise you."

"Unlikely." I'm just hoping this works, and Noah's not the villain I thought he was.

"Friendships have as wide a range as there are voltages in batteries," Ms. Curie says, exchanging a small smile with Mrs. Hodger. "There are many degrees between best friend and bitter enemy."

Lila and I are pretty quiet as the adults chatter. Our focus is locked on the tiny blinking dot on the screen creeping its way across the solar system.

"Are you nervous to see her again?" Lila asks. "Your mom?"

"I haven't really thought about it. I guess I haven't wanted to get my hopes up."

"Understandable." Lila leans back against the wall. "I wonder what life is like there. On the Old World."

"I bet it's amazing." I wrap my arms around my knees. "Plants growing everywhere, all over the place. No reason to hide your magic."

"I wonder what the Meteorons can do with the storms," Lila muses, twirling a curl around her finger. "I bet they work really well with the Botans, bringing rain when the plants need it, a windstorm when they want to scatter seeds, sunshine to make them bloom."

I nod. "It's the perfect partnership."

A beep chirps from the screen, and we scramble to our feet.

"It's time," Ms. Curie confirms. "The shuttle's about to pass by the Old World. Finch said they use this device to direct autoshipments across the sea to the school, but it should work for autopiloting the shuttle, too."

I hold my breath as Ms. Curie taps in a command. "What are you telling it to do?"

"Just a slight course correction," she says, not looking up. "To see if it responds."

We all stare at the blip as it blinks forward, and forward, and forward.

Then one notch to the left.

"It worked," Mrs. Hodger says through a sigh, beaming.

Ms. Curie clears her throat, then glances over at Mrs. Hodger. "I'm going to take over the controls. Can you calculate the new trajectory? We need it to land just off the shore of Fiona's region."

My stomach drops. My mother's region. Her home for the last ten years. What was it like, living in a garden at the edge of an ocean? A natural ocean that formed on its own, millions of years in the making. I can't wait for her to tell me about it. I can't wait for her to tell me anything.

"Let me test the equations first." Mrs. Hodger closes her eyes and rattles off a series of calculations and coordinates, and then repeats them. She pauses, computing without the help of magic, and then nods, repeating them once more, slowly.

Ms. Curie taps the coordinates into the computer, sending them across the galaxy.

Mrs. Hodger's eyes are once again locked on the tiny blip on the screen. Myra's ride home.

I don't dare ask if the shuttle redirected. I don't think I could survive hearing that it didn't. All the while, the dot flickers, moving closer to the Old World.

"It's working!" Lila shrieks.

Ms. Curie's eyes sparkle. "It is."

"Is MFI trying to regain control?" Mrs. Hodger asks. I can tell she's scared to hear the answer.

"They were, but they failed. I made it look like engine failure. The ship's listing to one side, like it's overpowered on the flank." She winks. "And it just happens to be the side facing the Old World."

"It's entering atmosphere," Mrs. Hodger says, her voice tight. "It's nearly there."

Ms. Curie leans in closer. "And right over the ocean, too. It should be a perfect landing with minimal damage."

Lila grabs my hand and squeezes. "They'll be home soon. All of them."

"We'll be able to meet more Botans," I murmur. I still can't let myself believe that it might be happening. Not until they're right in front of me.

Lila clutches my fingers tighter, like she knows what I can't say. "And who knows. Maybe they'll even bring some Meteorons with them."

CHAPTER THIRTY-TWO

MYRA

CHAOS ERUPTS AROUND US LIKE A HURRICANE, though that seems to have arrived on shore, too. The wind rages, blowing sand into tiny cyclones. I spit out a mouthful of grit, stumbling forward. The air whistles so loudly I can't hear, either. A heavy fog descends like a blanket, and I can't see which way leads to the beach and which is to the water. Human-shaped forms flicker around me. Whether they're friend or foe is impossible to tell.

I call upon my magic, and plants spring from the sand, wrapping around me like armor. As I race along the beach, searching for my friends, something hard and wet hits my cheek, then my chin, then my arms. Hail. The stems wrap around my head, thickening, the leaves multiplying. I can hear the ice pellets ricocheting off as I run faster.

A gust of wind tears at the fog, and for a moment I can see waves crashing in the distance and people fighting in the surf. As I change course to help, the vines curl around my arm, bursting with thorns.

Charlie's standing up to his knees in the churning water, dueling with a Meteoron a few feet away. He loses his footing and a wave sweeps him under. I rush forward to help, but he quickly reemerges, brandishing a vine like a whip. The end oozes sap, and as it connects with the Meteoron's face, the effect is instantaneous. Boils erupt along the man's neck and cheek, blocking his vision. A second vine bursts from the water like a sea serpent, snaring his legs, then dragging him onto the beach, secured and out of the battle.

Charlie finds a new opponent, and I go back to scanning the shores for other Botans who need help. Stillness in the chaos catches my eye. Hannah stands exactly where she was during the meeting, watching the combat unfold around her, her face pale and her eyes wide.

"Hannah!" I shout, but she doesn't hear or notice me until I slam into her.

She lurches back, and I remember I'm covered head to toe in vicious plants. I push leaves away from my face before hauling her up the beach, only realizing after a few moments that her feet don't seem to be working.

"Are you hurt?"

"I did this," she says, dodging my gaze. "Meredith told them about the shuttle."

I grimace, but it's pointless to talk about that right now. "We've got to find Bernard and Fiona. Maybe we can get a message to Ms. Curie. Tell her to stop the shut—"

With a blast like a sonic boom, something hits the water not far from shore. Through the sand and a sudden squall of what must be snow, I can see a giant wave cresting. Riding it is a ship.

"It's here!" someone shouts. At once, all the action seems to shift in one direction. Toward the shuttle. Our shuttle.

A group of Meteorons stand in formation along the beach, arms outstretched toward the ocean. At their center is a small, elderly woman with wispy hair the color of seafoam. Ophelia. The Meteoron leader.

Waves rock the ship and start to push it toward shore.

"They're going to take it for themselves!" I search frantically for Charlie. I don't see him, but I do catch a flash of red. A Meteoron woman leans over Fiona, a funnel of water spinning behind her like a cobalt tornado.

I bolt across the sand, my plant protections untangling themselves so they don't slow me down. I lunge at the woman, not caring what happens to me if she sends the waterspout in my direction.

The next moment, I'm sprawled on the ground. Charlie's thrown himself between us. A vine winds around the woman, curling tightly against her throat. She sputters and the funnel does, too. Fiona digs her hand into the sand and branches erupt around the Meteoron, forming a cage.

Charlie extends a hand to help Fiona up. The moment she regains her feet, a torrent of rain opens above them like someone turned on a faucet full blast. The water collects into puddles that quickly converge into a flood.

Charlie and Fiona are trying to wade through it, and up the hill to us, when another tree bursts from the beach behind them.

Only, it's not another tree. It's the one Fiona trapped the Meteoron inside.

"Look out!" I scream, but they can't hear me over the storm. I can only watch, frozen, as the woman, freed when the rainwater submerged the cage, tosses the sodden tree over her head and sends a flash of lightning directly into Charlie's heart.

He crumples to the ground, lying still in the sand.

Fiona snarls. Sharp branches erupt from the ground like spears, right through the Meteoron woman. She falls beside Charlie. Both are silent, motionless, gone.

Fiona drops to her knees and buries her face in her hands. All Hannah and I can do is look on, horrified and helpless.

"Hannah!" Meredith tears up the beach, her hair sticking to her face and neck.

I grab her collar before she can reach her sister.

"Get off me, Botan." She pulls out of my grip, shoving me away. "Hannah, come with me. You were right. We should go home together. I just couldn't leave the way you wanted me to."

"You told the Meteorons about the shuttle," Hannah says slowly.

"Of course I did." Meredith wipes water from her face. "I want to go home as much as you do, but the Botans would never have let me come with you in a million light-years."

"You never gave them the chance." I step between them. "You never gave us the chance."

"The chance to what?" Meredith demands. "Turn me in again? Cast me aside? No thanks. I make my own way now." A small smile pulls at her lips. "That's why I fit in so well with the Meteorons. They aren't afraid to carve their own path . . . even if it leads them right through their enemy."

"What's that supposed to mean?" I fire back.

"Just that the timing couldn't be better." Her smile turns taunting. "Remember how I told you they asked me to help track that storm? Well, it just so happens it's about to arrive in the Settlements."

"Where?" Hannah shakes her head. "The Moon doesn't have weather, and the other Settlements don't have much, either."

"That's not exactly true," Meredith says. "It doesn't matter. Solar storms aren't an Old World rain shower."

"What is it, then?" I ask.

"Oh, you'll find out," she says with a wink. "Now that you've repaired your ancient satellite—my sister's handiwork, I'm sure—your off planet friends can tell you all about it. *If* they have enough electricity left to power it." Behind her, the ship glides gracefully onto the shore, steered by the Meteoron-controlled storms and the waves.

Meredith glances over her shoulder, then at Hannah. "Let's go home. I'm your family, and I've never, ever betrayed you. You can't choose her over me. You won't. I know it."

"Hannah, this is wrong—" I start.

Meredith throws her hands up in the air. "The whole galaxy's wrong! Do you think anyone with any scrap of power cares about right and wrong? The ones who play by the rules are the only ones who get burned. And I'm done playing games, anyway." She grabs Hannah's shoulders. "Let's go home. Let's make our own rules."

"Hannah—"

My former best friend scans my face, then looks back at her sister. For a moment, I think she's going to tell her sister she doesn't believe her. That she doesn't believe in *this*.

"Meredith's right, Myra."

A chill seeps into my bones, even as the snow and ice coating the beach begin to melt.

Without another word, the two sisters join hands and make their way toward the shuttle.

CHAPTER THIRTY-THREE

CANTER

"WHY IS THE SHUTTLE HEADED TOWARD MARS?" LILA asks, watching the blinking dot tick across the screen.

My eyes follow the arc. There's no other destination besides Mars with the current trajectory. But why go there? It makes no sense.

"Try contacting them again," Mrs. Hodger says. "Maybe they misunderstood the rendezvous instructions."

"They aren't answering," Ms. Curie replies. "Something must be wrong."

"Were the comms damaged in the crash?" Mrs. Hodger asks, wringing her hands. "They weren't docked long. They couldn't have made repairs. Maybe they should have stayed longer, checked the systems more carefully."

"If they left quickly, they had a good reason," Ms. Curie argues. "And based on current orbits, Mars is a dozen or so million miles closer to the Old World. Maybe they're short on fuel."

"Then we should go to Mars," I insist. "What else can we do?"

The adults make the arrangements. It'll be tricky to get off planet to the Martian Settlement in time to meet the ship. Coming from the Old World, they're already halfway there, but thankfully, their shuttle moves a lot slower than the planet-to-planet transports, so even from Venus, if we leave right away, we should arrive first. We pile into an aquaxi and zip through the water to the transportation station.

"I've never been to the Martian Settlement," Lila says, watching the bubbles billow past the window as we cruise through the water.

"Me either. My dad was supposed to bring me once when he had to go to a Chemic conference, but there was a bad dust storm, so we didn't end up going."

"If they were worried about fuel, wouldn't it have made more sense to go to the Moon?" Lila asks. "It's so much closer."

"And a lot smaller. If they were trying to blend into space traffic, it would've been tough to land there."

"That's true." Lila tugs a curl around her finger. "I just wish they'd sent us a message letting us know they're all right."

"Maybe they wanted to tell us in person," I say, forcing

optimism I don't feel into my voice. Lila nods and turns back to the window.

I stare into the water, watching a school of fish dart away like they're being chased by a predator, and try to imagine how I'll feel when Myra and my mom walk off that shuttle. I can't.

It's probably just the series of disappointments, but for some reason, I can't seem to shake the feeling that something is wrong.

Hours later, I hurry down the high-speed transport's steps onto crimson Martian soil. Amber dust kicks up off my feet as I gaze up at the building rising behind the ship and the city skyline in the distance. Mars is the most populated planet in the Settlements, the first inhabited after the Moon. During our ride, one of the transport screens projected that sixty-five percent of the Settlements' population currently resides here, and seeing the rows and rows of buildings in the distance, I believe it.

"When's their ship supposed to land?" I ask Ms. Curie.

She squints at the screen in her hands. "Any minute. They're making their descent now."

I gaze up into the hazy red sky, hoping to see a ship approaching. There's nothing yet.

"Do we know that this is the landing strip they'll be using?" Mrs. Hodger asks.

"Based on their trajectory, it seems the most likely," Ms. Curie says.

We all quietly watch the rosy clouds.

"Is that it?" Lila asks, pointing to a glint in the sky.

It grows bigger and bigger. The knot in my stomach seems to grow, too.

"That should be it," Ms. Curie confirms.

The ship kicks up bloodred dirt and dust as it lowers to the ground. Even after it docks, the dust doesn't settle. If anything, more, huge crimson clouds billow around the shuttle, sweeping over us.

"Is this a dust storm?" Lila chokes on the grit. "I heard bad weather can come on fast here."

"It seems to be focused around the ship," Ms. Curie observes, shielding her eyes. "But that shouldn't be possible."

"The door's opening," Mrs. Hodger says.

I stumble forward. I'm not going to let a little wind and sand stop me from greeting my friends and family.

Mrs. Hodger's right beside me. The dust is so thick, I can hardly see two feet ahead, but I can make out two figures in the doorway of the shuttle. I recognize one of them: Hannah.

My heart leaps as I throw my hand up. It worked! They're really here.

She doesn't wave back, and neither does the other girl.

The other girl who isn't Myra.

She looks just like Hannah, but a few years older. It must be her sister.

"Hannah!" Mrs. Hodger chokes out beside me. "Meredith! You made it, thank the stars. Where's Myra?"

The girls don't answer as they descend the steps. Behind them, others file out, but no one I recognize. I strain, looking for the glint of Myra's glasses, or my mother's fiery auburn hair, but the only red is the crimson dust whipping around me.

"Hannah, where's Myra?" Mrs. Hodger yells over the storm.

Guilt flashes in Hannah's eyes, but she doesn't answer as she tries to pass.

I grab her arm. "Where are they? What happened?"

Hannah's sister shoves me. "Let her go!"

I grip tighter. "What's going on, Hannah? Where are the others?"

"Not here," she says quietly.

"What does that mean?"

Meredith grabs my arm and rips Hannah away. "They're back on the Old World where they belong. Now get out of our way, or you'll wish you were, too."

"You left her there?" Mrs. Hodger demands.

"Just like you and your family exiled me," Meredith snarls back. "Just like the galaxy threw all of us away. Now you'll understand what a mistake that was." Meredith sweeps her arms around. "Let's show them what we can really do. A little preview of what's coming."

I thought it would be impossible for the wind to blow any harder, but a sudden gust topples me to the ground. Mrs. Hodger coughs beside me, shielding her face with her arms.

"Enough!" someone bellows, and sparks glint through the amber haze. Ms. Curie appears above us, lightning dancing around the wires encircling her wrists. The ground ripples and the hairs on my body stand on end as a wave of electricity passes over us. Someone screams, and the wind dies down enough that I can wipe the grit from my face and mouth.

Raised voices echo in my ears, but I can't make sense of them. Then something falls beside me. I scramble back before realizing it's Lila.

"They're gone," she says, using her sleeve to wipe more of the dust from my face. "Are you hurt?"

I don't know how to answer.

"Here," she says, holding out her hands. She stays like that for a minute, eyes zipping across me like she's reading a book. Gently, she turns my palms over. They're scraped, but I don't feel any pain. Not in my hands, anyway. As I watch, the wounds knit back together, leaving behind shiny, smooth skin.

Mrs. Hodger is hunched over, sobbing. Ms. Curie wraps

an arm around her back. Lila starts to stand, but our former teacher shakes her head. "It's nothing you can fix."

"What happened?" I ask, climbing shakily to my feet, sure grit is permanently embedded in my throat and lungs. "Who were they?"

"Meteorons," Lila replies. "It had to be."

"So they took the ship from the Botans? Why would they do that?"

"I'm guessing the two Creers did not bond in their exile," Ms. Curie remarks.

"What are they here to do?" Lila asks.

Mrs. Hodger stares off into the distance, watching another storm bloom on the horizon. "Punish us."

CHAPTER THIRTY-FOUR

MYRA

Second Month, 2450

WE BURY CHARLIE BENEATH THE TALLEST TREE IN THE Coastal Region. A mound of wildflowers marks the spot. I haven't seen Fiona since the shuttle lifted into the sky and disappeared.

The sun streams through the leaves as we huddle around the grave. Someone's speaking—the older woman who spoke at the meeting, which now feels like weeks ago but really was only hours earlier. The storms vanished as soon as the Meteorons did, but now the weather doesn't match the mood. If anything, the storm should be raging. Instead, the air's warm and pleasant, the world cast in a cheerful glow.

It makes me uneasy, as if nothing's real.

Maybe this is a dream—a nightmare. I squeeze my nails into my palms until shivers of pain race through my hands.

Bernard glances at my clenched fists. "It's real."

I simply nod, unsure if he's asking me or telling me. At least Bernard is still here, and unharmed. He'd been battling with two Meteorons, trying to stop them from summoning the shuttle from the sea. They attacked him with hail the size of apples. I found him in the sand when I was looking for Fiona.

"What'll happen now?"

He shrugs. "I heard that they'll elect another leader this afternoon."

I shake my head. "No, with us. We have to warn the others the Meteorons are coming. And that solar storm..." I shudder. "We have to find another way home."

His pale blue eyes fall on the small hill of flowers. "The communication window won't open again for weeks."

"That'll be too late." I pace, withering grass marking each footstep. "Meredith said the storm's coming in days. We've got to stop the Meteorons."

"Or at least alert the others." Bernard waves a hand, and the burnt grass suddenly shifts to a shiny, glowing viridian. "We could ask Canter to send another shuttle, but we won't be able to coordinate anything until we can talk to them. And that's if they can even send another one. I'm sure the first wasn't easy."

I cross my arms and stare at him.

He sighs. "You don't care about any of that, do you?"

"You're finally getting to know me." A smile pulls at my lips. "We'll find another way. And fast."

"Can we find that other way somewhere else?" Bernard asks, nodding at the ceremony. "I don't think I can handle much more of this."

I nod, and we make our way toward the ocean. I'm starting to feel I can only think clearly when I'm near the sound of crashing waves, smelling the salty, balmy air. We crest the hill leading to the water. The old transports are still lined up like sentinels along the shore.

"The Meteorons were lucky the shuttle didn't need repairs," Bernard says, his gaze lingering on the row of ships. "They'd have had to hold off the Botans while they scavenged for parts."

"At least then we would have had a chance to take the shuttle back."

Bernard gives me a strange look. "Maybe there are enough parts here to put together a working ship."

"Wouldn't the Botans or Meteorons have done that ages ago if it were possible? Besides, we don't have anyone left to assemble it. Not with Hannah . . ."

Bernard sighs, slumping down in the sand. "I can't believe she left. You know, she actually seemed happy here."

"Happier than I've seen her in a long time," I agree, sitting beside him. "The Botans treated her more like a Tekkie than anyone would have in the Settlements."

"Who knows? Some of the people she helped might even develop Tekkie magic."

My eyes widen. "Or maybe they already have." I scramble up, turning back the way we came.

Bernard stands, too, though he doesn't seem as eager. "Their magic would be brand-new. Do you really think they could build a working shuttle?"

"I had no one to teach me, and I still managed to build a garden. It's worth a shot."

He hesitates, then nods. "You're right. Let's at least try."

It doesn't take long to locate a few of the potential Tekkies Hannah had been spending so much time with, and they help us find the others. In no time, we've got the whole group assembled. Unfortunately, they don't seem eager to help.

"We don't know enough yet to do something that big," one man says, with an apologetic shrug. "Maybe if we'd had more time with Hannah—more chances to practice, ask questions—but now . . ."

"None of us even have Inscriptions," a young girl adds. "We don't know for sure that we even *have* magic, as a Tekkie, or anything else."

"Sometimes Inscriptions take a while to appear," I tell her. "If Hannah was teaching you about Tekkie principles, it must have been because you were interested, right?"

The girl nods; the man just huffs.

"So that means you must have some skills already," Bernard adds. "Who builds things here, anyway? The structures that the Botans can't grow?"

"A lot of us help out," a teenage boy says. "But not with magic—"

"You don't need magic to matter! I get it. That's what the galaxy tells us, even here." I think of Meredith and how she felt rejected by the Botans because she didn't share their talents. "I know everyone seems to think magic is the most important trait you can have, but it's not. If you love what you do and you're good at it, that's what counts. And if you can accomplish something without magic, doesn't that make it even more amazing?"

"She's right, Vivian," a voice says from behind me. I turn and see Fiona, looking years older. Her face is pale and her eyes red, but her gaze is steely. Determined. She nods at the young girl. "When I was your age, I didn't think I had magic, either, and at first I was upset. But my friends made me see that I had so much to offer, even if it wasn't through magic."

"But you *did* have magic," the teenager says. "Botan magic."

"I know that here being a Botan might seem like the most important Creer, but out in the Settlements, it's worse than having no Creer at all," I explain. "Sometimes it's a matter of where you are, and who's there with you."

"Look, we want to help," the old man says. "Of course we do. We don't know enough."

I open my mouth to argue, but someone else beats me to it.

"Maybe we can learn while we're trying," the little girl says shyly. "Hannah said tinkering—taking the machines apart and figuring out how they worked—was way more useful to her than any teacher or text."

The man shakes his head. "If we fail—"

"Then we're no worse off than we are now," I insist. "But we've got to hurry. There's some massive storm approaching the Settlements. If the Meteorons are able to harness it . . . there might not be much left for us to go back to."

Vivian raises her hand. "I'll try."

The teenage boy nods. "Me too. Why not? It sounds kind of fun, to be honest."

More murmurs of agreement pass through the group.

"What do you say, Norm?" Fiona asks the older man.

He looks around, and then sighs. "All right, I'll do it. For Charlie."

I grin, looking from face to face. "Let's get going, then!"

CHAPTER THIRTY-FIVE

CANTER

WE RECONVENE ON VENUS TO FIGURE OUT WHAT TO do next, except this time, we meet at the Crumplers'. Ms. Curie's transmitter is essentially useless until the next communication window opens in three weeks. There's one person we can send a message to. He won't pick up if it comes from Sandra Curie's residence, though.

"Canter, is everything all right?" Dad asks when he accepts the call. "I wasn't expecting to hear from you so soon."

I shake my head, trying to figure out how to put everything into words. "Something happened. Something bad, but—"

"Canter, what is it?" Dad leans closer to the camera, his blue eyes crinkled with concern. It's strange: I feel like he never actually saw me before. Not like now.

"I need your help."

"Anything."

"But I don't—" I swallow, trying to clear my head. "It's a long story, and I don't know where to—"

Dad holds up a hand. "Just tell me what you need me to do. You don't have to give me the whole background if you don't want to."

Relief floods through me. "Have you had reports of missing MFI shuttles lately?"

Dad raises his eyebrows. "Yes, actually. One veered off course on a routine delivery and crashed. Did you have something to do with that?"

"Uh." I rack my brain for an answer that won't have him going supernova.

"Never mind," Dad says quickly. "Why are you asking?"

"What do they think happened to it?"

"It's highly unusual for a ship to malfunction that way." Dad rubs his jaw. "A few people here suspect that it wasn't accidental, but as far as I know, no one has any proof."

"Are they changing any protocols?"

"Yes," Dad says, and my stomach drops. "Now every delivery shuttle will have at least one pilot aboard so if the autopilot malfunctions, they'll be able to override it."

I run my hands through my hair. "Okay, then I have another question."

Dad hesitates like he wants to ask me more about the shuttle, then nods.

"Do Melfin or Warden Vander have any new leads on the rogue Reps?"

"Not exactly leads. . . . They haven't been able to track them down—that was their main focus until recently—but there has been some activity."

"Like what?"

"Raids, mostly. Perennial's group has been infiltrating MFI facilities."

"To steal weapons and food?"

"They were before, but not anymore. We think the Reps are stealing data."

"What kind of data?"

"We aren't sure, but they seem to always target control rooms or offices. They must be downloading something."

"Do you have an idea where they're based? Or where they might hit next?" If anyone could have ships at their command, it's Perennial. It might not be easy to convince her to sacrifice one if she does, but the promise of adding Botans to her ranks might be just the right incentive.

Dad shakes his head. "Nothing concrete." He studies me. "If I hear anything, I'll let you know. I assume you're trying to get in touch with them?"

I nod, opening my mouth to end the call, when another thought occurs to me. "You said finding the Reps was Melfin and Vander's focus *until recently*. What's more important now?"

"Something's going on in the Martian Settlement. It seems like some sort of storm knocked out communications earlier today."

I walk into the living room, where everyone is wound up, waiting to hear how my call went. "No leads," I say with a sigh. "Dad said he'd let me know if he hears anything. He mentioned something about MFI losing communication with the Martian Settlement today."

Ms. Curie's eyes widen. "The whole Settlement?"

"That's what he said. And if Meredith was telling the truth, there are worse things to come." I drop onto the couch beside Lila. "What are we going to do? We can't wait weeks—"

"We'll think of something." Ms. Curie is beside Mrs. Hodger, who's silently staring at the wall. "That will give us time to consider a new plan."

"We can't use an MFI shuttle again," I explain before describing the new protocols.

"That will make things difficult," Ms. Curie says, frowning. "They're responsible for most routine traffic crossing the Old World orbit."

While Ms. Curie and Mrs. Crumpler discuss alternatives, I tune out. The idea of trying this again—of building up hope only to be let down—is unbearable. "Where's Eli?" I ask Lila.

She points to her bedroom. "He said he's working on a project and needs to concentrate."

"Why'd he even come, then?" As soon as we set foot in the building, Eli materialized like he had a tracking device on us. I scan my shoes, making sure, but don't see anything.

"I think he's lonely. He doesn't have a lot of friends."

I remember him saying his closest friends were the Reps who worked here, and they left when Perennial flipped the switch. "There must be other kids, though."

"Not ones who want to play with a non-Creer," she says quietly.

"That's stupid."

She shrugs. "That's the galaxy we live in."

"Well, it shouldn't be." I overhear the adults say something about logistics and override codes. "Can't we at least make sure Myra and the others are okay?" I ask, louder than I mean to. "We're doing all this, and we don't even know— What if they . . ." I shake my head. "This could all be for nothing!"

"Myra is alive," Mrs. Hodger says quietly beside me. "So is your mother. And your friend, Bernard. We just need to get to them."

"I can't just believe that!" I lean back, my temples throbbing. "We need proof."

Lila lays a hand on my shoulder, and immediately, the headache eases.

"Canter's right," Ms. Curie says, and I look up. "Before we take any more risks, we need to confirm that the others are okay. We saw what the Meteorons are capable of, and I guarantee Fiona would have fought for that shuttle." Ms. Curie's glassy eyes meet mine. "I can't wait three weeks."

"Maybe there's a way," Mrs. Hodger says slowly. "Can I see the calculations you used to bounce the signal?"

Ms. Curie picks up a computer and taps on the screen, then hands it to her.

Mrs. Hodger studies the data, then points to something on the screen. "Why are you only using these satellites to relay the messages?"

"The others are too old to accept the transmission," Ms. Curie explains. "The rest date back almost a hundred years. Nothing made in the last fifty years operates on that frequency, and good luck finding devices older than that. I've tried. It's almost impossible. But I suppose . . ." She tilts her head. "We could go that route. We may get lucky."

"What sort of device would you need?" a small voice asks as Eli steps into the room.

At first, I think Ms. Curie's going to tell him to stop pestering us with questions, but she looks him right in the eye like he's a peer and rattles off a series of transmitters, antennas, and receivers. "If we found an old machine with those components, we'd at least be able to relay a basic message. Probably receive one, too."

"Do you have something like that, Eli?" I ask, fighting the hope brewing in my chest.

"Nope," he says, and my heart falls. "But you do."

"What are you talking about?" I ask, irritation flooding through me. "No, I don't."

"Yeah, you do." He flashes me an infuriating smile, then gestures toward Lila's door.

"Beep!" Bin-ro says, rolling into the room.

CHAPTER THIRTY-SIX

MYRA

THE OLD WORLD TEKKIES MIGHT NOT HAVE INTERgalactic training, but they make up for it with enthusiasm and curiosity. Before the tide makes its way back in, they've got half the shuttles disassembled, and another team scours the others searching for the best prospect to repair.

"That shuttle of yours is a gold mine," Vivian announces as I walk over.

I raise my eyebrows. "Really? They had to pilot it from Mercury. The control panel didn't even work."

"But everything else does," she says, cradling a bundle of parts. "The engines were intact. A little crispy from atmosphere entry, but still usable. The landing gear was totally cooked, but the propulsion systems and the climate-control centers only needed a little tinkering and—"

I laugh, holding up my hands. "I get it. The rest is interstellar."

She grins, then trots ahead, eager to show her armful of treasure to Norm, who's hunched over one of the still-intact shuttles. His eyes sparkle in the setting sun as he surveys the salvaged parts settled carefully onto a mat of woven grasses and leaves.

"There's an old saying Bernie used to tell me: 'One man's trash is another's treasure.'"

I turn. Fiona's scanning the shuttles, her blue eyes unreadable.

"That sounds like him." I watch as Norm high-fives Vivian. Hannah and I used to have a secret handshake that began and ended with a high five. We tried to teach the rest of our CHARM friends, but they never caught on.

"Friendships can be like machines," Fiona says quietly. "Sometimes the parts fit together perfectly and everything works as designed. Sometimes the pieces are completely incompatible, from totally different models. And sometimes, even though two pieces used to work well together, one gets worn down or is faulty or damaged, and the connection's gone."

"Hannah and I were best friends for years," I reply, sinking into the sand. "We did everything together. I told her everything, and she shared everything with me. . . . Maybe she shouldn't have."

"We all make mistakes." Fiona settles beside me. "But I think her recent actions far outweigh any wrongs you may have done to her."

"I can't believe she left." I say it so softly, I wonder if it was even aloud.

"Experiences change people," Fiona murmurs. She turns to look me in the eye. "When you were gardening, did you ever use a stake or a trellis?"

I frown. "Sure. Loads of times. Why?"

"What happened?"

"What do you mean?"

Fiona leans closer to me. "The plants. What did they do?"

I think back to the original moongarden, and the tiny replica, shoved into pots and pans in the abandoned kitchen. Then the seagarden, bursting out of the water and sprawling over the rail of the cove. "They grew around them, over them, through them . . ."

"Exactly."

I must look baffled, because she smiles. "Think of life as a garden. The plants in it are the people you know, including you. Some plants start off right next to each other, but put a stake in the ground next to one, and it'll cling to it, using it for support or as a bridge to somewhere new. The same is true in the wild." She gestures over her shoulder to where juniper bushes sprawl across the edge of the beach and dot the hills in the distance. "They grow over rocks and dead branches and even other plants. Those obstacles are like the experiences we have throughout our lives. Sometimes they make us stronger, and sometimes they force us to change. Modify our direction, make us adapt, even alter who we are and where we're going."

"So, even though Hannah and I might have started side by side, the different stones and sticks in our paths could have made us grow apart," I say slowly.

Fiona pats my knee. "It doesn't mean new experiences might not send you back together again."

I nod, staring out at the horizon.

"Still, you should be prepared for the possibility that they might not. And that's okay, too. Some plants shouldn't be next to each other for their own good. I'm sure you know that from working in your gardens."

"That's not Hannah and me."

"Maybe not."

There's a commotion on the path back to the village, and an older woman speeds toward us faster than I would have thought possible, her wispy white hair trailing behind her.

"What is it, Ruth?" Fiona asks, plants already budding on her palm.

"You need to come with me," the new leader of the community says, hardly even out of breath. "Both of you."

Fiona and I exchange a glance. "Come where?" I ask. "Should I find Bernard, too?"

"To the center of the village, and he's probably there," she calls over her shoulder, already darting back the way she came.

"But what is it?" Fiona asks, hurrying to catch up. "Another Meteoron attack?"

"No. Nothing like that."

I'm panting as my feet slam to the ground. "Then what?"

"A message."

Fiona and I take off, surging past Ruth and skidding to a halt in front of the satellite. Bernard has a strange expression on his face.

My eyes skim the words glowing on the screen and I gasp. "That's impossible."

"I thought you said Bin-ro was destroyed," Fiona says, her eyes wide.

"He was." I read the message again. My stomach swoops with hope. "Can it really be him?"

Bernard grins over at me, and a cluster of cherry blossoms erupts from the branch over his head. "Looks like we counted that little robot out too soon."

CHAPTER THIRTY-SEVEN
CANTER

BIN-RO ZOOMS AROUND MY FEET, WHISTLING HIS favorite show tune as I pace the room. I roll my eyes, then clutch my head. "I can't figure out if I'm about to laugh or be sick."

"If you're going to be sick, maybe you should steer closer to the bathroom," Lila says with a smile. "And I know what you mean. I couldn't be happier to have our best robot buddy back, all thanks to our newest friend." She beams at Eli, and he blushes.

"Or implode waiting to see if they answer his message," I complain. "We sent it hours ago. What's taking so long?"

"They probably aren't monitoring the satellite closely right now," Mrs. Crumpler says gently. "Remember, they aren't expecting a message for weeks."

"Let's just hope they check before then," replies Ms. Curie.

"Oh, don't say that." Mrs. Hodger sinks into a seat. "I can't take much more of this waiting."

"You might have to," Ms. Curie says, her voice grim.

Mrs. Hodger's head jerks up. "Do you have to keep reminding me? I understand perfectly well they might not reply right away."

"If you understand perfectly well, then why do you—"

A barrage of beeps and whistles cuts Ms. Curie off. As one, we all spin to take in Bin-ro turning in figure eights on the floor.

"Did they answer?" I ask.

"Beep!"

A half laugh, half sob erupts from my throat. Lila buries her face in her hands. The adults just look bewildered.

"What does that mean?" Mrs. Hodger demands. "Are they all right? Yes or no?"

"Beep!"

"One beep yes, two beeps no," I say, leaping to my feet and punching the air like I just scored the winning point in a hoverball game. "They're okay!"

The room erupts in cheers, sobs, and laughter. It's like a symphony of emotion.

I rub my hand across my face. "Ask them what happened. How we can help? Tell them we're trying to get them a new shuttle, but if they have any better ideas—"

"Canter." Lila places a hand on my arm. "We're kind of limited on what they can tell us."

"What are you talking about?"

"*One beep yes, two beeps no*, right?" Ms. Curie sighs as she sits.

"Err . . ." I hadn't thought that far ahead. "Maybe we can come up with some other communication system."

Mrs. Crumpler frowns. "That's going to be complicated."

We're all quiet a moment as we contemplate the next challenge.

"We'll come up with something," Mrs. Hodger announces, her eyes bright. "They're okay. That's all that matters."

Bin-ro whistles a cheerful tune, and some of my disappointment seeps away. "That's true. We'll figure something out."

We always do.

The next afternoon, I walk out of Noah's apartment building to my waiting aquaxi. I wanted to make sure Dad was right about the new protocols, and unfortunately he was. Noah confirmed that stealing another shuttle is out of the question, at least until the protocols relax, and it doesn't sound like that will be happening anytime soon. Especially not with the Meteorons causing trouble. The Governing Councils have kept the news pretty quiet, but the Martian Settlement is still unreachable. Noah said MFI can't even make deliveries there. With the Councils distracted, it'd be the perfect time to crash another shuttle on the Old World. If we can just get ahold of one.

It seems like our only hope now is Perennial and her small fleet of ships. Ms. Curie reached out to a contact, but no luck yet.

The door to the apartment building opens behind me and I whirl around, hoping to find Noah eager to share some brilliant idea that came to him in the time it took me to walk outside. Instead, I find myself face-to-face with Kyle Melfin.

"You're about the last person I'd expect to see here, Weathers."

"I could say the same for you. Shouldn't you be on the Moon?"

"My grandfather lives here," he says, gesturing toward the grand building behind him.

Of course he does.

"My dad has some meetings on Venus, so I stopped by to visit."

"And help him and your father plot what to destroy next? Or who?"

"The public could have pushed back on the new food. They didn't. That's not MFI's fault."

"When people start dying because their diet's nothing but Chemic junk, are you still going to say it's their fault? And what about whatever's next?"

Kyle glances away. "I don't make those decisions. Maybe someday. For now, that's my dad's department."

"So, you're okay with everything? All he's done."

"Did I say that?" Anger flashes in his eyes as he stalks by me. "You act like because he's my father, we're the same person. That we believe the same things. *Want* the same things. I barely know my dad. I don't expect someone like you to understand that, though. You've labeled me a villain since my first day at S.L.A.M."

I try to remember the first time I met Kyle. Instead, I'm hiding in the moongarden again as my father confronts Ms. Curie on the transmitter. She said something similar to him—about him being determined to make her the villain in his life—and she was right. My dad was so determined to blame her for everything that had gone wrong, he couldn't see that she was telling him the truth and trying to help him.

Could I be making the exact same mistakes?

"Actually," I begin cautiously, "I do understand what it's like having a difficult father. And I honestly don't remember the first time I met you. But clearly you do."

Kyle freezes, then takes a deep breath. When he speaks, his usual smugness has vanished. "I went to a JV hoverball game the first week of school. I was thinking about trying out, but I was late. My dad was visiting, and he always insists I go to dinner with him so he can look like this interstellar father to everyone else in the restaurant. It was the end of the second half, and I was walking to the stands when the ball bounced out right next to me. Or I thought it had. I grabbed it and tossed it to the referee, but apparently the play was still live, and the players had to reset because I interfered."

The memory comes flooding back. We lost that next point, and then the game. Afterward, I stalked over to where Kyle was sitting and tossed the ball at his chest. "I asked if you were a spy for the other team, since you'd sabotaged the game."

He nods. "My dad used to take me to games when I was younger, mostly just to keep me out of the way while he met with your dad. I'd watched your season the year before, and I knew you were the leading scorer. I—I'll deny this if you tell anyone, but I wanted to play with you." Kyle's shoulders fall. "But after that, I knew you'd sabotage any chance I had, like you thought I'd sabotaged your game."

"You didn't," I say quickly. "It wasn't your fault the score was so close. It was ours. Mine. *I* was the leading scorer. And I shouldn't have said that to you." I sigh and run my hands through my hair. "Myra used to say my ego needed its own gravitational field, and she was right."

Kyle studies the ground. "It wasn't right, what happened to her. She didn't deserve that, even if she was a— Never mind. I heard my dad talking." He shifts his weight. "Look, I know he's not a very good person, but I never thought . . . I didn't peg him as a murderer."

"Is that why you didn't turn me in back at the prison? You thought he'd kill me, too?"

Kyle shrugs. "Just because I don't like you doesn't mean I want you dead."

I study him. "Is that all?"

"You heard what was going on as clearly as I did. The Reps are planning an uprising."

"You don't seem bothered by it."

"I'm not." He shrugs again. "I'm not my father, and if he's going to ship people—*kids*—off to die, maybe the Settlements *should* rise up against him. Maybe he deserves that."

I watch Kyle as he watches me. Is he telling the truth or is this him trying to bait me like when we were at V.A.M.A.?

"You didn't seem to mind helping your dad on Venus."

"Figuring out if Director Weathers talked to the media about him is a little different than exiling people to the Old World. Besides, I didn't know then what I do now. If I had,

I would've refused to go. I never wanted to go to V.A.M.A., anyway."

"Myra said your dad was insisting you learn music?"

He rolls his eyes. "My dad and grandfather are obsessed with our Venusian heritage. They've been drilling me about chords and musical scales as long as I can remember."

"It must be handy for keeping secrets locked away."

"What are you talking about?"

I hesitate, then tell Kyle about the book we found in his father's office in the box secured by a musical code.

His eyes widen. "He has a log of all of them in his office?"

"Thankfully, Myra knew the notes to unlock it."

"She was always clever." His eyes cloud. "I'm sorry, for what it's worth. I'm sorry about what happened to her and for what my father did. If I could undo it, I would. I really would."

To my surprise, I believe him. "I'm sorry, too. For being an intergalactic idiot that day at the game."

He grins. "Forget it. Nowadays, I'd just tell you to go spark yourself."

"I'd deserve it."

Kyle turns toward a waiting aquaxi, then pauses. He whistles a few notes. "It really is clever."

"What is?"

"A musical code. You could even send messages with it,

if the words were simple enough." He whistles the tune again. "Those notes are *C, A,* and *D.*"

"*Cad?* What's that?"

He rolls his eyes. "It means someone who's rotten. A crook."

"Do you mean me or your dad?"

He chuckles. "I'll let you guess."

A thought occurs to me, and I argue both sides as I watch Kyle go. He's halfway to the dock before I call out to him. "Do you really want to help?"

CHAPTER THIRTY-EIGHT

MYRA

"THEY WANT TO WHAT?" I READ THE WORDS ON THE satellite again.

"Is it possible?" Bernard asks.

"Communicating using musical notes?" I sit back on my heels. "Technically, I guess. We'd be really limited, though."

"What letters could we use?" Bernard asks. "My original could sing, but he didn't play an instrument or read music."

"*A*, *G*, *D*, and *E*. Those are the main ones for a violin. But I think . . . I think there's *B*, *C*, and *F*, too." I shrug. "We could try it."

Bernard taps a response into the console, and we wait. After a few minutes, a question appears:

How did the Meteorons take the ship? Why did Hannah leave?

We exchange a glance. "Can we answer either of those?" I ask.

Bernard grabs a stick and scratches out our available notes, aka letters, in the sand. We play around with the combinations until we concoct at least a partial answer.

BAD DEED. GABBED.

We wait as Bin-ro translates. "Do you think they'll have any idea what that means?" I ask.

Bernard shrugs. "They should know enough on their own to piece together that Hannah gabbed and the bad deed was taking the shuttle."

"I don't think Hannah was in on it," I say quickly. "She decided when Meredith convinced her during the battle."

"I guess it doesn't matter. They should catch the gist."

I fold my legs under me. "We need to warn them about the storm."

Bernard frowns, trying different combinations. "That's going to be tricky." He glances at the screen. "Look, they replied!"

Going to be difficult to send another. Any other ship there you can use to come home?

We play around with the letters before responding.

GAGE.

"I'd kill to be able to do an *I-N-G*," I mutter.

Bernard chuckles. "They'll get it. And speaking of." He glances back toward the beach. "We should see how it's going."

BE BAC, I tap out quickly. We send the message and head back up the hill.

On the shore, we find the Tekkies clustered around one of the newer ships. Fiona stands off to the side, watching with her arms crossed.

"Is it good news or bad?" I ask as we rush over.

"Both." Norm wipes his sleeve across his face. "We swapped out the console innards and the ship's operational again."

My mouth falls open. "Already? That's great!"

"Replacing is usually faster than fixing," he says.

"So, what's the problem?" Bernard asks. "I thought most of the parts from our shuttle were usable."

"They are," Vivian says, shifting from foot to foot. "Mostly."

"It's the heat shield," Fiona growls. "It was working, then it just died."

"Better now than when the ship's in the air," Norm says gruffly. "The whole craft would have been cooked."

"Is there another we can salvage?" I ask, glancing around the group.

A teenage boy shrugs. "They're all fried. We think it's because they've been sitting in the sun all these years."

"And we definitely need one?" I ask, knowing it's a stupid question.

"Unless you want us to arrive in the Settlements as a fireball," Fiona says pointedly. She stomps a few feet away and drops down to the sand, her gaze fixed on the horizon.

"We'd better go tell them," I murmur, and her head whips around.

"I thought Bin-ro could only transmit yes-or-no replies."

"We found a way to say a little more," Bernard says slowly. "Using musical notes. It's limited, but it's something."

She bolts to her feet and is halfway across the sand before she answers. "I'll take it!"

GAGE BAD, I type back at the satellite.

We wait a few minutes before the screen glows with a reply.

The ship's still broken?

We send back a yes.

Which part?

"How do we translate that?" I ask, studying the letters scrawled in the sand.

Fiona hovers over them, scratching out words, erasing them, trying again. "Got it." She taps in a single word.

FAÇADE

"*Façade?*" I ask.

"It means exterior," she says. "At least it narrows things a bit."

The hull?

No.

Landing gear?

No again.

Heat shield?

We send a yes, then wait. I hum a few notes, my eyes fixed on the screen.

"What's that?" Bernard asks.

"*Façade*, I think. I'm better with the trombone, but Mr. Finch taught me a little about violin chords."

"Pretty handy," Bernard says. "Like a universal language."

"I never thought of it that way. I guess you're right."

"Music has a way of connecting people," Fiona murmurs, settling back to wait.

"I wonder how they're translating it," I muse. "Bin-ro can play the notes, I'm sure, but Canter and Lila don't know music."

"Maybe they got Mr. Finch to help?" Bernard says. "Isn't he friends with your dad?"

"Could be."

The screen lights up again, and we scramble over.

You can build a temporary exterior for the shuttle to protect it, but it has to be able to withstand the heat, and also fall away when you clear atmosphere. You wont be able to land anywhere but the moon. Everywhere else has another atmosphere you'll have to clear on arrival.

I bite my lip. "A temporary exterior? I wonder what we could use. It would have to be pretty strong."

"But still fragile enough that it'll fall away before it burns up and takes us with it," Bernard muses.

"Or something with multiple layers, so we can keep burning through them. And we need it fast. If we can't warn them about the Meteorons and the solar storm through Bin-ro, we'll have to do it in person."

Bernard shakes his head. "That's a tall order."

"We'll figure it out," I say with more confidence than I feel.

Fiona sighs. "I hate to burst your bubble, but if it were easy to repair these ships, many of the Botans would have left years ago."

A memory flashes in my mind. My first day of classes at V.A.M.A., when Mr. Kote asked the Chemic students to demonstrate their skills through art. I recall the paintings and sculptures . . . and the boy who used his Creer to form a series of embedded bubbles.

"Well, it can't hurt to ask the Tekkies," Fiona says, her shoulders slumped. "Maybe they'll have an idea."

"We don't need their skills for this," I say softly.

She pauses midstep. "What do you mean? What else could we use to repair the ship?"

I take a deep breath. "Chemic magic."

CHAPTER THIRTY-NINE

CANTER

"WHAT DO YOU MEAN, THEY FIGURED IT OUT?" I ASK Bin-ro.

He beeps once and spins around, then whistles the same three notes, over and over.

I glance at Kyle. "Translation?"

He frowns, squeezing his eyes shut. "B-A-C."

"Back? What does that mean?"

"They're coming back?" Lila says, her eyes wide and hopeful. "They fixed the heat shield and they're coming back!"

We type in a question to confirm.

"Beep!" Bin-ro chirps after a few minutes.

"But how?" I demand.

Kyle shrugs. "Does it matter? Still, you better get going if you're going to beat them to the Moon."

"What about you?" I ask. "Aren't you going back to S.L.A.M. with your dad?"

"He's already gone." Kyle rolls his eyes. "Urgent business on Mercury, or something. He arranged for a shuttle to take me back to school."

"Do you want to come with us?" Lila asks.

Kyle shakes his head. "If Dad gets an alert I'm not on the shuttle, he'll know something's up."

He turns to leave, but before he can, I grab his shoulder. I'm not sure what to say, so I don't say anything, but he still seems to get it. And then he's gone.

"We should head out, too," Ms. Curie says, slipping her computer into her bag. "We don't want them to beat us to the Moon. Besides, we need to make their landing arrangements."

As we're about to leave, my messenger buzzes in my pocket. I read the screen and frown.

"Who is it?" Lila asks.

"Noah. Can you pull up the Venusian newsfeed, Ms. Curie?"

"What's going on?" Mrs. Hodger asks as Ms. Curie removes her computer from her bag and powers it on.

"He said there's something we should see."

Our eyes flick to the screen. The lead story is a building collapse in the Lunar capital.

"How could it collapse like that?" Lila asks. "That apartment building was brand-new."

"It's MFI." Certainty washes over me like a Venusian rainstorm. "Noah told me MFI's experimenting with new Chemic materials."

"You mean, the construction equivalent of their imitation food," Ms. Curie growls.

"At least no one was living there yet," Mrs. Hodger says quietly, eyes fixed on the stream of the rubble.

Lila points to the news ticker, where the number of casualties rolls by. "People were still hurt. Crew members." She looks up, her eyes blazing. "Like my dad."

"Melfin's got to be stopped." Mrs. Hodger reaches in her pocket and pulls out her messenger.

"Who are you writing to?" Ms. Curie asks.

"Some old university friends. Colleagues. Former students. Anyone who might be able to dig up information linking MFI to this."

"That could be dangerous, Claire."

The glare Mrs. Hodger shoots Ms. Curie reminds me so much of Myra, my chest aches. "What have I got to be afraid of? Melfin's already taken everything I have. Maybe he should be afraid of me."

Ms. Curie grins. "I like this new version of you."

Mrs. Hodger chuckles. "More throwback than new. Ask

Val. She'll tell you some stories from before S.L.A.M." She sears Lila and me with a look. "But don't you dare tell Myra any of this."

"Never," I lie as Lila hides a smile behind her hand.

CHAPTER FORTY

MYRA

I'M IN THE SECOND ROW OF THE COCKPIT BEHIND Fiona and Bernard. They flip switches and test systems, preparing for takeoff. Excited babble rises behind me in the main hold, which is filled with the Botans who were supposed to come with us originally, along with a few Tekkies. After all their work rebuilding this heap of parts into a functioning ship, it didn't feel right leaving them behind if they wanted to come.

"Explain this to me one more time, Fiona," Ruth says from beside me. As leader of the Coastal Region, and a powerful Botan, she earned a place in the cockpit as well. Besides, we're going to need her powers.

Fiona nods at me. "Ask her. It's her brilliance."

My cheeks warm. "And yours. The only reason I even

discovered I had a little Chemic magic was because Director Weathers remembered that you'd researched the idea."

"Regardless," she says, stiffening at the mention of her husband, "this idea was yours."

"Fiona and I are going to use the solutions we created by breaking down plant materials to form heat-resistant bubbles," I explain. "When one bursts, we'll have another waiting within it to reflect the atmospheric gases and keep them from burning the ship."

Ruth raises an eyebrow. "And they'll be strong enough to protect the ship?"

"With our collective Chemic magic reinforcing them, yes."

"But none of us are trained Chemics," she argues. "We've never even dabbled in Chemic magic."

"Most of the things I've accomplished were things I never thought I could do," I say quietly. "In the end, it might not look exactly like you expect, but you find a way."

"I'm willing to try," Bernard says, putting a hand on my shoulder.

I smile at him gratefully.

"Just call to the plant materials in the solutions," Fiona says. "They'll answer."

Ruth studies us, then nods as she rises. "I'll go organize the others. Let me know when to start."

Fiona concentrates on the console and taps a button. The engines vibrate beneath my feet, and goose bumps erupt across my skin. "Get ready."

I rub at the Chemic Inscription tucked inside my elbow. I'd been terrified of it when it appeared, but now I hope the magic that created it is still in me somewhere. After a moment, I grip the armrests instead. Beside me, Bernard does the same. As the ship rises, I reach out and grab his hand. He squeezes back.

"Now?" he asks, and Fiona shakes her head.

We clear the trees and soar out over the ocean, cobalt waves crashing far below us. In a moment, the village is just a beige patch along the coast, and then it disappears. We climb higher and higher, my breaths increasingly quick and shallow.

The nav-screen tinges reddish orange, then yellow, and finally a violet blue.

"Now!" Fiona barks, and I jump. "Ruth, now!" she yells louder.

I shut my eyes and focus on sensing the bits of plant matter in the solution coating the ship's exterior, mentally reviewing the basic Chemic principles I explained to the other Botans before we left. I imagine the compounds merging and heating and bubbling, until one large, reflective bubble circles the ship.

Someone gasps, and my eyes flutter open. Through

the nav-screen a periwinkle haze glitters. *It's working.* The translucent edges of the bubble pull and stretch, and finally pop. Another bubble quickly takes its place, this one a deep violet. It bursts even faster, but an indigo one replaces it. And then a bubble the color of sunshine. Then tangerine. Cobalt. Magenta. Turquoise. On and on, the bubbles bloom like wildflowers, the prism of color glowing against the darkening sky.

The air is thick with magic. All of the Botans aboard work together, and the effect is almost like a song: a tide flowing through the shuttle. Fiona's eyes are shut, her lips moving as she murmurs to herself, and maybe to the plants. Bernard stares straight ahead, unblinking, his hands and knees shuddering with the effort of calling on his newfound powers.

And then the final bubble bursts and all I see are stars.

"We did it," Fiona croaks, turning her tear-streaked face toward us. "It worked. We're clear."

Bernard and I collapse back as she calls to Ruth's group. We stare dazed out the window, and still our hands remain twined like vines. Outside, as the ship turns, a familiar orb appears glowing in the distance. Home. It's never looked so beautiful. From here, the chalky gray dust I'm so familiar with glitters like polished silver.

Fiona stares at it, transfixed.

"Are you nervous to be going back?" Bernard asks.

She starts, as if she'd forgotten we were there. "Not nervous, no . . . I'm ready."

Slowly but steadily, the shuttle approaches the coordinates Canter sent to us, the Moon looming bigger and brighter. We fly over the large cluster of lights that make up the capital and a smaller patch that must be Apolloton, before a structure resembling a stretched-out Slinky slips into view.

Comings and goings of ships are logged, so docking in one of the cities is out of the question. Thankfully, ships docking in the S.L.A.M. hangar are overseen by the school director, and that now happens to be Ms. Goble. Despite her fondness for rules, I have a feeling this will be one she's okay bending.

A lone figure stands in the hangar waiting as the ship lands. Fiona's the first one off the ship, and she sprints across the room, throwing her arms around Ms. Goble. The two hug tightly, laughing and crying for a solid minute. I've never seen Ms. Goble so happy. She seems years younger, more like the girl I remember from the photograph in Director Weathers's office I saw so many months ago.

When they finally break apart, wiping their eyes and glowing with joy, Ms. Goble crosses to where Bernard and I are awkwardly waiting and, even more awkwardly, throws her arms around us. Though being hugged by a teacher was never on my list of life goals, I can't help but tighten my arms around her.

She lays a hand against my cheek. "Are you all right?"

"I am now."

The other passengers file off the ship hesitantly, gazing around awed at the vast chamber.

"Welcome." Ms. Goble greets them with a broad smile. "I know you've had a stressful journey, and I hope you don't mind staying here while we figure out our next move. As this is a school, the arrival of a large group of adults unannounced is sure to draw attention, which we definitely don't need at the moment. No other ships are due today, and I've stocked this area with everything I hope you'll need to be comfortable."

"That will be perfectly fine," Ruth says, stepping forward. "We're happy to help with executing next steps or planning when you're ready."

"What did you have in mind?" Ms. Goble asks.

A crease forms across Ms. Goble's brow as Ruth tells her about the solar storm.

"I read something about that on the open network," she says. "A once-in-a-lifetime phenomenon. But they say it's going to be far enough away that we shouldn't feel its effects."

"The Meteorons can use their magic to harness it," I explain.

Ms. Goble considers this new information. "They're in the Martian Settlement, or they were when Sandra and Canter had a run-in with them."

Fiona inhales sharply. "Where are the others?"

"In my office," Ms. Goble says gently. "I didn't want them wandering the halls. The other students would recognize them."

Fiona's already rushing to the hangar door.

Ms. Goble chuckles and links arms with Fiona as they exit the chamber. Bernard hurries after them, but I linger, taking in the familiar halls that suddenly look foreign. I feel like a ghost roaming a school I was never supposed to be in again, about to see friends I thought were lost to me forever.

A flash of gold where the corridor intersects with another catches my eye, and my mouth falls open. I stand frozen for a pair of heartbeats, unable to breathe, or move, or think as I watch another ghost wandering the halls.

Heart still pounding, I step slowly into the hallway. The blond-haired boy in front of me is clearly sneaking somewhere he isn't supposed to be. He doesn't see or hear me as I creep toward him.

I reach out and touch his shoulder. "Late as always, Weathers."

CHAPTER FORTY-ONE

CANTER

A HAND SQUEEZES MY SHOULDER AND I FREEZE, my mind racing with explanations for why I'm back at S.L.A.M., skulking around the halls.

"Late as always, Weathers," a familiar voice says, and I whirl around.

Myra is standing in front of me.

We stare at each other. Neither of us says a word.

"Are you real?" I finally choke out, and she nods, her eyes glassy.

"I feel like a ghost, though." She smiles, then her face crumples and tears cascade down her cheeks. "I'm *so* sorry, Canter. I shouldn't have said all those things on Mercury. I should've told you about your dad as soon as I found out. I've been running through the whole thing over and over.

How I never really got to tell you, properly, how sorry I am, before—"

"No." My eyes are wet now, too. I don't bother wiping them. "You don't need to apologize. Not to me and not for anything. *I'm* so sorry, Myra. For not saving you."

She shakes her head. "Not your fault. You tried."

"Not hard enough!"

"Canter—"

"Please," I say softly. "I need to tell you this. I've been imagining saying this to you since we found out you . . . survived. Honestly, even before that." She nods, smearing her face with her sleeve, and I take a breath. "I'm sorry for what I said at the prison. I didn't mean it, and you didn't deserve it. Not one nanobit of it. I'm sorry for everything. I'm—" My throat feels too tight for words, so instead I extend my hand.

She half laughs, half sobs, and takes it, giving it a sturdy shake. Then she throws her arms around me.

I stumble, then hug her back as our laughter echoes off the walls.

"Enough of that mushy stuff," Myra says, stepping away. "Did you at least avenge me while I was gone?"

"Working on it. I'm glad you're back so we can cause all sorts of trouble together again."

She beams at me. "We should probably find the others."

"Trouble, this way," I say, linking arms with her and heading back down the hall.

"Weren't you supposed to be there, waiting for us?"

"I got impatient, so I snuck out after Ms. Goble to try to find you guys."

Myra grins. "She's going to be so angry when she gets back to her office and you're not there."

A question burns in my mind, and I take a deep breath before asking it. "Who else was on the shuttle?"

Myra looks me in the eye. "She's here, Canter. Your mom's really here."

I rub my hand through my hair. "What's she like?"

Myra reaches out and pats my hair flat again. "She does that, too, when she's upset or anxious."

My stomach swoops. "What else?"

"Stop walking like you're wading through moondust and find out for yourself."

We pick up the pace, moving quickly and quietly through the deserted halls.

"What time is it?" Myra asks. "Must be after curfew."

"It's the middle of the night." I wink at her. "At least the curfew trackers are off. I used the last of my stash of reflector paper on Mercury."

"What's been happening?" Myra asks. "Fill me in on *everything*."

"All right—"

"As fast as possible."

I laugh. "I don't even know where to start."

"Pick a place and start there. Not knowing what's been going on has been killing me."

I fill her in on MFI's expansion, the rumored activities of Perennial's group, and my dad's deal to get Lila and me our magic back.

Myra raises her eyebrows. "So, he's a double agent?"

"Basically."

Out of nowhere, she slaps my arm, and I jump back. "What was that for?"

"You left out the most important development!"

I stare at her blankly.

"Bin-ro! How did you get him working again?"

"I didn't, actually," I say, before telling her about our newest ally, Eli.

She grins. "He sounds interstellar. I can't wait to meet him. Is that who decoded our music into words?"

I hesitate.

"What's with the fa—"

Heavy footsteps echo down a connecting hall, and we freeze, scanning for a place to hide. Myra races up the hall, waving her hand in front of the classroom door panels until one glows green. "Come on!"

I rush to catch up, heart pounding. Her fingers dig

into my arm as she pushes me inside before ducking into the room. From either side of the door we peek out the window.

And then the light flicks on.

I yelp. "They're on a motion sensor!"

"Shut them off!" Myra whisper-yells.

I slap the button, but nothing happens. "It must be a timer."

"Are you an Elector or not? Short-circuit them!"

"Oh, right." I send a spark into the panel and the lights die. "Oops."

"Oops, he says," she mutters. "How did you even survive this long without me?"

"Shh," I hiss. "They're coming."

We hold our breath as the footfalls come closer. A man walks past the door, head swiveling as he searches for something.

I catch sight of his face and my heart drops to my sneakers before I take a deep breath and crack the door open.

"Dad? What are you doing here?"

CHAPTER FORTY-TWO

MYRA

DIRECTOR WEATHERS DOES A DOUBLE TAKE. "I COULD ask you the same thing."

I slip into the hall behind Canter.

Director Weathers's eyes bulge. "How? What? How is this possible?"

Canter scuffs his shoe against the floor. "It's kind of a long story."

"Give me the short version," Director Weathers says, his gaze never leaving my face.

"The Botans on the Old World are alive," I explain, fiddling with my glasses. "They've been since everyone else evacuated for the Settlements."

Canter's dad takes a deep breath. "And those exiled there?"

I study him. The usual sharpness in his gaze is gone. "Most survived."

"And—and you escaped? Just you?"

"She's here, too," I whisper. "Fiona. In the school."

He stumbles, and Canter darts forward to catch his dad's arm and keep him from falling. "That's impossible."

"It's not," Canter says quietly.

"You've seen her?"

"Not yet," Canter admits. "We were on our way to Ms. Goble's office when we heard someone coming."

"Well, let's go, then." He meets Canter's eyes. "You've waited long enough."

We follow the former director down the hall. "What are you doing here?" Canter asks after a while.

"I came to warn Ms. Goble." Director Weathers's voice is grim. "Jake Melfin's on his way."

I skid to a halt. "What? Why?"

"The book. The log of the exiled Botans. Someone stole it. He thought it was me out to sabotage him."

Canter gapes at his dad. "How did you convince him it wasn't?"

"I didn't, but I managed to escape before he could have the warden throw me in a cell."

"Without magic?" Canter asks, his eyes wide.

His father smirks. "Jake may be a gifted Chemic, but he's not exactly creative. It wasn't hard to outmaneuver him, especially after the last month studying MFI's operations."

"But why's he coming here?" I ask.

"When he couldn't find the book, he assumed I'd sent it to an old friend, one who'd be as outraged about his role in your mother's . . . circumstance as I am."

"What are we going to do?" Canter asks. "We can't let him find Myra, or . . . or Mom."

"We'll figure it out," Director Weathers promises, and then we're turning into the corridor where Ms. Goble's office is located.

"But what about the book?" I press. "If you didn't take it, who did?"

"My dad has plenty of enemies," a voice says from behind us. Kyle Melfin stands in the middle of the hallway. "You should know that better than anyone."

I shift from foot to foot, escape routes and ways to silence him spinning through my mind. Seeds stir in my pockets as I raise a hand.

"Wait, Myra." Canter steps between us. "Kyle's on our side."

"Not in this solar system," I snap, magic humming in my fingertips.

"It's true," he says.

"Prove it." I plant my hands on my hips. "Tell us who stole the log."

Kyle reaches in his jacket and pulls out a very worn, very old black book. "Me."

"What in the name of Pluto are you doing with that?"

Director Weathers demands, lurching at him and pushing his arm down.

"I had to see if he was right," Kyle explains, jutting his chin at Canter. "Turns out my dad is an even bigger villain than I thought."

"What are you talking about?" I snap. "You're just like him."

"No, he isn't," Canter insists.

I turn and gape at him. "Since when?"

"Since he helped translate the musical notes so you could come home." Canter shrugs. "Probably longer than that, though."

I narrow my eyes at Kyle. "You really did that?"

His cheeks flush. "It was kind of the least I *could* do. Especially after all the damage my dad's caused."

"And what do you plan to do with that book?" Director Weathers asks carefully.

Kyle's eyes are like flint. "Whatever I have to."

Director Weathers studies him for another minute, then nods. "We should get to Ms. Goble's office. We need to warn the others Jake's on his way."

"Anything else change since I've been gone?" I ask while we hurry down the hall. "The planets still orbit the sun, right?"

Canter grins. "As far as I know."

CHAPTER FORTY-THREE

CANTER

I COME TO A STOP FEET FROM MS. GOBLE'S DOOR.

Myra comes up beside me, then rests her hand on my shoulder. "It's going to be okay, Canter. You got this."

"Are you sure it's real?" I whisper, nervous sparks dancing over my skin.

"It's real. I promise." She smiles, her eyes sparkling. "Now go meet your mom."

I reach out toward the panel, and the door slides open.

Lila walks by the entry, her arms full of Mending supplies that she drops when she sees us. "Myra!" she whispers, surrounded by bandages and ointments, before she throws her arms around both of our necks.

I hug her back—Myra does, too, even though physical affection has never been her thing. Lila's shaking with sobs, and thankfully Myra pats her arm, making several bad attempts at jokes. I hardly hear them. I'm too busy peeking over Lila's shoulder.

I scan the faces and see shock and joy on the familiar ones. Ms. Goble is glowing and Mrs. Hodger's already crying as she barrels across the room. I extract myself from the hug so I don't get caught in another that, by the looks of it, is going to be bone-crushing.

Lila darts away as Myra's mom throws herself over her daughter. Myra just nestles her head in her mom's shoulder.

I step farther into the room, sweeping my gaze over the desk and chairs, a small seating area with a couch—but I don't see my mother.

I turn to Ms. Goble, a question on my lips. Before she can say anything, the door behind the sofa slides open.

It's her.

Hair the color of fire cascades over her shoulders, flickering like flames in the light. But it's her eyes—the same shade as mine—burning bright, almost scorching me as she stares, frozen, that make my breath catch.

I take a step toward her, and that seems to set her in motion like I flipped a switch. She closes the distance between us in three steps.

"Hi, Mom," I whisper. There's no lump in my throat. No tears sting my eyes. I'm hollow. Numb. Maybe I'm the one frozen now—a statue afraid to move, afraid to breathe, afraid to do anything if it means shattering this moment.

She reaches out, laying a hand against my cheek. Tears fall down her own like rain. "Hi, baby. I missed you so much."

I don't remember embracing her. I can't recall who stepped forward first. Who reached for the other. But her arms are wrapped around me, and my head is resting on her shoulder, and everything is right in the galaxy.

For a moment at least.

Too quickly, I remember the news my father's here to deliver, and gently pull back, wiping my eyes on my sleeve.

"Robert," Ms. Goble says. "What are you doing here?"

Mom's hand stiffens and Myra's smile drops off her face like a Moon rock.

"I—I came to tell you. Warn you." He swallows hard. "Sorry. I just need a minute."

He takes a step toward us, and when Mom staggers back, he flinches. "I'm so sorry, Fiona. For a whole list of things we don't have time to go into right now. But I wanted that to be the first thing you heard from me after all these years. I'm sorry. You may never believe me, but I'm asking—begging you—to at least consider trying."

Mom doesn't say anything, but she doesn't back away, either. After a few moments, she gives a small nod. "I'll consider it. Once I hear the rest of the list."

A ghost of a smile flickers across Dad's face. He holds

her gaze for another moment, and a whole conversation seems to pass between them.

"Jake Melfin's coming here," he finally says, turning to take in the rest of us.

"For what?" Ms. Curie demands.

"This." Kyle moves away from the back wall where he's been lingering, holding out the stolen book.

As Dad explains, Ms. Curie takes the book and leafs through its pages. "This could be very useful. Especially if we can make the Settlements aware of its contents."

"But how?" Lila asks. "Broadcast it?"

"If what Perennial shared back on Venus is true, the Governing Councils control the airways," Myra reminds everyone. "They tried to use the open network to turn people against Melfin before. It didn't work."

"Maybe they've come up with a new approach." Ms. Curie squints at her computer screen. "Can't hurt to let them know we have it."

"Better make it fast," Dad says, watching her. "Jake will be here any minute."

An alert pings from Ms. Goble's pendant. She frowns, and when she reads the message, her scowl deepens. "There's a ship approaching the S.L.A.M. hangar."

"Can you deny it entry?" Mrs. Hodger asks.

Ms. Goble shakes her head. "It appears they have an access code and the landing is already in progress."

"The Botans! They're in the hangar!" Myra shoots up, dragging her mother with her.

Mom goes pale. "We've got to warn them."

"I'll go," Dad volunteers. "It's me he's after, anyway."

"No, it's that." Kyle nods at the book. "And you know as well as I do that he won't stop until he finds it. He'll tear apart this whole building if he has to."

"Then what do you suggest?" Mrs. Hodger snaps.

I throw my free hand up and a crack of electricity silences the room. "If we stand here debating much longer, it won't matter. I'm going."

"Not without me," Mom says, clutching my hand tighter. Despite the threat, I can't help the rush of joy from flooding through me.

"Or me," Dad says.

"Or me!" Myra's already marching toward the door, her mother trailing her.

We pile out into the hall and race toward the hangar doors. If we get there before Melfin docks, we can move the Botans. Direct them back onto the ship and send them to the other side of the Moon. Anything to get them out of Melfin's way.

I'm the first through the doors. Two ships sit in the cavernous room, along with lots and lots of people. The Botans are easy to identify, with their clothing woven from plants and vicious-looking stems curling across their arms, through their hands, and around their bodies like armor.

On the other side of the room, Jake Melfin faces them, his eyes flashing like a pair of nebulas. A small group hovers behind him. They aren't clad in green, and I don't recognize any of them. But they're restraining someone I do. *Eli.*

CHAPTER FORTY-FOUR

MYRA

I PUSH TO THE FRONT. IT ONLY TAKES A PAIR OF heartbeats to process the scene in front of me—a mixture of faces I know and others I don't. Clear allies, obvious enemies, and a little boy who seems entirely out of place.

"Eli!" Lila lunges toward the kid struggling in the grip of Melfin's goons. "What are you doing here?"

"I may have followed you and hidden on your ship from Venus," he says, before making another attempt to break free.

"Let him go!" Canter shouts. "He doesn't have anything to do with this."

"Really?" Melfin glares across the divide. "So it's a coincidence he was skulking around here with that very distinct robot?" He juts his chin toward a shiny something cradled by one of his men, and I gasp.

Without thinking, I thrust out my hand, and a vine propels out of my pocket, wrapping around Bin-ro and snapping him back to me like a lasso. "You'll have to exile me into a supernova before I let you hurt Bin-ro again."

Melfin's mouth falls open as his eyes trail the emerald line back to my hands. "What—"

Fiona steps in front of me. "She's the least of your worries."

He staggers back, his face paler than moondust. "You told me none of the Botans escaped," he growls.

"They must have sent another shuttle," one of the men holding Eli replies.

As I study Melfin's group, recognition blooms inside me. Meteorons. The woman who was holding Bin-ro is the same one who killed Charlie. Beside her is Ophelia, the leader of the Meteorons.

Fiona's eyes go wide as she recognizes the others. "Just when I thought you couldn't stoop any lower, Jake, you align yourself with a group of murderers."

"We could say the same of you." Ophelia sneers, nodding at the Botans filing in beside us. "At least he's promised us something you'd never even considered: equal power."

"I understand you're new to the Settlements," Director Weathers says coldly, "but let me offer you a piece of advice: Jake Melfin doesn't do anything to benefit anyone that doesn't benefit him first and most."

Ophelia smirks. "It seems our goals are currently aligned, so we're not worried."

When Fiona chuckles, the sound's like ice. "And what could you possibly want? Besides destruction."

"Exactly," Ophelia says. "And it just so happens an opportunity is hurtling toward us as we speak."

Canter frowns. "What are—"

"I'll explain later," I mutter.

Ms. Curie eyes Melfin. "I thought you were a businessman. Terrorizing the Settlements doesn't seem to fit with your corporate mission."

Melfin's chest swells. "That's where you're wrong. The more my new Meteoron friends destroy, the more the galaxy will need MFI's products to rebuild."

Canter snarls. "You mean your *imitation* products? If today's newsfeeds are anything to go by, they're even deadlier than your food."

Melfin shrugs. "Then the Settlements will need more."

"Melfin's playing you," I tell Ophelia. "He doesn't have power to give. Not as much as he used to, anyway."

"You've been out of touch for a while, Miss Hodger," Melfin says, with an infuriating flash of his teeth. "Thanks to that little bargaining chip you gifted me, I've made many more contacts than I ever had before, all ready to help me in any way I need."

"Then what are you doing here?" I counter. "Shouldn't you be, you know, destroying the galaxy?"

"We'll get to that soon enough," Ophelia says, her voice cold.

"And I had a small mess to clean up first." Melfin's gaze flicks to Director Weathers. "Give me back the book, Rob, and perhaps I can be convinced to keep your family together. Reunited on the Old World. For good this time." He scans the Botans. "Unfortunately, I can't make that promise to the rest of you. I understand there are grudges that need to be settled"—he motions toward the half dozen Meteorons flanking him—"and I'm not about to stand in the way of my new friends' retribution."

"You've made a terrible mistake," Ruth says from behind me. "The Moon doesn't have weather."

"Wait!" Eli yells. "That isn't—"

"It's all right, bud," Canter calls. "We won't let them hurt you. Their powers don't work here."

Ruth swivels to face the Meteorons still holding a struggling Eli. She digs into her pocket, then scatters a handful of seeds on the floor. Flowers erupt in a vibrant line, growing taller and taller until they reach the boy. A pair of trees sprout up on either side of him, breaking their grip. Eli bursts free and runs to Lila. He tries to tell her something as she clutches him against her hip, but her gaze is fixed on Melfin.

"Now I suggest you leave," Ruth continues. She glances over at Ms. Goble. "Or would you prefer we take them prisoner?"

"You won't be doing either," Melfin replies firmly.

"Give it up, Jake," Director Weathers grits out. "You're outnumbered. You may be a talented Chemic, but you can't take on all of us."

"Not alone, no. But I'm not alone. My offer still stands. You and your family can complete your reunion on the Old World. It's a better deal than you could have imagined a month ago. Just give me back the book."

"You mean this?" Kyle pushes through the crowd, lifting the book above his head.

The smile falls from Melfin's face so fast, it's like the Moon's artificial gravity generators yanked it away. "Where did you get that?"

"I found it in your office." Kyle casually turns the book over in his hands. "You're always telling me I need to learn about and respect my family history. I thought I'd start here. To be honest, it was kind of a disappointing read."

"Kyle." Melfin's voice has a dangerous edge. "You don't know what you're doing."

"Actually, I do. I'm not the failure you always tell me I am. I understand exactly what this is, what it means. And the galaxy will, too, once they learn what you've been up to. Exiling Botans from the Settlements while using plants for yourself." His eyes narrow. "Stripping people of their magic. You *and* the Governing Councils."

"Difficult decisions are often required to keep order," Melfin answers coolly. "To keep society functioning, some need to be at the bottom. Far more than at the top. Otherwise, the whole system crumbles."

"That's not true," Kyle says. "That's just what you tell yourself."

"In life, there are winners and losers, son."

"And it's up to you to decide who's who?" I snap, seeds vibrating in my pockets. "All because you own some company?"

"Because I *earned* it. Because I understand that sometimes what's essential is not always what's easy."

"That's your father talking," Ms. Curie says softly, and I swear Melfin winces. "You never used to believe that space junk."

"I grew up." He nods at Kyle. "We're leaving. I'll deal with you later. Give me the book."

Kyle tucks it into his pocket. "I think that's another of your tasks I'm just not up to, Dad."

"You're not taking anything or anyone from here," I say, pushing my glasses up and then stretching my hands forward. I call to the seeds Ruth scattered, and vines weave together like a snake, flashing thorns in lieu of fangs. "And you won't be leaving, either."

"Can we tap into the open network from the school system?" Ms. Curie asks. "I think it's time the galaxy sees what MFI has been up to." She meets Melfin's gaze. "And the monster you've morphed into."

Ms. Goble nods. "We can go live within the hour."

"Oh, I don't think you want to do that," Melfin says.

"I don't think we asked for your opinion," Director Weathers fires back. "Give it up. You're surrounded by magic."

Melfin fixes him with a cold glare. "Not yours."

Director Weathers's response is equally icy. "Not yet. Lucky for you."

"You'll find I have far more than luck on my side." Melfin nods at the Meteorons. "It's time to go." He nods at Kyle. "Get him on the ship with the book. I don't care what you do with the rest."

"Are you that delusional, Jake?" Fiona shakes her head. "What do you—"

A rumbling drowns out the rest of her sentence. It sounds like one of the capital trains roaring into the station, but there's no transport in sight.

My hair flutters around my face, then whips back, and the next second, I'm bracing myself against winds strong enough to rock the ships in front of me. "What is this?" I yell as the Botans spring into action, sending tree limbs careening after Melfin and his Meteoron bodyguards. "There's no weather here. How are their powers working?"

"Apparently, their magic didn't get the memo," Canter yells, fighting to stay upright.

Chaos erupts around us. Flashes of green are repelled by wind gusts. The Botan ship rocks and rolls, sending people scrambling out of the way. Ms. Curie calls a surge of power from the school's electrical grid, scorching the walls behind Melfin and the Meteorons.

As another bolt erupts from her palm, Ophelia leaps forward, snaring it around her wrist and whipping it back our way. Canter and I dive apart as it sears the floor between us.

"Don't use electricity!" Fiona yells. "They can control it, too."

The wind strengthens, whipping through the hangar, stirring up tools and furniture and sending them flying.

"How are they doing this?" I call, huddling beside Canter.

"The Moon *does* have weather," Eli insists from where he's crouched, shielded by Lila.

Canter flinches as debris whizzes by his head. "No, it doesn't. There's not enough atmosphere."

"There's solar wind!" Eli yells over the storm. "I read about it when I was studying satellite design. It's caused by particles from the sun. Normally, it's not strong enough to have much impact, but they must be channeling it with their magic."

"Couldn't you have told us that earlier?" I ask.

"I tried!" He glares at me. "No one was listening."

"Botans, ready your resources," Ruth barks over the howling wind, tearing at her sleeves. Seeds cascade from the fabric, forming a halo around her and every other Botan as they do the same. "Form a line."

"That's us." I grab Canter's hand and pull him back to his feet. "Lila, you should hang back in case someone needs your Mending."

"Good idea." She nods, taking Eli's hand. "You can come with me."

"I want to help!" he says, tugging away.

"You can't," Canter says. "Stay with Lila."

"Why?" he says, scowling. "Because I don't have magic."

"Crashing comets, no," Canter says. "I'm sure you could invent something in two nanoseconds and take half of them out."

A smile flickers across Eli's face before he forces back his frown. "Why not, then?"

"Because you're too young!" Canter shoves him toward the back of the hangar. "Now go with Lila and stay out of trouble."

Lila hauls Eli away, and Canter and I brace ourselves,

then push toward the fighting. The Botans are almost invisible in swirls of their green magic, branches whipping in every direction. Director Weathers braces himself against a large sheet of metal that must have blown off one of the ships, shielding Fiona as she hurls burdock bushes covered in oversized burrs at the Meteorons like massive taupe cannonballs.

Instead of slinging lightning bolts, Ms. Curie is directing her magic to sabotage the Meteoron ship. Lights flicker out one at a time, and something smokes beneath the hull. A Meteoron whips up a vortex, catching a large piece of machinery before sending the metal hurtling in her direction.

"No!" Fiona leaps out from behind the shield, summoning a cypress tree, which shoots up in front of Ms. Curie, shielding her. The metal smashes into the wide trunk, cracking it in half. One side tumbles toward Ms. Curie. Fiona shoves her friend out of the way, and the tree falls on her instead.

"Lila!" Canter and I scream as one before tearing over.

My blood runs cold as I sweep my arms to the side and the tree rises, dropping with a thud a few yards away.

A moment later, Lila is bent over Fiona. Lila's eyes are closed, and her hands hover over Canter's mother's chest, which isn't moving.

Canter is still, like the ice in my veins has crept over

him. Lila's hair billows around her face as her lips form rapid words, though I can't hear any of them over the wind.

No. No, this isn't fair. This isn't how Fiona's story ends. It can't be.

Director Weathers and Ms. Curie race over.

"Please. Please, Lila. You can't let her die." Canter's eyes are squeezed shut.

"Shh, Canter," I murmur in his ear. "Let Lila work."

The winds are stronger now, debris falling like snow. I tear my gaze away to scan the hangar and my mouth falls open. So many of the Botans are sprawled across the ground. The Meteorons have formed a circle, arms outstretched, commanding their storm. The remaining Botans direct their plants toward the ring, but most are sent hurtling back.

I realize I don't see Melfin near the Meteorons, or anywhere else.

"She's okay!" Canter shouts from beside me, and I swivel back around.

Fiona's eyes are open, her chest rising and falling in what seems like a normal rhythm. After a few seconds, she gingerly pushes to her elbows. "I feel like I got crushed by a tree."

Director Weathers drops his head into his hands.

"That's because you jumped in front of one, like an idiot," Ms. Curie chokes out.

"And I'd do it again." Fiona shrugs, then winces. She takes Ms. Curie's hand. "I'd do a lot for my best friend."

Ms. Curie squeezes back. "Until the end."

I glance between Canter and Lila, and know I'd do the same.

Lila carefully helps Fiona to her feet, giving her one last inspection.

Out of the corner of my eye, I see something silver glinting like a flash of lightning, but it's not electricity. It's metal. Part of an engine whipping by me.

Lila staggers, her gaze fixed, and drops to the ground.

CHAPTER FORTY-FIVE

CANTER

I'M STILL SITTING, PROCESSING THAT MY MOTHER'S okay, when something silver whips by me. My breath hitches as I take in Lila's still form beside me. My brain can't catch up. Can't figure out why she's not moving. Why her side's bleeding. Why she's not breathing.

Myra screams, and it snaps me out of my trance. Her hands curl into fists, greenery bursting from her like a deadly emerald aura. Plant shrapnel sizzles through the air, and distant shouts confirm that at least some of the weaponized flora finds its mark.

"We need a Mender!" Frantic, Myra glances around as bushes erupt from the ground, circling us like sentinels. "Are there any other Menders here?"

I jump to my feet, spinning as if one will materialize out of the building walls.

The *school* walls.

"There are Mender students inside!" I take off running, footsteps pounding behind me as Myra and I race to the hangar door.

A figure blocks our way—two figures. "Let him go!"

Melfin has Kyle by the collar and is snatching the book from his hands. "It doesn't look like you're in much of a position to be giving orders. Even with their limited powers here, you're no match for Meteoron magic."

"Maybe you rely on your magic too much," a small voice says.

We all turn, and my stomach drops. Eli's standing behind us, his hands shaking as he clutches his stun launcher.

"Eli, no!"

"Let them pass," he orders, though his voice sounds so small.

"Deal with that," Melfin calls to a nearby Meteoron.

The man turns, flicks his wrist, and a gust of wind whips by us, catching the stun launcher and smashing it against the wall. It shatters into a pile of bolts and twisted metal.

"We'll be heading back to the Martian Settlement," Melfin announces. "And I think we'll take you all with us." He narrows his eyes at Eli. "We've had a real shortage of Reps lately. You'd make a fine worker at one of my factories. And I'm sure we can find the rest of you a ride back to the Old World from there. Second time's the charm," he adds, winking at Myra.

"Not a chance," she growls.

Melfin uses the hand still clutching the book to open his jacket. An assortment of bottles, tubes, and vials lines the fabric. He uses his teeth to uncork one, and violet mist seeps into the air.

The purple fog drifts toward us, and Myra and I stumble back, scrambling away. It spreads, taunting us, coming so close I don't dare breathe.

"Inhale a little of that, and you'll do whatever I say," Melfin says quietly. "Follow any order, even if I told you to walk right into the sun, or launch your friend here"—he juts his chin at Myra—"into a black hole."

The violet haze drifts closer, like a hand reaching for our throats.

"Please," Myra whispers. "Let us go find a Mender. For Lila. She never did anything to you. It was all me."

"And me," I add. "Punish us. Not Lila."

Melfin tuts. "That's unfortunate. She seemed like a bright girl. Though I suppose if she was mixed up in all this"—he shrugs—"perhaps not."

"Dad." Kyle gapes at his father. "You can't just let her die. Any Mender student could save her. At least let them try."

"Why would I bring back an enemy, son?"

"She's just a kid!"

"A new plant's thorn is just as sharp as an old one's."

"You can't—"

Rumbling like thunder rolls through the room, and for a moment, I think the Meteorons have found more magic to tap into. But this is no storm. It's a ship.

"What in the Moon—" Melfin darts away, dragging Kyle along with him. The purple smoke trails them, and I wave my arm to clear any lingering Chemic magic from the air.

Overhead, a giant ship descends, pressing through the hangar ceiling and setting down between the Meteoron ship and the shuttle Myra arrived on.

For a moment, the whole room is still, and then the ship's main hatch slowly slides open and row upon row of people descend the ramp—a blur of unrecognizable faces. My eyes lock on one, and a shiver runs through me.

The hangar explodes with noise and magic. Chemic potions, spiked plants, crackling electricity, and makeshift walls and platforms erupt around us. In the center of the space, an older woman with pearly-gray hair and dark skin directs the attack, using her Number Whispering magic as smoothly as Mr. Finch conducted at V.A.M.A. Calculations stream around her like a funnel as she barks orders, directing her forces, executing her battle plan.

Myra and I exchange a glance and take off running.

"Perennial!" Myra shouts.

As she turns in our direction, recognition flares in her eyes.

"We need a Mender!" I call. "Please!"

More numbers float from her temple as she scans the room, then waves someone over. "Nora! Hurry!"

A middle-aged woman with brown hair and kind eyes races to us.

"Thank you!" Myra chokes out. We lead her to Lila, ducking machinery, vines, and magic flying through the air. Eli's huddled in the corner, gathering the pieces of his shattered launcher in his shirt. At least he's away from the worst of the fighting.

Nora drops to her knees and hovers her hands over Lila, her gaze zigzagging.

"What is this?" Dad demands. "Who are these people?"

"The rogue Reps." I push my hands into the ground and call to the plant particles scattered there. A hedge encircles us, forming a barrier. "Perennial's group. The ones Melfin's been hunting."

"We're not Reps anymore," Nora murmurs, pressing her hand against Lila's ribs, her eyes drifting shut as cracks of energy echo around us. The leafy wall holds, though.

"Melfin's escaping!" Mom shouts, her amber hair whipping around her as she jumps to her feet and bolts to the ships.

I catch a glimpse of him, racing toward his shuttle's door, dragging Kyle with one hand and clutching the book in the other.

Dad races after her, but Myra and I can't move.

"They'll get him," she whispers, her eyes still locked on Lila's face.

Right now, I don't care. My focus is on Lila and the Mender magic struggling to bring her back.

"She's okay, right?" Myra asks. "She'll be okay?"

"Shh," Nora whispers, eyes still closed. Her hand skims Lila's side.

Someone drops down beside me: Eli. I'm about to bark at him to be quiet, my mind already spinning with his stream of questions, but before I can say anything he lays a hand on my shoulder. He doesn't say a thing.

"Please," I murmur. "Please, please, please." After all the good luck we've had, I know it's not fair to ask for more. But this is *Lila*. She can't die. She can't. I yank my hair so hard it hurts and say a quick Worship Center prayer, willing her eyes to open.

Nora's hands are still frozen over Lila's body. Lila's eyelashes flutter, and then she takes a deep, shuddering breath and groans.

"*Lila!* She's okay!" Myra screeches, throwing herself at me.

"She's okay," Nora agrees, sitting back, looking exhausted. "But she should take it easy for the foreseeable future."

"I concur with that diagnosis." Lila grunts as Nora helps her sit up. "What's going on?"

Myra fills her in as I scan the room and sigh. "Melfin's gone."

"Did he take the book with him?" Myra asks.

"Unfortunately, yes." My dad comes up behind us, grimacing.

"He's headed to the Martian Settlement," I say as my mother and Perennial join us.

"The rest of the Meteorons will be there," Mom says grimly. "And given the Martian atmosphere, they'll be so much more powerful. The perfect place to harness a massive storm."

"It doesn't matter," Myra replies, looking more determined than I think I've ever seen her. "That's where we need to go, too."

CHAPTER FORTY-SIX

MYRA

THE DISTANCE BETWEEN THE MOON AND MARS ISN'T far, but the trip still feels like it takes eons. That could be because my mother is still following me around like a second shadow, pelting me with questions and endless hints that we should disappear in one of the other Settlements.

"You could've stayed behind with Ms. Goble," I tell her after the fourth time she suggests we leave the fighting to the Old World Botans. "I'm sure she could have used your help securing the school and making sure the injured get the care they need."

Mom waves the idea away. "If anyone can handle logistics, it's Val. Especially with my magic still dormant." She brushes a finger against her temple, testing to see if any numerals trail behind. Once we took off after Melfin and the Meteorons, Perennial instructed Nora to deactivate Mom's and Director Weathers's magic-suppression chips, but so far neither seems to have regained their magic.

"Anything yet?" Director Weathers calls. He's huddled on the other side of the cabin with Fiona and Canter, who's bent over a contraption that looks like a cross between a torpedo and a blender.

Mom shakes her head. "Hopefully, by the time we land."

"We'll need all the reinforcements we can get," Perennial adds from the cockpit. "We're racing a solar storm. This will be difficult."

When we boarded the ship, I told Canter and his father about the massive weather system hurtling across the galaxy and right into the Meteorons' hands. Comms on Mars are still down, but the rest of the Settlements are broadcasting the path of the storm, since it's veered so far off the expected course, straight toward the red planet.

"That's why we can all agree the children should stay behind," Mom argues.

I groan. "Perennial just said they can use everyone they can get."

"Every adult."

"That's not what she said," Canter calls back.

"I'll leave that up to you," says Perennial, squaring her shoulders "but I won't be turning away any help, though I'm hoping we'll get more reinforcements."

"From where?" Fiona asks.

"Everywhere, if we're lucky. I put out a call on the open network. The Lunar Governing Council took it down pretty quickly, but it's been reshared to the other Settlements. One of our Tekkies even managed to get the call out to all messengers and pendants in range."

I frown. "What sort of call?"

"For revolution." Perennial's eyes gleam. "The security cameras in S.L.A.M.'s hangar caught most of Melfin announcing his plans."

Director Weathers's eyebrows shoot up. "And you transmitted it to all the Settlements?"

"Not for long, but yes." Perennial clasps her hands. "We'll see if it's enough."

"The first time we met you, you said people don't care about things that don't affect them," Bernard says, walking into the room with Lila.

"This affects them. And even if it doesn't, who knows?" Perennial shrugs. "There are always exceptions."

Canter's still tinkering with the machine on his lap. "What sort of damage can the storm do?"

"Normally, a storm of this magnitude could wipe out power grids, spark electrical fires, and fry every device in a hundred-mile radius," Ms. Curie replies, "but with the Meteorons controlling it, potentially enhancing it . . ." She shakes her head. "Complete destruction."

Fiona watches Canter work. "We're going to need help. Let's hope your transmission worked."

"If the log in Melfin's book is accurate, there could be a lot more families siding against him than we'd expect," I say.

"Families *and* friends." Ms. Curie shoots Fiona a small smile.

I lean back in my seat. "If we can get the book back, maybe we can read the names on the open network, so the people who care about those listed will know the truth."

"What if we could get the Meteorons to turn on Melfin?" Canter muses. "Convince them that he'll betray them eventually?"

"I've got a few tricks up my sleeve that could help with that," Ms. Curie says.

Director Weathers shifts in his seat. "Like what?"

"You'll have to wait and see." She winks, and when he glowers, Fiona laughs.

Beeping echoes from the cockpit, and Perennial hurries back through the door. Ms. Curie, Fiona, and Director Weathers are right behind her.

"We're on our final approach and need to decide where to land," Perennial calls back to us. "I'd like to be out of sight, but within walking distance of where the Meteorons are camped out."

"Well, the average human can cover five to six miles an hour over short distances," Mom mutters from beside me. "Depending on the terrain, that means we should probably find a location at least three miles away, but you'd want multiple teams . . ." As her voice drifts away, something else floats into view. The misty 3 sparkles in the harsh overhead lights, but the way my mother looks at it, it might as well be carved from diamonds. "Myra, quick!" she says, leaping to her feet. "How many people are on this shuttle?"

I do a quick estimate.

"So if we create a perimeter around the Meteoron location, which is about a square mile, based on what Perennial shared earlier, we'd need three teams, evenly split between Creers . . ." She walks into the cockpit, numbers streaming behind her like a veil.

"Well, that was perfect timing," I say with a sigh when she's out of sight. "Good thing I wished on my lucky meteor."

"Whichever one that is today," Bernard adds, chuckling.

I beam at him as he and Lila settle in across from me and Canter claims the chair my mother vacated. I glance around at the familiar crew and feel a small pang in my chest.

Lila scans my face. "What's wrong?"

"Just missing Bin-ro," I whisper.

"Me too," Canter says, popping open a flap on the contraption and squinting at the mess of wires inside. "It was the only way to keep Eli from sneaking on board."

We told the kid we needed him to keep our robot sidekick safe and in perfect working order. He solemnly accepted the job like we'd ask him to guard the galaxy against an alien invasion.

"And your new project." Lila nudges Canter's machine, her eyes sparkling.

"What is it?" I ask.

"Eli's stun launcher." Canter wipes his forehead. "He wanted me to take it in case it could help, but I'm not sure I can fix it in time."

I eye the mishmash of parts. "Why'd you agree?"

"It seemed like it meant a lot to him. He was pretty upset we wouldn't let him come." Canter shrugs. "He wanted to help. Plus, he let me swap this project with another one I promised I'd help him with."

Lila beams at Canter, and I can't keep a smile from creeping across my own face.

"I like this new protective-older-brother thing you've got going on," I say, nudging him. "It's about time you showed some responsibility."

He tries to scowl but ends up laughing instead. "Someone's got to watch out for him, and after what he did for

Bin-ro, I feel kind of responsible for keeping him out of trouble."

"It still would have been nice to have Bin-ro here, though." *And someone else, too.*

"Do you think Hannah will be with the Meteorons on the Martian Settlement?" Lila asks quietly.

I sigh. "She must be."

"You'll convince her to rejoin our side," Lila says. "I know it."

I remove my glasses, rub the lenses on my shirt, then replace them. "Maybe."

Lila reaches over and squeezes my hand. "You know her better than anyone."

I'm not sure that's true anymore, but I keep the thought to myself.

"If all else fails," Canter adds, "you know what to do."

I raise an eyebrow. "What's that?"

"Nag her until she gives in."

I giggle. After a moment, the others join in.

My stomach lurches as the ship begins its descent.

Canter nudges me. "Time to settle the score."

I stare out the window. "All of them."

CHAPTER FORTY-SEVEN

CANTER

THE MARTIAN LANDSCAPE IS A LOT LIKE THE Moon's—dusty, barren. If I'm being honest, I think I prefer moondust. At least it doesn't cover you in a layer of grime the color of blood.

Based on Perennial's readings, Melfin's ship is docked exactly three miles from ours. We could see the vast encampment from the air. Melfin must have called in reinforcements, too. I just hope ours show up.

We file off the ship with the Botans, who are in fighting condition thanks to Nora's Mender handiwork. Even so, we're easily outnumbered.

"These odds are terrible," Myra mutters as three groups form and fan out.

I shrug. "Odds don't always matter. The last time the S.L.A.M. hoverball team played in the championship, our opponents ranked light-years higher than us and we still won."

"I guess that's true." She adjusts her glasses. "At least we have surprise on our side."

"We've got more than surprise," I say. "We've got passion. We're fighting for our survival. For justice."

Myra nods. "That's got to count for more than old grudges and profits."

"I guess we'll find out."

Myra and I join the party approaching the Meteoron camp from the east. My parents are in this group, too, which was the only way Myra's mother agreed to let her go. Number Whispering isn't really suited for the battlefield, so Mrs. Hodger's staying back with Perennial to strategize.

"See you guys on the other side," Bernard says, hurrying past with Lila. They're approaching from the west along with Nora.

Myra eyes them warily but doesn't say anything.

"What? No sarcasm?" Bernard asks, turning around.

Lila nudges me. "And what about you? Why aren't you trying to get us to bet on how many Meteorons we can take out? Winner buys dinner in Apolloton?"

"It's only . . ." Myra begins, then looks to me.

"We just got back together." A dull ache spreads across my temples. "I don't think I could handle it, if—"

"We'll be fine, guys!" Lila squeezes my arm, then grabs Myra's hand. "We always are."

"But what if our luck's running out?" I say softly.

Bernard shakes his head. "Impossible. The galaxy will never run out of lucky meteors."

"Still." Myra shifts from foot to foot.

"Stop worrying so much," Lila orders. "These nervous versions of you are freaking me out."

"Oh, fine." Myra rolls her eyes. "Don't die or I'll kill you."

We all laugh, and I feel some of the tension ease from my shoulders.

"That's better." Bernard scans the thinning crowd. "But we'd better hurry. I'm sure Mrs. Hodger wouldn't mind if we *accidentally* got left behind."

Myra groans. "Truth."

"See you in the victory parade!" I call over my shoulder as we run to catch up with the eastern group.

"Maybe Claire's right," my mom says to my dad as we join them. "Maybe the kids should stay behind."

"Don't you guys start now," I grumble, rubbing my hands through my hair. "We barely escaped Mrs. Hodger."

Dad looks uneasily between me, Myra, and my mother. When I cross my arms and Myra plants her hands on her hips, he sighs. "They'll just find a way to sneak in anyway, and we don't have time to lock them up."

Mom meets my eyes, her gaze a mixture of worry and pride. "I suppose not. But let's get one thing clear. If we tell you to run, hide, or do literally anything, you do it. Or I'll lock you in a cage of branches."

"And I'll mix a solution that'll knock you out for three days," Dad adds, eyebrow raised.

Myra and I exchange a glance. *They can try.*

We both nod enthusiastically, and they seem satisfied.

"Where's Ms. Curie?" I ask, glancing around.

"She's heading to the camp," Mom says. "She'll be fine."

"Not if we don't get moving to give cover." Dad prods us forward, while Mom slips to the front of the group to lead us across the grim terrain, her amber hair flashing in the Martian sun.

"Maybe the cities are nicer?" Myra says uncertainly. "They've got to be bigger than Apolloton and the Lunar capital." A shadow crosses her features.

"What's up, Mixture Myra?"

"Nothing. I never thought I'd say this, but I miss home."

"What was the Old World like?"

She sighs. "So much color. Blue skies and green grass as far as you can see. Plants growing everywhere. They actually live *in* them! The Botans, anyway."

"It sounds amazing."

"You'll see," she says, grinning at me. "After all this, we'll go back."

I hadn't really considered the after. What happens when this is over? The Meteorons defeated. Melfin punished. Botans free, living out in the open. "Is it really possible?"

"Look at what Perennial's accomplished." Myra nods toward the others around us, mostly former Reps. "Would you ever have believed the Reps could shatter the system and get their magic back?"

"When you try, who knows what sort of magic can happen?" I murmur, and Myra beams.

"Exactly." She focuses on a crater up ahead. The Meteoron camp is on the other side. "That's what we're doing. Trying to change things."

"Not just trying. We're doing it."

We crouch at the crater's ridge, surveying the Meteoron camp. Magic rushes through me, prickling across my skin. I can't make out Melfin from here, but I know he's down there. Once Ms. Curie's group gives the signal, we'll launch the attack.

We can't see them, which is good, because that means the Meteorons can't, either. But I know they're there, a few hundred yards away, hiding in the Martian landscape just like us.

"That's the first signal," Mom hisses as a lavender haze drifts toward us.

Lightning flashes across the sky, and the whole world

erupts. "There's the second!" Dad leaps over the ledge and careens down the hill. Our whole group follows, a few dozen people of all different Creers, backgrounds, and home planets.

Myra races beside me, her dark hair billowing over her shoulders, eyes narrowed behind her glasses. She turns to me and mouths, *Race you?*

I smirk and pick up speed. Buds curl around her arms as they pump at her sides. I call up my own magic. A thorny bloom sprouts in one hand, and in the other, I clutch a ball of electricity.

The central flank, which arrived at the camp before us, is already engaged in battle. I run through a rainstorm, shivering as the drops transform into flecks so cold they sting my skin.

"Watch out!" Myra screeches, sending a rope of firecracker vines hurtling ahead. It wraps around the legs of a Meteoron, sending him crashing to the ground. "After snow comes ice."

I duck as an icicle goes flying by my ear like a spear. "Good thing water's a conductor of electricity." I release the ball of energy in my fist, and it ripples across the wet ground, stunning everyone in its path.

"Nice job, hotshot!" Myra calls.

"Good work, son," Dad agrees. He's in a storm of his own, a rainbow of Chemic potions swirling around him.

Meteorons drop as fingers of fluorescent-orange smoke stretch out into the crowd. A violet stream of fog slithers across the ground like a snake, coiling around a trio of Meteorons wielding ice like daggers. The man in the middle hauls his arm back, a frosty cerulean blade clutched in his fist, pointed directly at us. Just as he releases it, the violet smoke smothers him and the ice evaporates.

"Did your Chemic mist melt their ice?" Myra asks, sending a cage of bamboo hurtling toward them.

"It melted their magic." Dad flicks his wrist, sending the smoky violet serpent into the crowd. "That mixture confuses their hippocampi, the part of the brain that stores their meteorological knowledge. It's temporary, but very effective."

"And slightly terrifying," Myra mutters, though she looks impressed.

The winds pick up, dispersing Dad's Chemic magic. I slip and slide, struggling to keep my footing as the ground transforms into a thick sheet of ice. Dad falls, and an instant later a Meteoron looms over him, an amber funnel swirling over his shoulder.

"Fire whirl!" Mom yells. "Get back!"

The heat hits my face like a fist, and when I stumble to my knees, Myra hauls me back. Sprawled on the ground, I summon my own electricity, ready to blast the Meteoron into the Martian desert, but Mom's quicker. Shafts of green bamboo burst up from the dust, shielding my father from the tornado of fire. The flames lick at the thick stalks, tingeing them umber, but they hold. Branches lash out at the Meteoron, drawing blood.

The wounded man rolls to the side, evading the bamboo's thick, meaty roots, which slither toward him like eels. His palm blazes silver, a ball of crystal glowing in his fist. It looks like a massive diamond, glittering in the blood-orange light, and for a moment, I'm transfixed.

He turns and hurls it at me.

I'm a beat too slow. I wince, waiting for the orb to smash into my skull. Something flutters by my cheek instead.

A massive palm leaf unfurls in midair, catching the ice like a ball in a glove, before flinging it back. It slams the man in the back of the head, and he crashes to the ground again. Gulping down air, I turn, expecting to see Myra.

Instead, Bernard claps me on the shoulder as he races past. "What happened to those hoverball skills I've heard so much about?"

"I'm a little rusty!" I reply, still scanning for Myra, and then I see her. She's locked in battle with a Meteoron woman commanding a small blizzard. Snow dumps down as ice fogs Myra's glasses, and she stumbles.

I drop my hands to the ground. A trail of thick grass bursts up, connecting me to Myra and melting everything in its path. She stumbles onto it, spinning as she regains her footing. A mound of burgundy erupts at the Meteoron's feet. Poisonous oak leaves crawl up her body like locusts. She howls, clawing at her skin as hives erupt across her face.

"That'll keep her distracted," Myra quips, jogging down my new greenway. "What about—" She freezes, her mouth hanging open.

I turn and gasp. Hannah's behind us, pinned to a tree, trying to wrestle away thorns that are intent on skewering her face.

Leave her, I tell myself. *She chose her side, and it isn't ours. Don't help her. Don't help her. Don't—*

"Blast it," Myra whispers before we both sprint toward the tree.

CHAPTER FORTY-EIGHT

MYRA

"STOP!" I YELL, THROWING MY HANDS OUT. "DON'T hurt her." My magic calls to the branches, and I will my own powers to overtake the other Botan's. A moment later, the limbs bend and Hannah breaks free.

"What are you doing?" a green-clad man snaps. "She's with *them*."

"She's with me!" I roar, moving in front of Hannah.

"We've got this," Canter says, sliding in beside me.

The man looks like he wants to argue, but a crack of thunder booms in the distance. He hesitates, then hurries away to find a new fight.

"I don't need your help," Hannah growls. "And he's right, I am with them."

A shadow falls across us. It's like someone flipped a switch, turning day to night. The sky's gone from pale butterscotch to inky black. Streaks of emerald dance eerily across it.

"Are those lights some sort of Botan magic?" Canter asks, his eyes wide.

Hannah barks a laugh. "As if Botan magic could command the sky."

"It's the solar storm." As I stare up, hypnotized, the wind blows my hair into my face. "And it's almost here."

Canter holds out his arms, face still upturned. "I can feel the electricity in the air, but it's pulling away from me like the storm is drawing a current."

"Building power," I whisper. "Like the tide."

"And the wave's coming."

A flicker of movement makes me turn. "That's not all that's coming!"

A couple of hundred yards away from us, the horizon has disappeared under a monstrous cloud of crimson dust.

I blink and the mound is higher, wider, closer.

"What is that?" I whirl around, searching for cover.

"A haboob!" Hannah yells over the suddenly roaring wind, her hair whipping in all directions. "A sandstorm."

"We need to find shelter!" Canter shouts in my ear. I can barely see him. "We're not outrunning that thing."

It's like being inside a tornado, and the haboob's still a hundred yards away. Grit coats my eyes, nose, and mouth. I cough and stumble, my knees skidding in the swirling dirt. I can't tell which way is up or down. The world is only sand and wind and sand.

A hand grabs me under my arm, hauling me to my feet. "We have to move!" Canter calls.

"There's no time!" I barely hear Hannah and see even less of her.

The ground rumbles beneath us. *An earthquake?* No. Boulders leap from the ground like fish, stacking higher and higher, forming a cave.

"The wind will topple them," I choke out. "We have to bind them together."

Pressed back to back to keep from being blown away, Canter and I call our Botan magic. Seeds I carried from the Old World stir in my pocket, and thick stalks of pampas grass stream away from me, weaving a chartreuse tapestry over and around Hannah's cave, securing it in place.

"C'mon!" she barks, and the three of us dive inside.

I hold my breath, partly to keep from inhaling the thick dust seeping through the cracks and partly to keep from screaming. Roaring fills my ears as the structure shudders.

Canter grips my hand. I reach for Hannah's, but she pulls away, pressing her palms into the stones over our heads, her eyes drifting shut. The rocks around us quake until even my bones seem to be vibrating. I silently recite multiplication tables.

A stone shifts overhead and a stream of sand pours in.

I tighten my fingers around Canter's, staring at our interlocked white knuckles. Hannah watches us but remains still.

After what feels like light-years, the stones settle and the howl fades. Still, we don't dare leave our shelter. I take a few long, deep breaths.

"You're not with the Meteorons," I say to Hannah when the storm's quieted enough to speak over the wind and my heart's no longer racing like I'm on a hover coaster. "You're with your sister. And I—I get that. But you're not with the Meteorons. Why would you be?"

"Why wouldn't I?" she asks, shifting rocks and sand so she can crawl out. "They never tried to kill me or steal my magic. They don't care what powers I have, or if I have any at all. Only that I'm on their side."

"That's because they're using you," Canter counters as we emerge after her. The dust clouds of the haboob are already shrinking in the distance. "You're another weapon in their arsenal."

"At least they think I'm valuable."

"I think you're valuable," I say quietly, watching the glowing green lights dancing closer. "And that has nothing to do with your magic."

Hannah winces. "We need to go our separate ways, Myra. But we don't have to be enemies."

I swallow hard. Nearby, others are emerging from makeshift shelters and from behind barriers, all coated from head to toe in thick dust. They barely pause before the battle restarts. "If you're fighting my friends, then that's exactly what you are."

Hannah scoffs. "These people aren't your friends. You hardly know them. Or the Meteorons."

"I know who the Meteorons are fighting *with*," I snap, clenching my fists. "How can you side with people working with Jake Melfin?"

"They don't care about him," she says. "They're using him to get to the Settlements."

"Melfin's using them, too!" Canter shakes his head. "He wants the Meteorons to destroy everything so MFI can swoop in and 'fix it' with their garbage products."

"And then he'll turn on the Meteorons," I plead. "That includes you and your sister."

"So, let them fight among themselves." She shrugs. "My family can finally go live somewhere in peace. Maybe it'll be good for the galaxy, to suffer a little."

"Who even are you?" I ask, taking a step back. "How can you say that?"

"Because she's smart." Meredith strolls toward us, some sort of canister resting on her shoulder. "She *is* my sister, after all. It runs in the family."

Canter laughs coldly. "If smart means oblivious, sure."

"You're one to talk," Meredith bites back, tossing her sleek hair over her shoulder. "Like you know anything about how the galaxy works outside your little Lunar bubble."

"I haven't lived on the Moon for a long time," Canter says quietly. "And I know plenty."

"What's that?" I ask, pointing at the metal contraption, which resembles Eli's stun launcher but far more lethal.

"This?" Meredith lifts the cylinder from her shoulder. "My brilliant sister invented it. Want to see how it works?"

We don't answer, and she doesn't wait for a response anyway. After tucking it under her arm, Meredith aims the device at the quickly growing crowd and clicks a lever on the back—a trigger. There's a loud *whoosh* and a flash, and then fifty yards away, a woman collapses. Nora.

I stand stunned, but Canter jolts into action, diving on top of Meredith to wrestle the tube from her hands.

"Let her go!" Hannah screeches. Rocks and gravel from our cave rise and surge together, re-forming as a barrier that knocks Canter and Meredith apart.

Blood trickles from Canter's forehead as he rolls away. Meredith climbs shakily to her feet, the weapon still clutched in her hands, as she stalks around the wall toward him.

I step between them. "Point that thing somewhere else."

"Or what?" She positions the tube under her arm again. I flick my wrist and a shrub bursts up from beneath her feet, knocking her to the ground. The weapon flies out of her grasp and rolls toward Hannah, who scoops it up, though she doesn't point it at me.

"*She* is not your friend, Hannah," Meredith grits out.

"And these people are?" I snarl as I haul Canter to his feet. "Melfin tried to have you and your sister killed."

"Because of *you*!" Meredith's eyes flash. "*Both times.* Because of you."

"*He's* the enemy, Hannah!" I stare at my oldest friend, trying to find a trace of the girl I used to know. The one who would sneak into our apartment café with me for snacks, plan elaborate sleepovers, and help me hack the secret codes in our favorite holo-games.

But she's gone.

Too much debris has been thrown in our paths for us to grow anywhere but away from each other. And now we're too far apart to even recognize the girls we used to be.

Still, Hannah is silent. She chews her lip, her gaze flicking between me and Meredith. *I hope she's still in there somewhere.*

Meredith narrows her eyes. "Maybe Melfin doesn't have to be our enemy," she says. "Maybe it's our turn to betray you." She snatches the weapon from Hannah, redirects it at me, and pulls the trigger.

I hear the click and see the flash.

I steel myself, waiting for the ball of light to slam into me.

It never comes.

The ground shakes and the world goes white as the tube explodes in Meredith's hands.

CHAPTER FORTY-NINE
CANTER

MEREDITH SINKS TO THE GROUND AND THE REST OF us stand as still as stone, like the fog radiating off the battlefield has frozen us in place, clouding over everything except her crumpled form in front of us. Hannah is the first to snap out of it. With a sound that's part shriek, part sob, she hurtles toward her sister, throws herself over her, and screams for a Mender, but I can tell it's too late. Even for magic. Meredith's gone.

Myra hasn't moved, either, but she's not looking at the sisters. She's staring over my shoulder. I turn and find Ms. Curie waiting behind us, her hand still outstretched from whatever magic she unleashed to save Myra.

"Leave them," she says quietly, taking our arms and leading us away.

Myra looks over her shoulder. "Shouldn't we—"

Ms. Curie shakes her head. "They made their choices."

"But she's my best friend," Myra whispers.

"When's the last time she acted like it?"

"She's right, Myra," I say quietly. "Just because you and Hannah used to be good friends doesn't mean she deserves to keep you as one."

"Fiona told me that friends fight," Myra says, her tone pleading. "That true friendships can survive anything."

"Not anything," Ms. Curie says. "Most things. If both friends want it to. If they both are willing to put in the work. But that's not what's happening here."

Myra can't tear her eyes away from the sisters. "We grew apart, and lots of things got in the way, but we could—we could come together again. We could try—"

"You're trying to save your friendship while she's trying to drown it, Mixture Myra." I squeeze her arm. "She literally just tried to kill you."

"That was Meredith."

"I didn't see Hannah do much to stop her," I snap, a wave of fury crashing over me. Myra winces.

Ms. Curie puts a hand on my arm. "Canter—"

"I don't care," I snap, jerking away. "I almost lost *my* best friend today. Because of *her*."

Myra's shoulders slump.

"You can mourn your friendship later," Ms. Curie says.

"And you should," she adds more gently. "Right now, let's focus on not having to grieve anyone or anything else."

Fighting rages all around us. Meteorons are scattered everywhere. Mahogany clouds swirl overhead and thunder booms so loud, it shakes the earth. The Botans are fighting back, lost in storms of flowers and leaves and thorns. Branches sharp as spears whistle through the air while a forest of trees roams the perimeter of the field like soldiers.

In the chaos, I catch glimpses of my parents and Bernard fending off various forms of Meteoron magic. Lila materializes like a ghost, healing fallen Botans with her Mender magic, only to slip away again. Thankfully, they all seem okay.

But as I scan the combat, our side looks increasingly outnumbered. Overhead, the streaks of emerald have shifted to ruby red, flowing like lava across the sky. I call my Elector magic and feel energy pulsing all around me in rhythm with the lights, building, strengthening, into a final wave.

"What about the atmospheric generators?" Myra asks, watching the storm. "Won't it knock out their power?"

I shake my head. "They're buried deep underground."

"Deep enough to protect them?"

"Probably, but I don't know for sure."

"The Meteorons wouldn't destroy their own oxygen supply," Myra reasons.

"Isn't this the biggest storm in history?" I run my hands through my hair. "What if they can't control it?"

"We've got to stop them."

"I know."

The ground shudders again. I assume it's thunder, only it doesn't stop. The rumbling grows louder and louder.

"Get out of the way!" Ms. Curie yells, shoving us behind her.

The dark clouds overhead have spun into a funnel, and it's raging straight for us.

Myra grabs my shirt, yanking me back. We crash to the ground, and she thrusts her hands into the dirt. A massive tree bursts out of the dust, its trunk as wide as an Anti-Grav Chamber. It bends over us, twisting into a U-shaped barrier.

Screams erupt around us, but we don't dare move. Myra's hair whips into my face, and I can hardly breathe through the grit and sand coating my nose and mouth.

"Hold on!" she calls over the howling wind. "It's almost here."

We grip the branches and press ourselves into the tree's bark. Wood creaks as the trunk lifts slightly, and for a second I think it might be blown away. But then the tree settles. The wind dies down and the howling slowly fades to a whisper and then eerie silence.

I peek over the trunk, and my stomach drops at the

sight before me. Half of the Botans who were locked in combat with opponents moments before are laid out across the ground, though the rest still valiantly struggle against the fully intact Meteoron army. I spot Ms. Curie wielding what has to be an electromagnetic field, metal weapons flying to her from all over the battlefield, heaping around her like meteors around a moon. A red form flits from body to body sprawled in the dust. With a gasp of relief, I realize it's Lila, and the crimson is dirt, not blood.

"I don't see my parents," I say. "Or Bernard."

"Bernard's over there with Lila." Myra points across the field, to where he's channeled his Botan magic into a shield-shaped cactus that looms over them, blocking her from any Meteoron attacks. I still don't see my parents. It's hard to identify anyone when red dust coats everyone and everything.

I can't deny, though, that the funnel cloud fueled a tide that was already turning. Less and less green cuts through the haze of red as the Meteorons press the line forward. And once the Botans are defeated and the Martian Settlement's leveled by the solar storm, what will stop the Meteorons from continuing their war across the galaxy?

"This is our last chance," Myra says, reading my mind. "It has to end here."

We rise together and run into the battle. Even in the chaos, we manage to stay close, summoning all the magic we can muster. Around us, a storm of plants erupts. Bushels of poison sumac, thorny branches, and spools of bittersweet whip around us, tangling between legs and around arms, hauling away enemies. With my Botan magic, I call on my Elector powers, using the faint electricity humming in the plants to build a web of energy that crackles in the air, searching for its next mark. Lethally sharp hawthorn trees burst from the ground, twining into living cages, and we catch Meteoron after Meteoron, stunning them with electrical surges. It's not enough.

I spin, trying to decide who to engage next, as leaves curl around my arms and chest, coating me in emerald armor. Beside me, Myra wields roots like a net, ensnaring a group of Meteorons nearby. She hauls back another tangle, and freezes.

"What's happening?" She holds out her arms, the tiny hairs on her skin standing on end. Her hair floats up from her shoulders, hovering around her like a chestnut aura. "Are you doing this?"

I shake my head, not bothering to smooth down my own hair, as I stare into the carmine sky, which flashes and pulsates like a beating heart.

Myra tilts her face upward, going rigid beside me. "The storm . . ."

"It's here."

CHAPTER FIFTY

MYRA

THE SKY'S ON FIRE. ALL AROUND ME FLAMES FLICKER across the sand, casting eerie amber light and umber shadows as the inferno dances closer and faster. Even the air seems to be ablaze, scorching my throat and coating my skin in sweat and ash.

"I can't breathe," I croak to Canter as we stumble toward what I hope is our camp. It's almost impossible to tell one direction from another. "Is it the atmospheric generators?"

"If they were destroyed, we'd be dead already," he says, coughing. But he drops to the ground anyway, digging his hands into the dirt. "I still feel them. They're working."

"For now." I rub my eyes beneath my glasses, then scan the horizon. In the distance, trails of black smoke drift from what must be the Martian cities. Electrical fires. "We've got to get back to the others."

We take off running again, traveling in zigzags to avoid the flames. "How are these fires forming?" I call. "There's nothing to burn but sand."

"There are chemicals in the air from all the fighting," Canter pants. "Decaying plant debris and moisture and probably some lingering Chemic mixtures. The energy from the storm is flash-heating them until they combust."

The closer we get to the main battle, the thicker the flames become. The ground's littered with debris, but I realize the Meteorons and Botans are no longer fighting. Not one another, anyway.

A trio of Meteorons are huddled together, arms outstretched, gray clouds swirling above their heads. Rain is pouring down, but the water turns to mist just above the blazing ground. A haze of steam and smoke blankets everything, warping my vision. It's like a dream I wish I could wake from.

But the blistering heat assures me that this is no dream. It's a nightmare.

I squint, trying to find anything to do, any way to help. A solution. Nothing seems to be working. Some Meteorons direct snow squalls, while others try to trap the fires in ice. One's even concentrated on blanketing the ground in a thick layer of frost. The flames eat through it all.

Alongside them, Botans summon plants in the hope of

suffocating the flames, but the new growth is incinerated so quickly, it's like it never sprouted.

"What are you kids doing here?" a hoarse voice snaps. Fiona rushes over, grabbing us both by our collars. "You have to get out of here!"

"And go where?" Canter staggers, and we all nearly topple.

"There's got to be something we can do," I gasp out.

"*They* brought it here!" Fiona points at a trio of Meteorons, still trying desperately to call down enough rain to douse the blaze. "They can fix it."

I sweep my arms, taking in the flood of weather magic struggling against the out-of-control storm. *"They're trying!"*

"It's their fault," she insists.

"We can argue about who's to blame and end up dead." Canter swipes his sleeve across his sweaty forehead. "Or we can try to help."

"Botan magic is powerless against this." Fiona nods toward the struggling Botans. "But if we all join forces, maybe we can create a path out of here before the plants burn away."

I pause. "What about plants that *need* heat?" I dig in my pockets, praying to every Worship Center I still have them.

"What are you talking about?" Canter asks, before dissolving into another coughing fit.

The Meteorons and Botans press together as the flames inch closer. If this doesn't work . . .

"Some seeds only grow after being exposed to extreme heat. Wildfires can spur new growth on the Old World." I check another pocket, twisting through the fabric, searching. "If we can get them to bloom, they could sprout more plants once they're scorched by the fire, and on and on."

Canter's eyes widen. "And you have some?"

I pull my hand out of my pocket and uncurl my fingers. A few seeds rest on my palm. "I had more, but I must have used them earlier." I take a deep breath, even though it burns my lungs. "Hopefully, it's enough."

"Maybe the others will activate, too, if we call to them," Canter says gazing across the destruction. "Wherever they are."

"It can't hurt to try." My hand shakes as magic courses through my veins, then chills to ice, going still.

"What's wrong?"

"It doesn't feel right," I whisper. "Making them bloom just to die."

"But if we don't do it, then *we* all might die."

Images flash through my mind so fast, it's like a Meteoron tornado whipping my memories around.

The charred stretch of land on the Old World, destroyed by Meteoron magic.

Plants curling through the remnants of a building, taking the world back for their own.

Pots and pans hidden in a dark cupboard, sprouts curling over their edges.

The rounded leaves of an oak tree, bursting through the cobalt-blue sea.

A lone yellow flower, rising out of the ashes to say goodbye. To say thank you. Because we tried. Because we cared.

Because we wanted to help.

Maybe the plants want to save us now.

"Please can you help us?" I whisper. An answer stirs in my mind and my heart and my hand.

The seeds on my palm explode like a firework, gold and fuchsia and coral petals filling the air as banksias bloom in a halo around us. Eucalyptus leaves follow, silvery-green vines weaving a tapestry over our heads and under our feet, linking together the army of lodgepole pines that burst from the ground and surround us like soldiers.

The plants clash with the flames, flashing brightly as they burn. My heart clenches as the blooms are destroyed, but from the ashes a new garden rises in a prism of color so bright and vibrant it makes my eyes water.

Beside me, Canter's arms are outstretched, adding his magic to mine. Over and over new growths spring from the flames until wildflowers spread as far as we can see, covering the burgundy Martian landscape and smothering the flames.

Fiona and the other Botans stare at us, gaping. The Meteorons are quicker to recover, wielding their storm clouds with renewed energy, washing away any ghost of a spark. And for a moment, it's like being on the Old World again, color and greenery as far as I can see.

"What did you say to the seeds?" Canter murmurs beside me, gazing at the garden born from ashes. "Right before they started to grow."

"I asked them to help." Water glistens on every leaf and petal. The landscape looks enchanted. Kissed by magic.

I suppose it is.

He shakes his head. "Why did they?"

"Partly because they wanted to," I say, gazing up at the leaves brushing the pale copper sky. "And partly because they wanted a chance to grow among the stars."

CHAPTER FIFTY-ONE

CANTER

THE PLANTS GLEAM IN THE SETTING MARTIAN SUN, glittering under the rainstorm the Meteorons managed to summon. But moments later, they begin to wilt. Without flames to spur new growth, the garden fades away like I'm waking from a dream, until just ashes remain.

"Is that it?" Myra asks beside me, gazing sadly at the endless rows of barren dunes. "Or do we have another phase of the solar storm to look forward to?"

I close my eyes, reaching out with my Elector magic. "The energy's dissipating. I think it's passing us."

She exhales loudly. "Interstellar."

"Hopefully, we smothered the fires before anyone got hurt," I add. "And it stopped the fighting."

She shakes her head, glancing behind me. "Try again, hotshot."

When I look over my shoulder, my stomach drops. I thought our brush with death would be enough to end the fighting, or that at least it would've cooled it a bit. But it's like it never happened. Botans whip eucalyptus vines and pine branches while clouds collect over the Meteorons, lightning flashing ominously. Even Mom is a blur of leaves and thorns.

Myra's already running into the conflict, throwing her hands up, and a blanket of wildflowers knocks the closest group of Meteorons off their feet.

I call my Botan magic, but all that responds are the pine trees. "The fires destroyed all the seeds except the ones spurred by fire."

"I noticed!" Myra knocks a blade of ice out of the air with a silvery-green lasso.

Meteorons are everywhere, and the rain they summoned to douse the remaining flames has grown into an endless torrent. A gust of wind hits me like a sonic blast, sending me sprawling. I fight to get up, but the surge is too strong. Myra skids in the sand beside me, barely keeping her feet, as hail the size of hoverballs pummels the ground around us, spraying sand and ice fragments toward our faces like shrapnel.

"It's a derecho!" Mom yells above the howling wind as she disappears into the gale. "Linked storms that feed off each other. We've got to break them up."

Overhead, a ridge of gray has gathered.

"How?" Myra calls back, brandishing tree limbs like swords.

"Overwhelm the Meteorons controlling them." Fiona spins, wildflowers swirling above her like a rainbow tornado. The stems braid together into a rope that she hooks around the ankles of a silver-haired man nearby.

"There're too many of them!" Myra hollers over the wind and rain. I don't know how she can see through the streams of water running over her glasses. She flicks her wrist and a thorn the size of a knife whips through the air.

"Just keep going." I toggle between my Elector and Botan magic, but neither seems to be enough. The rain's so heavy now, I can't see anyone.

Myra and I tense, waiting for the whistle of hail or the flash of a strategically placed bolt of lightning. But then a cloud so white it seems to be made of light floats toward us.

"What is that?" I call.

I feel Myra tilt her head. "I think it's Chemic magic." Her shoulders press into my back as she turns. "It must be your dad."

I squint through the rain, which seems to have let up a little, but I don't see him. A dark-haired boy runs by, his hands conducting the pearly cloud.

"It's drying out the rain!" I watch him maneuver the fog into the path of the derecho storm. "Who is that?"

The boy spins, and Myra gasps. "Noah."

His head jerks toward us. Our eyes lock and he gives us a quick nod before turning back to focus.

"What the meteor?" I stare as the ivory cloud overtakes the storm.

"Where did he come from?" Myra asks.

I do a double take. "The same place as the rest of them, I guess."

So many new faces, young and old, have joined the fight, and they aren't wielding weather magic. Sparks flash on the wrists of Electors. Chemic potions fill the air. Tekkie barriers pop up everywhere, shielding the surging forces from the Meteorons' magic. Some don't use magic at all; instead, they weave through the crowd, pushing back Meteorons or helping the wounded.

"Non-Creers," I say, awed.

"Mom!" Myra calls when Mrs. Hodger pops up in the crowd, numbers swirling around her head like a crown. "What are you doing here? Who *are* all these people?"

Mrs. Hodger slashes her hand through the calculations, erasing one half and multiplying the other. "Reinforcements."

"Have you seen my parents?" I ask. "Are they all right?"

She nods, hauling us behind a massive cypress tree that's sprouted nearby. "I just passed them on my way here.

They're dealing with some lingering Meteoron magic but doing fine."

"But where did all these people come from?" Myra asks, eyes wide as she peers around the trunk.

"All over!" Mrs. Hodger tugs Myra back. "They saw Perennial's message on the open network and came to help."

Myra and I exchange a look of shock.

"Some of my university contacts managed to mimic the signal. They got it out over the airwaves again and again. Every time the Councils shut it down, it popped up again in three new places." She narrows her eyes. "And now that we have all of these supporters, you kids should get back inside."

We both roll our eyes.

"Okay, Mom," Myra says, in a tone I'm sure she thinks is placating. "You win."

Mrs. Hodger crosses her arms. "Myra Josephine Hodger, this isn't up for debate."

"*Josephine?*" I can't stop the chuckle from bubbling up. "Your middle name's *Josephine?*"

Myra plants her hands on her hips. "Yeah, so what?"

"We used to call her Myra Jo when she was little," Mrs. Hodger adds.

I'm laughing so hard, tears are streaming down my cheeks. Myra looks ready to turn into a human fire whirl.

Mrs. Hodger presses a finger to her chin. "Just like your parents used to call you Canter Francis."

The laughter dies in my throat as quicky as the Chemic cloud evaporated the rain.

Meanwhile, Myra looks like she just found a trove of Trickering candy. "Canter *Francis*?"

"Don't even—"

"*Can Fran* has a nice ring to it."

Horrified, I turn and glare at Mrs. Hodger, who shrugs. "We received the announcement when you were born." She points between branches toward the horizon, where Perennial's ship is docked. "You two can talk about your middle names all you like *inside*. Now."

Though it looks like the fighting on the ground is turning in our favor, this is one battle we won't be winning.

"Keep behind the trees on your way," she barks, shoving us toward the forest that sprang up while we were talking.

Myra and I hurry from trunk to trunk until we're out of Mrs. Hodger's sight.

My best friend shoots me a look. "You don't tell, I don't tell?"

"Deal. And we're not really leaving, right?"

She barks a laugh. "Of course not. We'll duck over the ridge, then double back."

"Sounds gre—" From the corner of my eye, a familiar stocky frame sweeps past us.

Myra's head whips around, following his path. "That's Melfin. He's trying to escape."

Without another word, we follow him.

CHAPTER FIFTY-TWO

MYRA

MELFIN FOLLOWS A FEW OTHER SHADOWY FORMS, disappearing around the side of a massive, circular sand dune. We creep after him, the battle forgotten.

"Where are they going?" I whisper.

"Maybe they have a ship hidden out here."

We pick up our pace. No way am I letting Melfin blast off Mars like a shooting star so he can continue his reign of MFI destruction.

"We've got to get that book," I say. "We need proof of everything he's done."

"I'm sure he has it on him," Canter replies as we edge around the dune. It's massive, almost as large as S.L.A.M.

We walk all the way around, but there's no sign of Melfin. The air's still. Too still. I stop, scanning the barren landscape.

Boom!

Canter and I jump back, my heart thudding in my ears. "What was that?" I whisper.

"It sounded like an explosion." Canter nods at the mountain of sand towering over us. "Chemic magic."

"But what did it do? Wait, I hear something."

"It sounds like running water," Canter says after a moment, searching for the source.

"It's not water!" I grab Canter's arm and haul him backward. "The dune's collapsing!"

We sprint, the avalanche of sand racing at our heels, but we can't outrun it. An instant later, the surge washes over us, flattening me to my stomach. I manage to find Canter's hand and latch onto it. We kick and push, trying to claw our way to the surface for a gasp of air, but there's nothing but never-ending sand.

A memory flashes through my mind—passing through the wall at the weather-monitoring station on Venus, Hannah's magic the only thing standing between me and suffocating in the gritty walls—and I wonder if that was a preview of this moment, and if it will be my last.

My lungs scream as I dig with one hand, still clutching Canter's fingers with the other. The pile on top of us gets heavier and heavier. Beneath me, the sand shifts and I slide, Canter's fingers slipping from mine as I sink deeper.

We can't die here. Not like this. Not after everything.

My body shudders, demanding air I can't find. Something stirs in my chest, burning from my heart to my fingertips. Beneath my eyelids, the darkness is cut by a golden glow, and instead of sand, I feel the familiar scratch of twigs and branches pressing against my skin, pushing me up and up and up.

Sand sprays everywhere as I burst through the top of the dune, Canter beside me, riding a boxwood blooming like a leafy throne.

A half dozen people stare at us from the ground, and in the center of the crowd, a heavyset man searches his pockets, cuff links glinting in the setting Martian sun as he extracts a glittering vial.

"His Chemic magic can't reach us up here," Canter tells me.

"We're still kind of outnumbered." I remove my glasses, wiping them on my equally dusty shirt. "I could send a burst of flowers into the air like a flare. Maybe someone would notice and—"

The bush shudders beneath us, an earthquake rattling it from the ground below.

"Is that Meteoron magic?" Canter asks.

"Seismology isn't related to weather." The boxwood rattles from root to stem, but the dune beneath us hardly moves at all. "It's the plant!" I grab onto the branches, trying to steady myself, but it only shakes harder.

And then it begins to sink.

"What's happening?" I reach out with my magic. Canter does, too. It's not working.

Leaves curl back to buds, branches retreat, and the bush retracts to nothing. We hit the sand and slide, skidding down the dune. I dig my heels in, but we're moving too fast.

A few feet off the ground, we jump, aiming to land as far from Melfin as possible. It's not far enough.

"How did you do that?" I call out.

He smirks. "I'm not sure what you mean."

"How did your Chemic magic make our tree rewind?" Canter demands.

Melfin nudges the pale-haired woman beside him—Ophelia. "You were right. The Botans are weak."

"Not all Botans, Jake. Just you."

And then Ms. Curie is there. Fiona isn't far behind.

The clouds overhead darken.

"Don't even try it," Fiona growls, thorns the size of arrowheads clustering in her hands. Ms. Curie's bracelet of wires hisses with electricity. Across from them, Canter and I summon our magic, digging our heels into the sand.

Ophelia pauses, assessing the situation, then nods at her companions. The clouds overhead clear. "What were you saying?" she asks, nodding at Melfin.

"He's always been full of secrets," Ms. Curie says, her voice like acid. "And a hypocrite."

"Hypocrite?" Fiona looks back and forth between them.

"I think most of us know how MFI's really survived all these years," Ms. Curie seethes.

I glare across the gap at Melfin. "They've been growing plants illegally to keep the food cloning formulas working."

"Plants?" The Meteoron leader takes a step forward, lightning flashing in her eyes.

"MFI had a secret garden all along?" Canter's mouth falls open. "Where?"

Ms. Curie's gaze never leaves Melfin's face. "The better question is, *how* did he get them to grow."

"It's not impossible to grow plants without magic," Canter says.

"Not impossible, but also not easy. Especially out here."

"And Jake Melfin always takes the easy route." Fiona's eyes narrow. "All these years, I thought he'd only inherited the seeds."

I reach into my pocket and pull out the small emerald box. I'd almost forgotten I had it. As I turn it over in my hands, light catches the engravings.

Fiona turns to Ms. Curie. "You never told me."

"I promised I wouldn't tell anyone." Ms. Curie's eyes flicker to Melfin's face. "Jake and I were friends, and then more than friends. And by the time I realized we weren't anything at all," she says, her expression hardening, "it was too late."

"What are you saying?" Ophelia presses.

"Jake Melfin is a Botan."

The Meteorons freeze. Overhead, the clouds again grow dark.

Goose bumps bloom across my skin. "You didn't use your Chemic magic to rewind our boxwood. You used *Botan* magic."

"Lies," Melfin spits. He scowls as he yanks up his sleeve, displaying dozens of Chemic Inscriptions. "I'm well known in my field. This is a pathetic ploy to turn my new allies against me."

"You haven't had seeds to practice your Botan magic for a long time," I say, gripping the box so tight it cuts into my palms. "Not since Ms. Curie stole your family's stash."

"Ancestral Botans?" Ophelia's eyes flash, focusing on me. "Can you prove it?"

"No," Melfin barks. "Of course she can't."

I toss the box to Ophelia. "The list of initials carved into that proves otherwise."

"Jake Melfin, Bradford Melfin, Frank Melfin, Walter Melfin," Fiona rattles off.

"Karl," Ms. Curie adds, taking over, ticking them off on her fingers. "Then Zacharias, Jayden, Patrick, another Walter. Oh, and George. The Melfins are incredibly proud of their heritage. They had portraits plastered everywhere when we were kids. Probably still do. A whole family tree of Botan magic."

"That's how you kept our garden going on Venus," Canter says. "Noah told me it was thriving. You were using your own magic."

"Just because my family passed down Old World seeds to keep our business flourishing doesn't mean I'm a Botan!" Melfin snarls.

"Then how do you explain the tree shrinking down a few minutes ago?" Canter argues.

Melfin glowers at us. "My Chemic compound overwhelmed their powers, obviously."

"The children's powers didn't appear weak in battle," one of the Meteorons murmurs to Ophelia. She nods, her gaze never leaving Melfin's reddening face. "And the plant was retracting before the vapors could have reached them."

"We will never align ourselves with a Botan," Ophelia finally says.

"What?" Hannah steps out from behind the dune, her sister's weapon in her hands. "What do you mean *Botan*?"

"Treachery," a Meteoron man spits. "Typical Botan betrayal."

Fiona's gaze is ice. "We did warn you about Melfin. Back in the Moon hangar. You should have listened."

The man scoffs. "To a Botan?"

"To someone trying to help you," I snap. "You've been

fighting each other for so long you've forgotten who the real enemy is. The type of people who left you behind in the first place."

"And the one who kept sending more to join you," Canter growls, "just for having Meteoron or Botan magic." Canter takes a step toward Melfin. "Especially when he had it, too."

"You sentenced me and my sister to death for having seeds," Hannah says, her voice shaking, "when all this time, you were a Botan."

"Look around us," Melfin snaps, sweeping his arm toward the battle, which is winding down behind us. The Martian desert is littered with the debris of magic war. "Having Botans and Meteorons in the galaxy is dangerous. Certain magic has no place in civilized society."

The Meteorons beside us stiffen. Ophelia's eyes are darker than the storm clouds.

"Except for yours," I spit.

Melfin shrugs, eyes gleaming. "Just because I don't play by the same rules as the rest of you doesn't make me the bad guy. It makes me smart."

"And this is where your intelligence got you." Tears are streaming down Hannah's face as she points the weapon at him and pulls the trigger.

I hear the click and see the flash, and then a ball of light erupts from the muzzle.

CHAPTER FIFTY-THREE

CANTER

MS. CURIE IS A BLUR OF MOTION AS SHE LAUNCHES herself in front of Jake Melfin. The blast catches her in the chest.

"Sandra!" Mom rushes to her friend's side.

Myra runs, too, but back toward the battlefield. She returns a few minutes later with Lila. The girls fall to the sand and Lila holds her hands out over Ms. Curie's body, her eyes squeezed shut.

When she opens them again, they're glassy. She shakes her head and my stomach sinks.

Mom's sobbing. Jake Melfin stands there frozen. He hasn't moved since Hannah leveled the weapon at him.

Myra's cheeks are blotchy as she walks over to me. "Why would she do that?" she whispers.

"I don't know. Maybe she thought she'd have time to divert it. But why would she even try to protect him?"

Myra's gaze drifts to Hannah. The metal tube lies forgotten in the sand. "Because they used to be friends. And sometimes you can still love the memory of someone, even when you don't recognize who they've become."

Hannah slowly sinks to the ground and wraps her head in her hands. Melfin still hasn't moved.

"What's going on?" Kyle jogs up, then jolts to a stop and gasps as he takes in the scene. "I thought you said to go— What the meteor?"

The sight of his son seems to snap Melfin out of his daze. He extracts a small remote from his jacket and clicks a button. "I told you to wait on the ship."

"Did *you* do this?" Kyle hisses.

"Of course not," Melfin snaps. A hum fills the air, and a sleek silver shuttle glides toward us, setting down in the sand, sending crimson dust swirling. "They did."

Kyle takes in the rest of us, all in various states of shock and grief, and then focuses back on his father. "It was you."

"Get on the ship. Now."

"I think I'm done listening to you." Kyle pulls something out of his pocket. "Like how you told me to hide this on board."

In Melfin's split second of hesitation, Myra and I call

our magic. A web of English ivy unfurls from our hands, ensnaring the book. As Melfin lurches toward us, Mom leaps to her feet.

"One inch closer and you're stardust," she growls.

Melfin meets her gaze, weighs his options, then turns and stalks toward the waiting ship.

"Should we go after him?" Myra asks.

I untangle the book from our greenery and riffle through before handing it to Myra. "There are enough names listed with Jake Melfin's that the whole galaxy will have turned on him by morning."

"I'm not taking any chances," the Meteoron man growls, heading after him.

"You don't have to," a young voice says. "He's not going anywhere."

"Crashing comets! Eli!" I gape at the small boy sliding from under the wing of Melfin's ship, Bin-ro tucked under one arm.

"You two aren't supposed to be here!" Myra tries to look angry, but can't hide her grin.

"How did you even get here?" I demand, and Eli blushes.

"I might have hidden a tracker in the stun launcher I gave you to fix, so I knew what part of the Martian Settlement you were in." Before I can react, his face brightens. "And did you know Bin-ro can pilot a ship!"

"We're aware." Myra glares at Bin-ro, who promptly whistles.

I scowl at him. "You could have been hurt or worse."

"But we wanted to help."

"Beep!" Bin-ro agrees.

I shake my head. "Help how—"

The hum of Melfin's shuttle shifts to a whistle, then a squeal. Black smoke pours from the hull.

Eli beams. "We made some adjustments to his exit strategy."

Myra frowns. "If Melfin had found you messing—"

"Melfin would never have caught these two. They're way too savvy for him." I wrap an arm around Eli's shoulders, and the kid looks like he won the galaxy's largest Jupiter Jackpot.

"What will our deceitful friend do now?" Ophelia asks, cocking an eyebrow.

A moment later, Melfin appears at the ship's hatch, his face as red as the Martian desert. He takes one look at us, then bolts in the opposite direction.

Mom sighs. "Run like the coward he is." She reaches into her pocket, flinging a handful of seeds. At the same time, Ophelia sweeps her arms wide, the air suddenly arctic.

In a perfect ring, cerulean-blue roses sprout, thorny

stems weaving tightly together, their petals glittering silver in the setting Martian sun.

Melfin spins in a circle at the center of the magical cage, throwing himself against the towering blooms, but they're as strong as stone, or more accurately, ice.

"Frost flowers," Bernard murmurs, coming up behind us. "I've seen these before. Or my original did."

"How do they form?" Myra asks, staring in awe at the shimmering sculpture.

He nods to Mom and Ophelia. "A combination of Botan and Meteoron magic."

"I never knew different Creers could blend together that way," Lila says.

"Most can't. Or don't." Bernard flashes a small smile. "But Botan and Meteoron magic complement each other in a way others can't. It gives them a special bond."

"Or it did," I say, my voice low.

Everyone is quiet for a moment. "What are your plans now?" Mom finally asks.

Ophelia shifts, but doesn't answer.

"I don't think a revenge tour of the galaxy will be in your Creer's best interest," says Myra. "Even if you manage to escape Perennial."

"Then what do you propose?"

Mom stares at Ms. Curie's form lying in the sand. "I'd suggest something that doesn't include doing any more harm." She meets Ophelia's gaze. "The Settlements owe both our Creers quite a bit. Maybe enough to be lenient about whatever damage yours caused, at least for those who weren't responsible for serious injuries. And with MFI out of the picture"—she nods at the icy cage—"they're going to need a new solution for their food dilemma. It's going to take a lot of work to grow food for the Settlements, even for a crew of Botans."

Ophelia stares at the frost flowers. "I suppose the Meteorons may be able to help with that." She glances back at the battlefield, where the fighting has all but ended. "And it appears our other bargaining chip may be lost." She exchanges a glance with her Meteoron companions before refocusing on Mom. "Maybe we can work something out."

Myra beams, and a few sunshine-yellow daffodils sprout at her feet. But I can't bring myself to trust these people. Not yet. Maybe not ever.

"What about him?" I ask, gesturing toward Melfin. "And the book."

"I can give it to Perennial," Lila says, carefully taking it from Myra. She turns to Kyle. "You might want to have a conversation with her, too. About what you should do next, if you're sure about not going with . . ."

Kyle's gaze is steely. "I'm sure."

Lila pauses a few steps away. "Hannah, maybe you should come, too."

Hannah doesn't answer, but she follows silently behind them.

Ophelia sighs. "I suppose we should plot our next move as well." She nods at Mom, who returns the gesture before the Meteorons turn and follow.

A few minutes later, Dad rushes up, looking frantic. "What happened? I overheard Lila talking to Perennial."

Mom turns to him, tears shining in her eyes.

"I thought they were mistaken." He kneels down next to Ms. Curie's body. "Did she really try to save him?" he whispers.

Mom nods, unable to find any more words.

I swallow hard. "Is the fighting done?"

Dad tears his gaze away. Even though he and Ms. Curie despised each other for many years, I see old memories, happier times, playing in his eyes. He wipes his hand across his face and takes a breath. "It's over. Perennial is organizing the wounded, and the Meteoron prisoners."

"That might be more complicated now," Mom says, filling them in.

"What about the Governing Councils?" I ask. "Won't they have to decide what happens to them?"

Dad gives me a weary smile. "I have more faith in Perennial. The Councils are dealing with a lot at the moment."

"Like what?" Myra asks, adjusting her glasses.

"Perennial just posted photos of the book on the open

network. She'd already distributed . . . other information that made the entries even more impactful."

Eli snickers. "I saw the transmission when Bin-ro and I were messing with Melfin's ship. People are going to go supernova."

Bin-ro whistles his agreement.

Myra shoots me a puzzled glance. "Someone tell us what you're talking about already!"

"Remember how I said her group was stealing data?" Dad says. "It was contracts. The ones for the Reps working in MFI factories. And it just so happens that a lot of them were formerly people with Creers."

"Enemies of Melfin?" Myra asks.

Dad nods.

"And the families of the people exiled to the Old World," Eli adds. "Mostly turned in by him." He juts his chin toward the frost-flower cage, then shrugs. "That's what the comments I read said, anyway."

"The Governing Councils will shut down the posts," Myra says grimly. "They always do."

"Not this time," Noah says. He has dark circles under his eyes, and a gash on his cheek, but appears otherwise okay. He lingers on the edge of the group, as if he's expecting us to bark at him to leave. I glance at Myra, trying to gauge if she's about to tell him to jump into the sun, but her expression is unreadable.

"What do you mean?" she finally asks, her voice stiff, but with the way Noah's chest swells when she speaks to him, you'd have thought she'd announced an incoming Neptunian diamond storm.

"The Meteorons destroyed the Martian comms systems," he explains eagerly, "but Perennial's people were able to create a patch—a single line out. I overheard them talking about it back at base."

"Won't the Governing Councils just shut it down?" I ask.

"If they could find the source channel," Noah says, his eyes sparkling. "But so far, no luck. And that's not the only thing she's broadcasting."

"What do you mean?" Bernard asks.

"I may have also provided some footage of a certain seagarden."

A smile creeps across Myra's face, and Noah's cheeks go pink.

Dad slips wearily to the ground. "It's all coming out, then. The magical suppression. The Botans. All of it."

"Good," Myra whispers. "It's about time."

I squeeze her shoulder.

"We should get you kids back to the base," Dad says after a moment, glancing sideways at Mom. "I'll stay."

"No," Mom whispers. "She's gone." Her eyes drift shut, and she lays her palms on the crimson sand. Sprouts push through the gravel, leaves unfurling to form an emerald halo around Ms. Curie. They rise higher and higher, weaving into an arc over her, until her body disappears from sight. Wisps of white flutter and bloom as bushels of pearly hydrangea petals cover the green. The flowers glisten, so pale they're almost silver, glowing in the light of the rising twin Martian moons.

Mom rests her hands on top of the mound of blooms. "Until the end," she whispers, then turns to go. Dad drapes an arm around her, and they walk slowly away.

Myra and I pause next to the flowers.

"Thank you," she whispers.

"For everything." I take Myra's hand and squeeze it, and then we turn to leave, too.

CHAPTER FIFTY-FOUR

MYRA

Fourth Month, 2450

LIGHT STREAMS THROUGH THE OPENING AT THE TOP of our tree house. A pair of black-and-white birds perched on the ledge chirp a melody as I climb down the ladder to the main living area.

Dad adjusts his glasses, studying the birds. "They must be a migrating species. I haven't seen that breed before."

"You should log them," Mom says, looking up from the table. "It could be useful to know their arrival and departure schedules."

"You're one hundred percent correct." Dad bends to make a note on his computer. "We don't want to disturb their habitats when we plan the new Settlement communities."

I rub my eyes. Leave it to my parents to turn a bird song into a math equation.

Mom smiles as I enter the kitchen. "You're up early."

I yawn, stretching my arms out, mirroring the wings of the birds as they fly away. "I have a vid-call with Canter before he goes to class."

Dad studies me. "You know you could go back if you want. I'm sure you miss your friends."

"Ms. Goble would enroll you in a nanosecond," Mom adds.

I shake my head. "Everything I need to learn is here."

"Fiona would love to have you in her class," Mom presses. "She's sent me about a dozen messages saying so."

"Maybe I will someday." I considered going back to the Moon—to S.L.A.M.—with Canter and Lila, but now that I have the option to stay here on the Old World with the plants growing wild and free, I can't imagine settling for tending a garden on the Moon. Even if it *is* allowed now. Though attending Fiona's Botan classes was definitely tempting.

"All right. If you're sure."

I nod, grab my computer, and head outside, walking for a bit until I find the perfect spot, then settle under a pink weeping willow.

At a snap of my fingers, a pile of peonies blooms at my feet, and I settle carefully on top of them, switching my video feed on.

Canter's face fills my screen, his hair sticking up in all directions. He groans. "You did that on purpose."

"What?" I ask innocently.

He jabs a finger at the screen. "That!"

I glance at the small box on the corner of my screen reflecting my video feed, taking in my face surrounded by a rainbow of flowers. "Oh! You mean this?" I pick up the computer and pan it around so it captures the pink-and-white blossoms trailing from the tree overhead, the forest behind me, and the ocean just visible in the distance. "It's all right here, waiting for you to come visit."

"I'll be there in two weeks," he says.

"To stay?"

He laughs and shakes his head. "Mom really likes her new job. Plus, I think it's nice for her to be able to grow a garden in the open here after everything that happened. She said it's like coming full circle. I'll keep working on her, though. I'm sure she'll miss the Old World eventually."

"You'd better not forget to bring Bin-ro with you," I warn. "It's my turn to have him."

Canter grins. "Bin-ro told me to tell you he doesn't want to come."

"BEEP BEEP!"

"Liar," I say, laughing as Canter scoops up Bin-ro and places him on the bed so I can see him. "One beep yes, two beeps NO."

I wave at my first friend, his blue light flashing a greeting, as I settle back. The flowers form a pillow behind my head. "How's your dad? Is he still in the apartment next to yours?"

"For now." Canter shrugs. "They said they're trying to rebuild their friendship before they think about anything else. But besides me and Ms. Goble, Mom spends more time with him than anyone."

"Goble must be busy. Running the school and taking the Number Whispering position on the Lunar Governing Council is a lot."

After the battle on Mars, and all the revelations that stemmed from it, the public demanded that the Governing Councils be dissolved and re-formed, this time to include nonmagical representation.

"Does your dad miss being part of it?" Canter asks.

I shake my head. "He likes it here, plus there's plenty for him to calculate, especially with new people requesting to join the Old World Settlement all the time. He'd have liked to work with Lila's dad, though."

"Pretty interstellar he's the first non-Creer chosen to be on the Lunar Council."

"It still doesn't seem all that fair. There's a Chemic representative, a Number Whisperer, a Mender, a Tekkie, an Elector, and now a Botan rep . . . and *one* non-Creer. If you look at it as magical versus nonmagical votes, they're outnumbered six to one."

"You sound like Perennial," Canter scolds. "But you're right."

Perennial was elected to the Number Whispering position on the Venusian Governing Council, the first former Rep ever to hold a council position, though I'm sure there will be others now that they've officially ended the entire Repetition program. She's been advocating for additional non-Creer seats ever since taking office. "They may as well give in now," I say with a grin. "Perennial won't rest until she convinces them. What about the Meteoron position? Have they filled it yet?"

He shakes his head. "Not until they repair the damage they caused at S.L.A.M. and on the Martian Settlement. And some other conditions they're still negotiating. I heard Mom talking to Perennial about it the other day."

I raise my eyebrows. "Do they talk a lot?"

He nods. "Perennial wants her to apply for the Botan spot on the Lunar Council."

"She should. She'd be great."

Canter waggles his eyebrows. "Then we'd *never* leave the Moon."

"Scratch that. She'd be awful," I say quickly, and Canter laughs.

We're both quiet for a minute.

"It's weird being at school without you," he says softly.

A pang ripples through my chest like a pebble tossed in a pond. "At least you have Lila."

"And you have Bernard."

"But still, when it comes to adventures . . ."

"And getting into trouble . . ."

"And getting *out* of trouble," I finish, grinning. "No one outmaneuvers us."

"The OBs. Original Botans."

I snort. "How's Kyle? I heard my dad mention he's back at S.L.A.M."

"Quiet. He keeps to himself, mostly, except when he's visiting his grandfather on Venus. I had him bring Eli the invention we're working on together the last time he went." He pauses. "And I gave him the tryout info for next season's hoverball team."

My eyebrows shoot up. "Really? That was pretty interstellar of you."

"Seemed like he could use a distraction with his dad locked away in the Mercurian prison. Plus, I kind of owed him. Long story."

"Tell me about it when you get here."

"Have you heard from Hannah?" he asks after a moment.

"No. Noah mentions her sometimes. They're both at V.A.M.A. now."

It's Canter's turn to look surprised. "I didn't know you were talking to him."

"We've been playing *Space Pirates V* on the open network," I say with a shrug. "We chat while we game, and he has some classes with her."

"Are you going to reach out to her?" Canter asks.

"I—I don't think so. Too much has happened."

"You could say the same about Noah."

"I know, but at least he's tried to fix things. I think Hannah and I are too far past that. But you never know. Friendships are funny sometimes."

Canter stares offscreen, lost in thought. "They renamed the auditorium after her," he finally says.

"Ms. Curie?" I ask, and he nods. "That makes sense." I touch an ivory peony and the petals turn periwinkle. "I guess it would be weird if it was still called the Fiona A. Weathers Auditorium now."

"True."

He's quiet and so am I, my gaze drifting up to the azure sky. I should get off the call. I'm supposed to meet Bernard at the beach in a little while, but I don't want to say goodbye. It's not like I'll see Canter in the cafeteria at the end of the day.

Canter's image suddenly shrinks. Another face fills the other half of the screen. And it does not look happy.

"Uh-oh." I try to smother my giggles. "Canter, you're in trouble."

"Did you or did you not agree to meet me at breakfast

before Goble's class?" Lila's eyes flash, but the edges of her mouth tug into a smile.

He rubs his hands through his hair. "Uh, did the breakfast block start already?"

Lila points her messenger camera over her shoulder, showcasing the nearly empty cafeteria, then back to her scowling face.

I raise my hand. "For the record, I would have shown up on time."

"I know you would," Lila says, beaming at me. Then she sighs. "I miss having you to help keep this one on track."

"It's a full-time job," I agree solemnly.

"Hi." Canter waves. "I'm still here."

I scoff. "Like any of this is news to you."

"Punctuality isn't your thing," Lila adds. "Thankfully, me and Myra are on it."

"And I'll definitely be on time for our catch-up call tonight," I tell her.

"Can you grab me an apple before the caf closes?" Canter asks.

Lila rolls her eyes, then reaches behind her and plucks something scarlet off a shelf. "Fine, but if you're not in Goble's class in five minutes, I'm eating it." She grins at me. "Talk to you later, Myra!" And then she's gone.

"I guess I'd better go, too," Canter says.

I nod, still not wanting to end the call. Light streams through the branches, and something silvery white glows in the sky.

"Wait!" I sit up abruptly. "Do me a favor first. Go to the window in your living room, okay?"

"Sure." Canter raises his eyebrows, then pushes off his bed. The video feed swirls as he makes his way through the apartment. "Now what?"

"Can you see the Old World?"

A smile pulls at his lips. "Yup."

"Good." I stretch my arm toward the sky. "Sometimes on the Old World, you can see the Moon, even during the day. And I'm looking at it right now and waving."

He laughs. "I'm waving, too."

I study my old home, the glowing disc barely visible against the pale blue. In a few hours, it'll disappear. Until dusk, at least. But that's okay.

I may not always be able to see the Moon, but sort of like friendship, I can always feel it, floating in the air. Like magic.

ACKNOWLEDGMENTS

To Jared, Julia, and Jensen. No story means more to me than the one we are writing together. Thank you for being by my side in mine, and I'm so thankful to be a part of yours. These books would mean nothing, and would likely not exist, without the three of you.

To my editor, Alison Weiss, it's been an honor to work on these books with you and an even bigger one to know you these past several years. Thank you for helping me to be a better writer, for championing Myra's story, and for lending your magic to this series. It glitters on every page.

As always, a huge thanks to Derek Stordahl, Bethany Buck, and the rest of the Pixel+Ink team—Terry Borzumato-Greenberg, Michelle Montague, Miriam Miller, Erin Mathis, Saskia den Boon, Tiffany Coelho, Mary Joyce Perry, Melissa See, Alison Tarnofsky, Sara DiSalvo, Carmena Jarrett, Melanie McMahon Ives, Courtney Hood, Jamie Evans, Raina Putter, Jay Colvin, and Arlene Goldberg—I am so lucky to work with you all in connecting this story with readers.

To my agent, Moe Ferrara, I am forever grateful for your advice, savvy, (gifs!), and support. I did not think I could adore you more . . . until we discovered our shared *Ted Lasso* and EPL enthusiasm! Working with you has been a joy and I'm so excited to see what we can accomplish together next!

To Sarah Coleman (a.k.a. Inkymole) and Sammy Yuen—each cover created with your brilliance has exceeded my wildest dreams. They are truly works of art, and I could not love them more. Thank you for bringing Myra (and Bin-ro and Canter) to life.

Community has been a huge part of my writing journey, ranging from the writing community to my local community and everything in between, and I could not be more grateful for the support and inspiration I have found in mine:

A massive thank-you to my local school district and libraries and the incredible teachers and librarians who work there, especially Mrs. Smith, whose love of books shines to all who meet her. And a special thanks to Ms. Baldis and Mrs. Janssen for sharing these books with your classes—hearing about their reactions, questions, and theories are experiences I will never forget.

To the lovely booksellers at my nearby bookstores, especially the ones I frequent on lunch breaks to write new words and discover new stories—thank you for keeping me supplied with amazing books, friendly conversation, and plenty of writing fuel in the form of coffee and grilled cheese sandwiches.

Thank you to the local farms and parks and forests I'm lucky enough to have nearby for being a perfect muse for these books about a magical garden.

To my family and to the friends that feel like family, to my fellow soccer moms and book club moms, to my work friends and bookish friends, from the bottom of my writerly heart, thank you for all the love, support, and encouragement throughout this journey. It's worth more than a million Jupiter Jackpots.

And finally, thank you to the readers who have found a friend in Myra. You will always have one in me, too.